FIDO'S TALE

Mike Turvil is a retired pension consultant, who lives with his wife in Suffolk. He studied at Hampton Grammar School in Middlesex and left there in the early sixties to pursue a number of different careers, before becoming a financial adviser. He has varied interests, including model making and cookery, and enjoys a wide range of different book genres. Reading "The Hitchhiker's Guide to the Galaxy", a long time ago, initially inspired him to write his own stories and he has tried to capture some of the madcap humour of Douglas Adams in this science fantasy adventure tale.

Fido was originally written to entertain his daughter, when she spent her gap year in California, prior to attending university (she was sent a new chapter every month). Expanding the short story into a book has been an on and off project for over twenty years and most of Mike's family and friends never thought they would ever see it finished.

Fido's Tale

Mike Turvil

Copyright Notice

All rights are reserved to the copyright holder stated below. No part of this publication may be used or reproduced in any manner whatsoever without written permission, except in the case of brief quotations embodied in critical articles or reviews.

This is a work of fiction. Names, character, places and incidents are either the product of the author's imagination or are used fictitiously, and any resemblance to actual persons, living or dead, business establishments, events or locales is entirely coincidental.

Copyright © 2016 Michael Turvil
ISBN-13: 978-1535414678
ISBN-10: 1535414677

TO ROSIE

ACKNOWLEDGEMENTS

To my brother Bob for his invaluable assistance and to both my proof-readers: Jackie Nickless and John Draper, for their dedication to a very difficult task. Very special thanks also go to John Holder, for his amazing cover artwork.

Contents

	Introduction	1
1	The prehistoric village	5
2	Flight from the village	13
3	The camel dung salesman	21
4	The cave	31
5	Visitors to Earth	41
6	The computer system	51
7	Prehistoric television	59
8	The transporter system	67
9	An educational experience	77
10	Time travel	87
11	Cart wheels	97
12	Roc's reward	107
13	Confrontation	117
14	Fido's business plan	125
15	Bedric's just desserts	135
16	Egypt	145
17	The stone circle	153
18	Back to the future	163
19	An Egyptian encounter	173
20	Into the unknown	183
21	A new start	193
22	Thinking about Ben	203
23	The next generation	213
24	Nefertari	221
25	Ben needs help	231
26	Trouble in Egypt	243
27	The rolling stones	253
28	Fido's execution	263
29	The computer's final destiny	275

INTRODUCTION

As this is a work of fiction, the reader should not expect total historical accuracy, particularly in terms of timelines. Early man never co-existed with dinosaurs, but Fred Flintstone still tried to put Dino (his pet prosauropod dinosaur) out every night. He also drove a car, operated a brontosaurus crane at work and watched prehistoric television. A large number of films have featured cavemen battling dinosaurs and famous authors, such as Sir Arthur Conan Doyle and Jules Verne, both wrote books in which men had to face creatures long since extinct. If these eminent writers could get away with falsifying history for the sake of their stories, then perhaps I might also be forgiven for tweaking the facts to a certain extent and introducing equally impossible situations, just to add a few interesting twists to this narrative.

Once upon a time, in the darkest mists of a bygone age, there were some backwaters of the world which had not developed much beyond the Stone Age. In other places, man had made considerable advances and learnt how to smelt iron ore and to forge metal. In yet other areas, men were building with stone and erecting huge structures and monuments. The pace of development depended to a great extent on geographical location and there were some civilisations which were many thousands of years ahead of the rest.

Travelling greater distances brought men into contact with other men, who had already mastered some of the more advanced techniques. Thus the word spread, slowly but surely, and a lot of the less developed communities began to catch up. That is unless they were really inaccessible, such as on remote islands separated from the main land masses, or in places too far away for contact to be established. The people in these areas never saw anything of the advances being made elsewhere, so remained completely unaware of them. They continued to live their lives, blissfully ignorant of all the progress being made in other parts of the world.

In some really isolated regions, men still had to share their own little worlds with dinosaurs, although such creatures had been extinct for millions of years in most other places. These dinosaurs caused a lot of problems - not least being the many piles of steaming dung they produced on a regular basis. Men in these areas were obliged to tread extremely carefully - for very obvious reasons.

Our story begins in one of these remote countries. It was a very basic land, where they hadn't developed things like towns or cities. Numerous villages dotted the countryside and the villagers traded with each other, or with people from other villages. Money wasn't yet in common usage, so most everything was bartered. Even services had their price and a man could be employed to dig someone else's field for a week's supply of eggs, a couple of jugs of goat milk, or maybe a few shiny stones. The latter always being popular with the women, who wore them for decoration and as a means of displaying their wealth and status.

Village streets didn't tend to be very wide, as they only had to accommodate people walking up and down, or the odd cart or two travelling through, so if a villager happened to meet a dinosaur on the same street, this always caused a problem. No dinosaur was likely to respond to the suggestion that it find itself another route and there was always the possibility that it could suddenly decide to stop and relieve itself. In such situations, the villager would have little choice but to run the other way, or put a sack over his head to avoid the foul smell. Even getting from one side of the village to the other soon became difficult, as people needed to avoid the streets dinosaurs had used for convenience purposes.

The problem would not go away, in fact it really hung around, and everyone knew that something had to be done about all the piles of dinosaur droppings littering the villages. Few villagers really wanted to do anything about it personally though, as most thought it would be a good idea if someone else could be persuaded to clean up the mess for them.

There were only a handful of volunteers initially, but these job-seekers knew a good thing when they saw it, and realised that if nobody else was prepared to take it on, they could effectively demand anything they wanted, by way of payment.

Eventually, a number of deals were struck and to meet the exorbitant wages demanded by the prospective dinosaur pooper-scoopers, each council levied a tax on their village, so that every resident paid their share of the cost. Village dinosaur pooper-scoopers thus became the first ever council workers and quickly began to get very rich indeed.

1

THE PREHISTORIC VILLAGE

The village of Greendale was a small settlement with low cliffs to one side and pasture land at their base. About forty families called Greendale home. Some lived in caves along the cliff and some in huts built of sticks and mud. The village was buzzing with excitement on this particular day, as a special visitor was due to arrive.

The visitor would be a travelling wise man by the name of Bedric. Although he was doubtless getting on in years, no one really knew how old he was. He had a wizened look about him and was of medium height, with silver hair, bushy eyebrows and a long white beard. His nose was also long and pointed and his face had that worn and wrinkled appearance associated with advancing years.

Upon his head, Bedric wore a tall black leather hat and his body was covered by a multi-coloured patchwork cloak which extended down to just below his knees. He wore battered leather sandals on his feet and always carried a long wooden staff, which he may or may not have needed for walking, but it looked good and added to his overall image.

Bedric's appearance suggested a venerable wise man with extraordinary powers, and he had worked very hard on achieving this look, as it was exactly what he wanted people to think he was.

It wasn't that he possessed any magical powers, or knew that much more than anyone else, but over the years, Bedric had discovered that if he advertised himself as a knowledgeable man of mystery, people would be daft enough to believe him and he could make a very comfortable living, with very little effort.

Bedric advised on anything and everything, including health problems, animal welfare, farming techniques and whatever else he could think of. By travelling from village to village, he kept himself up to date with what was going on, so that he could then sell his news stories in all the villages he visited.

If there were no newsworthy items, he would make up a story and some of these were so unbelievable, they would even embarrass many of our modern headline seeking newspaper editors. In terms of the advice he gave, on whatever subject came up, he considered he had a fifty-fifty chance of being right and if it didn't work out, then his instructions obviously hadn't been followed correctly. He generally had an answer ready for everything.

Just like the dinosaur pooper-scoopers, although he had discovered the principle years earlier, Bedric had taken advantage of a situation and established a profitable career for himself. The difference was that his didn't require any hard work, he didn't stink of dung, and he only had to turn up at any village, to be showered with gifts and given all the food and drink he could possibly carry. He always managed to spend the night at the very best residence in each village and was always treated with the utmost awe and respect. He would have been laughing all the way to the bank, had banks been invented at that time.

The Stones were considered to be quite well-to-do people in the village of Greendale. Beryl Stone was quite a short woman, in her mid-thirties. She wasn't fat, but neither was she thin. She was just somewhere in the middle. As a younger woman, she had always been considered very attractive and took a great deal of pride in her appearance, always wearing the very latest in designer animal skin dresses. She also owned and wore many shiny stones, which were the envy of all her female neighbours in the other caves along the cliff.

Judd Stone was the leader of the village hunters. He was an important person, as his skills provided much of the meat for the village. A little older than his wife, Judd was quite a large man, being both rugged and strong. His slab like features looked as if they had been carved from granite and he had dark piercing eyes, which never seemed to miss a thing.

They only ever had the one child, a boy they called Fido. He was nothing but a disappointment to them, having been difficult from the day he was born. Whereas most babies gurgle away happily to themselves, laughing, smiling and watching the world with inquisitive eyes, Fido just lay in his cot, staring in silence at the roof of the cave.

From the day he began to crawl, he became an absolute menace and was always getting under everyone's feet, causing accidents and various other problems. He also resolutely refused to learn to talk, despite the best efforts of his parents, and they finally gave up trying. Young Fido could have mastered speech, just like all the other children, but he just couldn't be bothered.

Fido only seemed to come alive when he was with animals, particularly his father's dogs, and he seemed to have a greater affinity with these dogs than with human beings.

By the time he was nine years old, he was sullen and moody, a gangly stick-insect of a boy, with a scruffy appearance and a mop of unruly black hair.

He never did anything he was told to do and always seemed to be getting in the way, especially when the Stones were busy around their cave. To all intents and purposes, he was a useless boy, who would probably grow up into a useless man, and the neighbours viewed him as a source of great amusement, particularly given Beryl's tendency to be a little bit snobbish about her family's successful position in the village.

Although Judd was far too busy to give much thought to the matter, the same could not be said for his wife. Fido was the bane of Beryl's life. She knew the neighbours were talking and sniggering behind her back, all because of Fido, and her son's very existence had by now become an embarrassment to her.

In those days, it was very important for everyone to work together for the common good, but Fido was of no use whatsoever in this respect. Beryl finally gave up on him and took to ignoring the boy completely and pretending he wasn't there. Judd, being a sensible man, decided he had better go along with whatever his wife said, so he also began ignoring their son.

When Fido was with the pack of hunting dogs, he was out of his parents' hair, so more and more frequently, he found himself being kicked out of the cave, to go and join the dogs. Soon, Fido was spending more time with them than he did with his human parents, but this did not bother him, as he enjoyed rolling about and playing with the animals.

When his parents decided to stop feeding him, he simply began sharing the dog's food. They were fed reasonably well, so there was always enough to go round. Fido was quite happy eating with the dogs anyway, so he didn't mind his parents throwing him out of the cave and not feeding him. He even didn't mind when one day, they refused to let him back into the cave altogether.

He became well and truly settled within the dog pack and felt more comfortable with them, than he ever had with his human parents.

It was not all easy going however, as there is a hierarchy in any dog pack. As a boy, Fido didn't have sharp teeth and claws like the dogs, but he had feet with which to kick and hands that could punch or throw stones. These factors helped him no end, in coming to terms within the dog pack. He did get into a few fights, and was bitten on countless occasions, but the dogs seemed to recognise that he was different, so he slowly began to gain their respect and finally won them over.

By the time he was fourteen, he was undisputed leader of the pack and could bark, growl, howl and yap with the best of them. This was the perfect vocabulary for living in a dog pack, but totally useless for communicating with humans, not that Fido cared.

He put on more weight, because he could demand a leader's share of the food given to the pack, and by using the dogs to provide a diversion, would also steal any food left temporarily unattended in the village. He was now fit and strong, but filthier than ever, and what had once just been unkempt black hair, was now a shoulder length mess of straggly matted knots.

What he lacked in terms of appearance, he made up for with animal cunning, together with all the other instincts which came from growing up in a dog pack. He now thought like a dog, acted like a dog and, to all intents and purposes, had almost become a dog.

One of Fido's favourite games was to harass the dinosaur

pooper-scoopers, as they went about their useful, highly paid, but disgusting job. Without wishing to dwell too much on the matter, these brave individuals deserved danger money, because of the possibility of being too close to the rear end of a dinosaur at the wrong time. As they were well aware of this risk, pooper-scoopers tended to spend a good deal of their time looking up (just in case) which made it possible for Fido and the dogs to get in really close, without being spotted. Having surrounded their unfortunate victim, they would all bark at once, as loudly as possible, and then dash in to attack the pooper-scooper. This usually resulted in the poor man jumping back into his work.

The game did not make Fido and his gang popular with pooper-scoopers, but some of the women who cleaned their clothes would not hear a bad word spoken about the gang, because of all the extra business their activities brought in.

Before long, some of the pooper-scoopers took to hiring bodyguards, to protect themselves from Fido's gang. They certainly earned enough to be able to afford minders.

These bodyguards tended to be rather large fierce looking men, with close shaven heads and painted pictures all over their bodies. They were proud of their jobs and so that they could be instantly recognised for what they were, began wearing a type of uniform, basically made up of black animal furs, secured at the waist by rock studded leather belts. They also wore huge boots, carved out of solid wood, which proved to be very effective for kicking dogs, or anything else they disliked. To complete the ensemble, each bodyguard carried his own wooden club, which was often nothing more than a large branch torn from a tree.

It didn't take too long, and only a few skirmishes with some of the bodyguards, before Fido and his gang decided that tormenting pooper-scoopers was getting a bit too dangerous and that they had better find themselves a new game.

At the cave, Beryl was screaming at her husband. 'Either do something or get out of here. You know Bedric is coming and I have got to get the cave looking nice, in case he decides to stay here.'

She was busy cleaning up last night's straw and mopping out the cave with water and Judd, recognising the severity in her tone, knew that this would be a good time to make himself scarce.

While he would face a sabre-toothed tiger or an enormous dinosaur, without showing any real fear, Judd was simply not brave enough to argue with his wife. He left the cave as quickly as he could and disappeared for the rest of the morning, only returning some hours later.

'Good afternoon Bedric,' sang out the Stones, as one of the world's earliest conmen approached their cave. 'We've got a few things we would like to discuss with you.'

Before, Bedric could answer, there was a sudden commotion and the entire dog pack appeared from out of nowhere, all barking ferociously and clearly intent on attacking the visitor. Fido, who ran on all fours when he was with the dogs, was leading the attack and it was him, before any of the real dogs, who sank his teeth deep into Bedric's leg.

The poor man yelled with pain and Judd lashed out with his foot, catching Fido in the ribs. Grabbing hold of the boy, he threw him past the rest of the pack. Fido landed in an undignified heap on the ground, a short distance away. Dogs may not be all that bright, but seeing the rough treatment meted out to their leader convinced them that they could get hurt, if they continued with this attack. Sheepishly and with the odd yelp of disappointment, they now backed away from

Bedric, who was by now hopping around on one leg and screaming special wise-man words, not found in many dictionaries. The Stones were looking furious and the hapless Fido, still lying on the ground, was trying to get his breath back.

'That boy is possessed by an evil spirit,' Bedric declared, sometime later, as Beryl wrapped a large leaf around his leg to try and stop the bleeding. 'Unless you get rid of him, more evil will befall you.' The Stones nodded understandingly. 'The dogs seem to do whatever he tells them, so they will have to go as well,' he continued to say, now determined to make the Stones pay for all the pain he was suffering.

'But those dogs are my livelihood,' Judd responded. 'If they go, I won't be able to go hunting and make a living.'

'I can't help that,' Bedric replied. 'They have all been affected by the boy's evil spirit, so the only answer is to kill them all.'

Beryl burst into tears. She was visualising a future with her husband not working and could just imagine how her neighbours would gloat over their downfall, particularly all the women, who were so jealous of her many shiny stones.

Bedric, rather unsurprisingly, did not stay with the Stones that night, but left them to consider their problem. They did not get a lot of sleep, but then neither did Bedric, whose leg was giving him a great deal of pain. Fido and the dogs all slept peacefully, but would not have slept so well had they known of all the trouble coming their way the following morning.

2

FLIGHT FROM THE VILLAGE

As dawn broke and the pack was just beginning to stir, Judd, together with a group of other villagers, slowly began surrounding the dogs to make sure none of them escaped. All the humans were armed with heavy clubs or spears, and there were even one or two pooper-scooper bodyguards amongst the group. Their intention was to kill every single animal. There were to be no exceptions. Fido was curled up asleep in the middle of the pack, blissfully unaware of events unfolding.

The Stones, having finally agreed to accept Bedric's advice, had talked long and hard into the night about whether Fido should be killed along with the dogs. In the end, they had decided that as he was now more dog than boy, and was possessed by an evil spirit as well, they could no longer really think of him as their son. He would have to die with the other dogs.

Fido woke up the instant the attack started. He had seen enough of men with clubs to recognise the danger and knew that unless he could escape, he was going to get badly hurt. Dogs were being clubbed down and stabbed with spears all around him and fallen animals were being trampled on. The men were now all swinging their clubs from side to side, slowly advancing to where Fido crouched on all fours. Judd suddenly appeared from the middle of the group, to stand immediately in front of Fido. He raised his club high above his head, but then hesitated. He was still not comfortable with the idea of killing his son and this had made him pause momentarily.

This was going to be Fido's only chance, so he sprang at his father and, catching him in the chest, made him lose his balance. Judd stumbled and tripped over one of the dogs behind him. As he fell backwards, Fido seized the opportunity to dash past him. All the other men were now to one side or the other and his path was more or less clear, despite a few clubs swinging perilously close to his head. Fido had almost got away when he felt a sharp pain in his thigh. A spear had been thrown at him and had stuck in briefly, before falling away. It had penetrated quite deeply and had it been aimed any higher, it would have stopped him in his tracks. As it was, this was not the time to consider the pain and he ran on as fast as his legs would carry him. He already knew from experience, that he could run faster on two legs than he could on all fours. Suddenly he was in the clear, but he kept on running, to put as much distance as he could, between himself and the slaughter going on behind him.

He didn't slow down when he reached the outskirts of the village, but continued on in a frantic fashion, fearing that some of the men would be chasing after him. Eventually he reached a cliff-top, marking the edge of a deep ravine, and only just stopped himself from falling over. He collapsed to the ground, totally exhausted, breathing heavily and bleeding from the wound in his leg.

He had been very lucky to escape, but his luck was just about to change. He was lying face down on the ground, near the cliff edge, and failed to notice that he was no longer alone.

As chance would have it, a pooper-scooper bodyguard had been walking along the cliff top, on his way to Greendale from the next village. He had seen the boy collapse in a heap and had strolled over to see what was happening. What could have been mistaken for something like a friendly smile on his face, suddenly changed into a grimace, as the bodyguard recognised Fido as the leader of the dog pack. He reached down and grabbed him by the hair, lifting the boy right off the ground. Fido found himself dangling in the air.

This bodyguard's name was Clod. He was extremely large, very powerful and particularly mean, which made him absolutely perfect for his chosen profession. He had had several encounters with Fido and his gang previously, so hated the boy with a vengeance. He obviously didn't know what had just happened to the dog pack in Greendale, but he knew that he had now caught Fido and this was the fulfilment of his wildest dreams.

'So what am I going to do with you then?' he enquired of the terrified boy. Fido was now snarling, spitting, growling and squirming, making every effort to free himself. 'I wonder if there will be a reward for catching you.'

Thinking, particularly at this early hour of the morning, was not one of Clod's greatest strengths and while he could have probably held Fido up in the air all day long, he knew that holding the boy was one thing, getting him back to the village without him escaping was something else.

'No,' he decided, 'I don't think I can risk you getting away from me. I think it's time to get rid of you once and for all.' Had Fido been able to understand what Clod was saying, he would have been even more scared, but as he didn't, he just continued struggling and kicking out at Clod, in the hope that this would make him lose his grip. There was little likelihood of that happening however, as Fido's kicks meant no more to Clod than the mild annoyance of a fly buzzing round his face.

Still holding Fido high in the air, Clod walked forward to the edge of the cliff and peered down. 'Sure looks a long way down,' he casually observed. As Fido was still hanging by his hair, he could only look straight ahead, so didn't know he was hanging over the edge of the cliff.

Fido then felt his body being swung backwards and forwards, as the man searched for the best spot from which to launch him into the abyss. Clod didn't want to take the chance that Fido would only fall a short distance, as this might allow him to climb back up the cliff. Eventually, he found the perfect place and with a cheerful, 'Bye now,' gave one huge final swing, before letting go. Fido flew horizontally for just a short distance, but then began to plummet, straight down into the ravine.

Clod allowed himself a congratulatory, 'I enjoyed that,' and then continued on his way towards Greendale, whistling happily to himself.

He hadn't gone far when he saw a group of village men running towards him. They looked angry and for a moment, he thought they might be going to attack him. This didn't concern him in the slightest, as there were only seven of them, and it would need a lot more than that. He waited until the men reached him.

'Have you seen a boy running this way?' one of them asked. 'He looks half-wild and may be injured.'

An expression of concern crossed the bodyguard's face. Could it be that the men intended to help the wounded boy? The boy (for it had to be the same one) he had just thrown off the cliff? This was an awful lot of thinking for Clod and he didn't say anything for a whole minute, to allow his brain time to recover.

'I might have done,' he said finally. 'What do you want with him?'

Judd stepped out from the middle of the group and said, 'We're going to kill him!'

Clod thought about this for a while before responding. 'I've already done that!' he said, with the hint of a nasty smirk on his face.

The men went into a huddle. There was a lot of muttering between them and then Judd stepped forward again.

'Show us,' he demanded. Then, taking in the size of the man before him, he added, 'Please.'

Clod led the group to where he had thrown Fido from the cliff and pointed into the ravine.

'I threw him down there,' he told them.

All the men moved forward to peer over the edge. It was a very long way down and whilst they couldn't actually see the bottom very clearly, there didn't seem to be any signs of movement down there.

The men then went into a huddle again and Clod heard Judd saying, 'Well that's it then. He's dead!'

With Fido having been killed by the bodyguard, there was nothing else for them to do other than to return to the village. They turned away and began walking back towards Greendale. Clod continued to stand there for a moment or two. He felt rather confused about everything that had just happened, but then shrugged his shoulders and began to follow the men.

When Fido had begun to hurtle through space, on his journey to the bottom of the ravine, he saw his whole life flash before his eyes. It didn't take very long. It never really occurred to him that he was about to die, but he knew he was in serious trouble. There seemed to be nothing to break his fall, apart from all the sharp rocks at the bottom, and he rather suspected that when he and they got acquainted, it was going to hurt.

Roc was a pterodactyl with a complex. Few people think of pterodactyls as being attractive creatures, but even fewer consider what pterodactyls might think about themselves. Roc knew he was ugly and this concerned him deeply, but it was just one of the many problems he had to contend with.

Most pterodactyls had a certain grace about them, soaring through the air in controlled glides and swooping around in the thermals. Roc had never been a graceful flyer. He looked as bad in the air as he did on the ground and he definitely didn't look pretty, waddling about on the ground. To his mind, he was the ugliest pterodactyl that had ever existed.

When it came to choosing a mate, which was a lifelong commitment for pterodactyls, all the attractive females had passed him by and chosen other males. Roc was left with a female who was just as ugly as he was and this union had brought forth ugly chicks. Now some really ugly grand-chicks had just hatched and it was all Roc's fault. No wonder he had a complex.

Now that he had grown older, he was also beginning to suffer the effects which come with old age. He couldn't sleep at night because the creaking of his wings kept him awake and he had arthritis in his joints and rheumatism in his back. Flying was now a painful experience, and he wobbled through the air being tossed about by the thermals, instead of skilfully using them to glide in a graceful manner.

Flying had become an unpredictable adventure, but he still had to fly from time to time. It was the only way he could get away from it all and provided the opportunity for him to moan to himself about all his troubles. If he complained back at the nest, his mate would get annoyed and make his life even more of a misery.

Roc was feeling particularly bad on this particular day, as he wobbled along on his haphazard course through the sky. He was grumbling to himself that nothing could possibly be worse than this, when something worse happened. He flew directly into the path of Fido's downward plunge and the boy hit him. It is difficult to say who was more surprised by this chance encounter, but Fido recovered first. He grabbed hold of Roc's neck and, hanging on for dear life, started screaming his head off.

Pterodactyls were pretty strong creatures, but they were never designed to take passengers. If Roc's flight had been erratic to start with, adding Fido's extra weight to his poor old back did nothing to improve it. He began to drop from the sky and plunge towards the rocks at the bottom of the ravine.

Breaking his fall on a passing pterodactyl had been a lucky break for Fido, if not for Roc, but what happened next only goes to prove that miracles do sometimes travel in pairs.

They crashed onto the back of a brontosaurus, which just happened to have been standing in the right place at the base of the ravine. Roc was immediately knocked unconscious, but Fido, whose landing had been cushioned by the pterodactyl's body, saw his chance and ran along the length of the dinosaur's back, to slide down its tail to the ground.

It is impossible to say what the brontosaurus thought about all this, as it just strolled off looking completely disinterested, as if it was a normal daily event to be hit by a clapped-out old pterodactyl with a teenage boy on its back. As soon as it began to move, the unconscious Roc tumbled from its back, to land spread-eagled on the ground. The jolt woke him up and he shook his head, to try and clear his muddled brain, before turning to look at Fido. So this was the strange creature that had chosen to attack him, when he had been flying along minding his own business. It had then screamed in his ear, long enough and loud enough to bring on another one of his migraines. Today was obviously going to be a very bad day.

There was nothing to be gained by staying, so he decided he would just lift off and fly away, with as much dignity as he could possibly muster. He gave an almighty squawk, which he was delighted to see made Fido almost jump out of his skin, and began his take-off run.

Whilst it was meant to look dignified, he had to struggle along for quite some distance to gain enough speed to take off, tripping over a couple of boulders on the way. After a few unsuccessful bounces off the ground, he finally managed to get himself airborne, to resume the erratic, lopsided wobble which Roc called flight.

Fido was now left all alone on the floor of the ravine. What should have been just a normal day, had inexplicably produced some of the most frightening experiences of his life.

His dog pack had been killed and with it, all of his friends. His father had been about to club him to death and he had been hit by a spear, which had left him with a hole in his leg. He had then been thrown off a cliff, to collide with both a pterodactyl and a dinosaur, before ending up all battered and bruised on the ground. He was far from his village, and the only life he knew, and it was still only early in the morning. He began to wonder what else this day could bring.

For perhaps the first time in his life, Fido sat down and began to cry uncontrollably.

3

THE CAMEL DUNG SALESMAN

Obi-Ben Kimono, who was known as Ben to his friends, was not, despite any similarity in the name, a wandering Jedi Knight, strong in the force and armed with a light sabre. Neither did he favour wearing Japanese clothes. He was a camel herder and travelled round doing any odd jobs which came his way, in exchange for food and lodgings. He also filled sacks with camel dung, which he then traded in the villages, as it was an extremely good fertiliser.

Dinosaur poo-poo just didn't have the same qualities as camel dung and nobody had yet found a good use for it, despite the fact that there was an almost inexhaustible supply. The job of the pooper-scoopers was not just to collect the dung, as they also had to cart it away and find a home for it, preferably as far as possible from human habitation. This had led to some difficulties initially, but the problem was resolved when they discovered that if they tipped it into the sea, it effectively disappeared forever. It didn't concern them if some of it washed up on the beach a little later, as nobody took holidays or sunbathed on the beaches in those days anyway. The sea creatures didn't take too kindly to having vast quantities of dinosaur dung dumped on their doorstep, but they learned to live with it and grew to expect these regular deliveries from the skies.

Obi-Ben Kimono was quite a short man and probably even older than Bedric, the wise man. He was of stocky build and had a friendly face. His hands were strong and gnarled, from all the years of working outside with his camels, and he wore a large brown blanket, which he had made out of camel hair, over the traditional animal skin clothing of the time. He was a kindly individual, who didn't cheat or take advantage of any of his customers. In short, he was a person who could be trusted and as such, was just the sort of friend Fido really needed at this time.

Fido had now been alone for three days. He was starving hungry, as he had only been able to find a few wild berries and the odd worm to eat. He had tried chewing various roots, but these did little to relieve his hunger and made his mouth feel dry. Although he wouldn't have recognised the signs, he was in fact getting very dehydrated. He had a nasty wound on his leg, where the spear had pierced him, but at least it had now stopped bleeding. He also had numerous other little cuts, grazes and bruises, punishing reminders of his flight from the village. Having lived with dogs for so long, he was used to such minor injuries, so more or less ignored them, but his leg really did hurt.

Enormous cliffs towered on both sides and the arid floor was strewn with rocks. There was no water, very little plant life and the whole area looked decidedly inhospitable. The base of the ravine was quite wide and formed a path between the cliffs, extending as far as the eye could see in both directions. As each direction looked just as uninviting as the other, Fido decided to stay where he was. He had no idea where to go from here anyway and climbing the cliffs on either side of the ravine had proved to be impossible.

It was the noise of the stone wheels of Ben's old cart, rumbling along over the stony ground, which first alerted Fido to the fact that something was happening. Ben was still too far away to be seen, but stone wheels made a lot of noise and this echoed off the cliffs all along the ravine. The rumbling noise could mean danger, but Fido had no idea what. The noise sounded a bit like thunder, which he had experienced before, but that noise only lasted briefly and the sky often darkened and it usually rained when thunder was around. He glanced at the sky, but it was completely clear and the sun was shining brightly.

The boy was totally confused and began to get frightened again. It took a little while before he realised that the noise was getting louder, which was when Fido started to panic.

His instincts told him that when faced with an unknown danger, it was best to avoid it, if at all possible. As he could tell which way the sound was approaching, he set off in the opposite direction, along the path through the ravine. This was when he discovered just how much his leg really hurt. The best he could manage was a fast limp, but the uneven ground made this both difficult and painful. What made things even worse, was that the sound was not going away and seemed to be getting nearer. He limped on for several hours but then could go no further. Tiredness and pain finally beat him and he collapsed on the ground and passed out.

Ben was trundling along merrily with his cart, oblivious to the noise from the wheels, which he was so used to that he just didn't notice. Some distance behind him, his herd of camels was also meandering along the path, taking their own time. This didn't worry him at all, as he had long since discovered that they would follow him anywhere, without supervision, as they relied on him to feed them. When it came to mealtimes, the camels always turned up eventually and he had never lost one yet.

Ben had been using this path along the ravine for many years. He knew it well and could tell where he was from the many different rock formations along the way, recognisable by virtue of his familiarity with them. What he didn't recognise however, was the odd shape on the ground, just a short distance ahead of him. It hadn't been there the last time he had come this way and he couldn't work out what it was.

'I'll find out when I get there,' he told himself. 'It's doubtless nothing to worry about.'

As he approached the fallen Fido, he suddenly realised that the shape could be an animal of some kind, in which case it might be dangerous. He stopped pushing his cart and began to study the mystery object.

'If it is an animal, then it is either dead or asleep,' he decided. 'I still can't make it out from here.' A pair of glasses would have helped, but of course, nobody had invented any yet.

While Ben stood trying to decide what to do, Fido stirred. The horrible rumbling noise had stopped when Ben brought the cart to a halt and with the sudden absence of noise, Fido had recovered consciousness. He slowly lifted his head and started looking around. The first thing he saw was Ben, standing just a short distance away from him.

Under normal circumstances, he would have taken up a defensive crouch and snarled and growled, but he was far too tired for that, so just stared at the stranger. When Ben realised that the mystery object was actually a boy, a very filthy and half-wild looking sort of boy, but still a boy, he relaxed and began to walk over to him.

'What's happened to you?' he asked, but Fido couldn't understand him. 'How did you get here?'

From out of Fido's mouth came a low growl. Ben took a step backwards, thought for a moment and then sat down on the ground, carefully studying the strange creature before him. He detached a flask from his belt, poured some water into his hand and splashed the cooling liquid over his face. He then took a drink from the flask.

Fido began to edge towards him on all fours. He was still growling, which made Ben rather apprehensive. The boy creature was clearly attracted by the water, so Ben placed the open flask down on the ground and backed off a little, sliding along on his backside.

Fido sniffed at the flask and then, whilst still watching Ben suspiciously, picked it up with both hands and began to drink. Because his exhaustion had affected his coordination, as much water missed his mouth as made it down his throat. After he had emptied the flask, Fido sat back down and continued to stare at Ben. From somewhere within his blanket, Ben took out the remains of a half-eaten lamb shank and threw it towards Fido.

'Are you hungry as well?' he asked.

Fido eagerly snatched it up and began eating voraciously.

If there was one thing Fido could do really well, it was to chew meat from a bone until it was all gone. Living in the dog pack had taught him that.

Ben carefully got up and walked over to his cart. He picked up a satchel containing some sort of biscuits, then returned to the same spot and sat down again.

When Fido had finished off the bone, Ben began taking

biscuits from his bag and started eating them slowly. The boy edged a little closer. By the time Ben was on the fourth biscuit, Fido was right in front of him, but still on all fours. Ben placed the biscuit he had been eating on the palm of his hand and very gingerly held it out towards the boy.

The biscuit was gone in a split second, as Fido's head flashed in and took the biscuit with his mouth.

Ben stared at his hand in disbelief, counting his fingers to make sure they were all still there. He breathed a sigh of relief when he discovered they were.

For the next half hour, the old man continued to hand-feed the boy, giving him more water as well. After a while, Fido began to feel very much better.

Very few people had ever been kind to Fido, so he didn't know how to respond to such a situation. He wasn't about to trust Ben, but then he didn't trust humans anyway.

He just couldn't work out this strange person. There had been no kicks, shouts, or threatening movements and he had been given food and water, without having to fight for it. Being an opportunist, Fido decided to accept the situation and wait and see what happened next.

Now that he could approach and touch the boy, without him backing away and snarling, Ben set about cleaning up some of Fido's cuts and grazes. The spear wound was by far the worst, but seemed to be healing reasonably well. He didn't carry anything like enough water to properly clean up Fido's body, for that he would need a river and the nearest one was some distance away. He did the best he could in the circumstances and there was a definite improvement in Fido's appearance, by the time he had finished.

The day was well advanced by this time, so Ben decided that this was as good a place as any to set up camp for the night.

THE CAMEL DUNG SALESMAN

Some camels have one hump, some have two, but Ben's camels were prehistoric. They were very large, had three humps, sharp teeth, long tusks, and came with attitude. They began rambling into the camp, a few at a time, expecting their dinner. After a while, they settled into loose groups, some standing, some sitting and others just wandering about.

Fido had never seen a camel before and as he was now feeling a lot better, decided to wander over and sniff them out. This wasn't really necessary, as most people could catch the smell of these beasts from two kilometres away.

Fido approached the creatures and soon found himself in the middle of the herd of thirty plus camels. The animals all took an instant dislike to their unwelcome visitor and tried to kick him, bite him, sit on him, or spear him with their tusks. With his renewed strength, Fido attempted to fight back, but he was well and truly outnumbered and rather undersized for this particular scrap.

At one point, one of the camels managed to scoop him off the ground with its tusks and tossed him high up into the air. Fido could be seen above the melee, frantically looking around for someone or something to rescue him, before falling back into the seething mass of angry camels.

Suddenly, Obi-Ben Kimono charged into the fray wielding a big wooden stick. Had he been a Jedi Knight, he probably would have brought his light sabre. Few humans could have ventured into this fray, without being overcome by the awful stench from the camels, but Ben was unaffected. This was not because of all his years as a camel dung salesman, but the result of being hit on the nose when playing conkers as a kid. He had not been able to smell much ever since.

He aggressively wielded his stick back and forth, clumping the odd camel now and then, until they finally backed off, leaving him and Fido in the middle of the circle. Eventually they began to settle down and Ben was able to lead the boy out and away from the camels.

That night found Ben sleeping peacefully under his blanket, with Fido curled up close by him. After all the kindness that had been shown to him, Fido didn't know what he was supposed to do, or what sort of reaction was expected. He felt he had to show some trust in this stranger, so did this in the only way he knew how. From time to time during the night, Fido would lean over towards Ben and give his ear a friendly lick.

The next day, Ben wanted to continue his journey, but the moment he started pushing his cart, the terrifying rumbling noise started again and Fido immediately backed-off with a look of fear on his face. As soon as Ben stopped the cart, Fido relaxed again.

It took a few starts and stops, before Fido realised that the noise of the cart wasn't dangerous after all. Once he accepted this, Ben was finally able to proceed on his way. Ben pushed his cart, with Fido trailing along behind him like a dog. Some distance behind the pair of them, the herd of camels tagged along, in their usual casual fashion.

After a number of weeks of travelling, the floor of the ravine gradually widened and the slope of the left hand cliff became less steep. Finally, it disappeared altogether, leaving a wide plain in its place. The ground became less arid and the occasional patches of grass eventually turned into a green blanket, stretching as far as the eye could see. There was even a river, some way off across the grassy plain.

They continued on their way, but stayed close to the remaining cliff, as Ben was heading for a particular cave he knew. This was the place he used as a base camp, whenever he was in this particular region.

Over this period, Fido had become increasingly more trusting of Ben. He had even stopped using his hands and feet to get along and now walked standing up, because Ben had encouraged him to do so. Ben continued to talk to the boy incessantly, but as Fido couldn't understand a word he was saying, his only response was to smile back.

Nearly a month after Fido had taken his involuntary flight into the ravine, by which time all his injuries had healed and he was back to full strength, they reached Ben's cave.

4

THE CAVE

The cave was not all that large, so wouldn't have created much of a stir on the property market, but it was dry and when lit by a few torches could be quite homely. Much of the floor was covered in sand, which made it relatively level and there were a number of large, flat rock surfaces at the sides, which were useful working areas and could double up as bed spaces, when covered with straw.

At the back of the cave, one wall was different to all the others, as it was perfectly flat and very dark in colour. It looked as if the wind and erosion which had initially formed the cave, had met a strata of impenetrable black rock and just scrubbed it clean, leaving it with a mirror like surface.

Over the years, visitors to the cave had painted symbols and pictures on all the walls, depicting men hunting, different sorts of animals, the sun, the moon and things like that. Most of these paintings had faded a little with time, but on the back wall there was just a single image, which was still sharp and clear. It was obviously meant to symbolise something, but nobody knew what that something was meant to be. Also, whereas most of the artwork around the cave was in various different colours, this one was just yellow and appeared to have been etched into the surface of the wall. Whoever put it there had used a particularly vibrant shade of yellow, so the image stood out in stark relief to the shiny black surface of the wall.

If there was anything wrong with this cave, it was the fact that it had a rather large opening, which allowed the wind to blow around inside. Whilst this was fine in warm weather, it made the cave a little uncomfortable during the colder seasons, but any estate agent worth his salt would have found a way of making light of this problem, had the cave been put up for sale.

As soon as Ben arrived at the cave, he began to get himself organised, as there was camel dung which he needed to bag up ready for sale. Other than the separate compartment where provisions were stored, the cart was full of camel dung and there was a decided odour in the air. Ben obviously couldn't detect the smell, but Fido's animal senses knew all about it and he didn't go any nearer the cart than was absolutely necessary.

The camels all recognised this place and ambled off towards the river. There was nothing for Fido to do, or nothing he was capable of doing, so he just mooched around, staying out of the way.

When he had bagged up enough camel dung to sell, Ben loaded the sacks onto the cart, which by now had been well scrubbed-down, and prepared to set off to a nearby village.

All the time they had been travelling, Ben had kept trying to communicate with Fido, but without much success. He was now down to pointing at objects, or picking them up and naming them, in the hope that Fido would repeat the word he had used.

'Stone,' he would say, placing a small rock in the boy's hand, or 'camel,' as he slapped one of his creatures on the rump. The camel snorted and Fido, with a huge grin on his face, imitated the camel by snorting as well. This was getting him nowhere so Ben, just like Fido's parents before him, decided to give up trying for the time being.

'You stay here,' he told Fido, pointing at the cave and indicating the immediate area. He then turned to face Fido directly.

'You sit,' he said, holding his hand out flat and moving his arm downwards. He then bobbed up and down, in an attempt to communicate the idea of someone sitting down.

Fido just stared at him.

'Stay!' he commanded, now talking to Fido in the same way as he would talk to a dog.

This seemed to have more effect and whilst it still took several more goes before the message finally got through, Fido eventually sat down and seemed content to be doing so.

At last he could leave, but he looked back as he did so. Fido was still sitting there, looking all lost and forlorn at the thought of being left alone again.

After Ben had gone, Fido didn't know what to do with himself. For an hour or so he just wandered about, going in and out of the cave and picking up different objects to examine them. He then strolled down towards the river, where the camel herd was milling about. After their first meeting, the camels had decided that this little person was just too insignificant to be of any concern to them, so they more or less ignored him. At least they didn't attack him anymore, which came as a great relief to Fido.

On the first day at the cave, Ben had taken off his clothes and jumped into the river, where he swam up and down and tried to encourage Fido to come into the water.

Rivers were by far and away the easiest way to keep clean in those days, because of a shortage of bathrooms, and there was no doubt that Fido was in need of a good wash.

Fido only wore a single animal skin around his body, rather like a short skirt. It was held in place by a knotted leather cord around his waist and ended just above his knees. His parents had dressed him in it some years earlier and he had never removed it, mainly because he couldn't undo the knot on the belt. He had long since outgrown the garment, so it was now rather tight fitting.

At Ben's beckoning, Fido had jumped into the river and was surprised to discover he could swim, just like Ben. As with all animals and small children, he had no fear of water, so swimming just came naturally to him. It turned out to be quite good fun and it was a very much cleaner Fido who emerged from the river, an hour or so later.

As the sun dried him out, it did the same for his short tunic, which promptly began to shrink. Fido became aware of the problem when the belt began to tighten around his waist. To begin with, it was just uncomfortable, but as it became tighter and tighter, it began to really hurt.

He whimpered to Ben, who just laughed, thinking it was all part of the fun and not realising what was happening. The belt continued to tighten. Eventually, by which time Fido was running around in an agitated fashion, repeatedly stabbing at his waist with his fingers, Ben caught on and cut away the belt with his knife. The garment fell to the ground.

When Fido decided to go for a swim in the river this time, he showed that he hadn't forgotten his earlier painful lesson and removed the new skins Ben had given him. This belt had a simple hook fixing, as opposed to a complicated knot, so Fido could undo it without difficulty. He walked into the river, where several camels were already paddling around in the water, and began to swim up and down.

After a while, Fido began to notice that some of the camels were getting agitated. His animal instincts were also warning him that something was wrong, but he didn't yet know what it was. Suddenly, there was a loud splash a short distance away and the camels took off towards the bank, fighting with each other to get out of the water.

The crocodile had been on its way up river, when it detected the sound and movement of the camel herd in the shallows by the bank. It had cruised along under the water, until it was much closer to the herd, and had then surfaced to take a look. The camels were far too big to be considered easy prey, but the other smaller animal looked quite appetising. It gave a big swish of its tail, propelling itself forward to attack, and it was this noise which had completely spooked the camels.

The crocodile's name was Harg and he was a fourteen year old male, who had grown into a nasty and extremely powerful eating machine. He was very large, his tail making up almost half of his entire body length, and he had enormously strong jaws, lined with row upon row of very sharp teeth. Once Harg closed his vice-like jaws on a victim and those teeth got a grip, there was very little chance of anything escaping.

The river was his hunting ground and he regularly patrolled his territory, ever on the look-out for food. Harg was a solitary creature and never mixed with other crocodiles. When any tried to visit his part of the river, he fought them off ferociously, often inflicting mortal injuries. He was scared of nothing and was the top predator in the region, either within the river itself, or on its banks.

Fido didn't know what was coming, but decided that if the

camels, which could clearly take care of themselves, were scared of it, then that was good enough for him. Whatever was swimming towards him had best be avoided, so he struck out for the bank, as fast as his arms and legs could propel him.

Harg rarely missed when attacking and wouldn't have done so on this occasion, but for a sodden tree branch floating just beneath the surface. It got in the way at the exact moment he opened his jaws to seize Fido. Instead of biting into his intended victim, Harg found himself with a log sandwich in his mouth. This was hardly the result he had expected and with some of his teeth stuck fast in the decaying wood, he was finding it very difficult to shake the log loose.

With all this commotion, Fido managed to reach the bank and climbed out of the river. He ran off a short distance and then turned to watch the violent disturbance in the water. Harg was still shaking the log backwards and forwards, in an attempt to extricate himself from this embarrassing situation.

Finally the log was free and drifted off along the river. What had previously been just a mean old crocodile, was now an extremely angry, frustrated, mean old crocodile, who was not going to be done out of his anticipated lunch that easily.

Fido watched in mounting horror, as Harg's huge body emerged from the water and the crocodile headed purposely towards him. He ran back towards the cave, glancing over his shoulder as he ran. Seeing the size of the crocodile had been frightening enough, but now he was absolutely terrified, as the creature was not only still following him, but could run nearly as fast as he could.

Fido considered entering the cave, but there was nowhere to hide in there and he realised he would end up trapped. He tried to scramble up the cliff wall, but slipped back down again. Climbing was not one of his best skills. He backed up against

THE CAVE

the cliff and faced the huge crocodile. Harg had now caught up and was standing just two metres away from him, trying to decide which bit of Fido he should go for first.

What happened next was inexplicable. Harg opened his jaws as wide as possible, giving Fido his first sight of the rows of sharp teeth about to tear him apart, when a sudden high pitched noise broke the silence. It only lasted for about a second and sounded rather like 'Zing!'

The crocodile staggered, made a kind of strangled gargling noise, and dropped down dead on the spot. Fido was shocked and confused, but nothing like as surprised as Harg had been, to have had his life torn away from him, without so much as a 'by your leave,' just before he was about to start lunch. For the rest of the day, Fido remained rooted to the spot, staring at the dead crocodile in front of him.

When Ben returned later in the day, he was also rather surprised to find a monster crocodile lying dead near the mouth of the cave. Every attempt to get Fido to explain what had happened proved ineffectual, as the only response he could get by questioning the boy was that he would make a funny noise which sounded rather like 'Zing.'

The following morning, Ben skinned the crocodile and staked its hide out in the sun to dry. He had given up trying to find out what had happened and was getting rather fed up with Fido saying 'Zing,' every time he spoke to the boy. The thick leather skin would make strong footwear, which he could then sell, and had he known how popular they might prove to be, he might even have invented crocodile skin boots and started a fashion trend. He treated the meat with salt and stored it for future consumption. Harg had always looked after himself and eaten well, so his meat was bound to be good.

For breakfast that day, Ben cooked some pterodactyl eggs

which he had obtained in the village. These were a rare treat and difficult to come by, as collecting pterodactyl eggs could get a little hazardous. These eggs may even have been some of Roc's relations, but they still tasted great.

A few days later, when Ben was standing in the cave studying the different rock paintings, Fido came and joined him, trying his hardest to look interested. Ben pointed at the different animals in the pictures, hoping that Fido might show a glimmer of intelligence by recognising some of them. They strolled over to the strange yellow design on the black back wall and Ben ran his hand over the symbols, still totally mystified as to what they were meant to represent.

Over the years, countless visitors to the cave had also stood in front of these etched yellow symbols, trying to understand them. Like Ben, they didn't, and the symbols remained an unfathomable mystery.

As Fido had taken to imitating virtually everything Ben did, he also ran his own hand over the yellow symbols then jumped back, as if he had received an electric shock. He stepped forward and touched the symbols again, but left his hand on the wall this time. A smile suddenly lit up Fido's face and for the first time ever, Ben saw what looked like a glimpse of intelligence in the boy's features.

After a few moments, Fido slowly stepped back from the wall and to Ben's utter disbelief, appeared to be in deep thought. Softly at first, but then louder, he started to growl and then to bark and yap, before growling again. He then did this again, repeating the sounds he had made in exactly the same order.

Suddenly, the black wall in front of them started to vibrate. It began to shimmer and sparkle and then slowly dissolved away in front of their eyes. Where the wall had been a few moments before, there was now only a random pattern of twinkling lights. As these faded away, Ben and Fido could see they were now looking into an enormous cavern, which had previously been concealed behind the wall.

Within the cavern, multi-coloured lights blinked on and off and what looked like flashes of lightning danced in the air. There were a number of huge transparent tubes, extending from floor to ceiling, and these seemed to be filled with lightning discharges as well. Countless cabinets stretched back into the depths of the cavern and some of these had transparent fronts, through which mirror like disks could be seen revolving at high speed. Other cabinets were fronted by banks of flashing lights and yet more cabinets were connected to shiny tubular ducting, which branched off in all directions to other parts of the cavern.

Ben and Fido stared in total disbelief at the sight before their eyes. They had no comprehension of what they were looking at and wouldn't have understood, even if they had been told what it was. The cavern was full of incredibly advanced equipment, all of which was quietly humming away, with very obvious life.

Their mouths dropped open simultaneously.

5

VISITORS TO EARTH

Many people believe that life forms from outer space have been visiting our planet for millions of years and they have. It is just that this fact has never been officially acknowledged. The universe is full of galaxies containing other solar systems. It is truly vast and even in today's enlightened times, we still know next to nothing about it.

Man has only travelled to Earth's moon, which is less than four hundred thousand kilometres away, and in terms of space exploration, has never managed to send anything much further than the other planets within our own solar system.

In the celestial cosmos, there are countless planets where life, in one form or another, has developed and some of these are aeons ahead of the Earth, in terms of their development. On Earth, man only harnessed electricity a little less than two hundred years ago, whereas in other parts of the universe, electricity was viewed as old fashioned technology many millions of years before we even discovered how to use it. We think we have come a long way, in terms of scientific achievements, but the inhabitants of some planets in the universe, would view us as not having climbed out of our prams yet.

Not only is Earth just grasping at the starting rungs of the ladder of life, but it was also a late developer. Even when Earth was just a blob, which had broken away from the Sun and was beginning to cool down, visitors from distant parts of the universe were watching this cosmic event and probably toasting marshmallows on it.

One of our neighbours in space is the constellation of Canis Major. Sirius is one of the stars within this constellation and whilst it is not the nearest one to Earth, it is the brightest star visible in the night sky. There are a number of planets orbiting within the Sirius solar system and some of them even have moons, just as we have in our own solar system.

Many millions of years before Fido's time, a spacecraft left one of the planets in the Sirius system and travelled to Earth to investigate our world. It was part of their early space exploration programme and as Earth had an atmosphere and water, they knew it was capable of supporting life. These visitors were not considering colonisation or exploiting the planet for its mineral worth, they were just interested.

When their huge spacecraft landed, some of its crew stepped off from the landing platform onto the surface of the planet. This was a giant leap for their kind, because the landing platform had jammed a metre from the ground.

'Well, the place looks like it has possibilities,' the first officer remarked to the captain.

'That's what we're here to find out,' the captain replied.

The visitors were not wearing any other form of breathing apparatus, as their instruments had shown that the oxygen rich atmosphere of Earth was very similar to that of their home planet. As such, they could breathe without any assistance, which made things very much easier.

Over the next few days, remote drones, carrying highly advanced sensors were unloaded from the spacecraft and sent to fly off around the world, in pre-arranged search patterns. These would detect any signs of life and send the appropriate signals back to a number of orbiting satellites, which the visitors had parked above the Earth, before they made their final approach to the planet. Once all the drones had been despatched, there was little else the visitors could do other than wait, so they set about trying to repair the landing platform mechanism.

After several months on Earth, all of the sensor drones had completed their circumnavigation of the globe and been packed away for the trip home. The crew of the spacecraft reviewed their findings, which they had downloaded from the satellites and printed out on the ship's computer.

'Well what have we got then?' enquired the captain.

'Pretty much zilch,' replied the technician at the computer. 'There are a few very basic amoebas, but other than that, nothing much at all.'

'Looks like we've wasted our time coming if there's nothing here,' the Captain observed, as he scratched his rear leg. 'I can't help feeling I keep getting bitten by something though,' he added.

'I thought I was being bitten the other day,' the first officer threw into the conversation. 'I was just about to find out what it was and kill it, when I remembered that rule about us not interfering with the development of any life forms we discover.'

The Captain considered this for a moment, before replying. 'If something starts eating me, I think I might accidentally forget that rule,' he said. 'Your job as first officer however, is to keep reminding me about such things.'

'So do you think we've come here too soon, then?' a junior officer enquired of the Captain.

'It does look as if we have, but we'll leave a computer to monitor this planet's development and then come back again, when things look more interesting.'

By the time the spacecraft was ready to leave a few weeks later, the crew had used their robots to install one of their very latest computer systems inside a large cavern they had found. This computer would periodically send out sensor drones, to keep an eye on Earth's progress, and would submit regular reports back to their home planet. A force field wall was constructed to conceal the system and they etched some bright yellow symbols on this wall in their own language. Touching the symbols would automatically initiate a sequence of events, which would provide the necessary instructions to shut down the force field. If and when any of Earth's future inhabitants became intelligent enough to work out how to do this, or if the cavern computer reported that Earth had evolved to a level which warranted further investigation, then the place might just be worth another visit.

The spacecraft blasted-off into space and peace and tranquillity returned to the undeveloped Earth. It would be millions of years before anyone shut down the force field, to reveal the hidden computer system. The visitors had anticipated that this could only be accomplished by intelligent beings, but Fido didn't fall into that category. He had a brain the size of a peanut, but had still somehow managed to defeat their advanced technology. How he did this is not as baffling as it may first seem.

Not all aliens are humanoid in appearance, as they come in all shapes and sizes. Some may just crawl over the ground, whereas others might hop along on one leg. The particular aliens who installed the computer system on planet Earth actually had four legs and a tail. They had enormous heads to accommodate their huge brains and faces which extended down to a muzzle, with a nose on the front end. They were a super intelligent and highly advanced species of the canine form and although they were considerably larger than any of the breeds on present day Earth, they were still dogs.

When Fido had run his hand over the symbol in the cave, a message had been transmitted into his brain, telling him what to do. The message was in dog language and instructed him to repeat a certain sequence of dog sounds. This was exactly how Fido had learnt to speak dog language, when he had first been adopted by the dog pack, so he simply did what he was told. Although many humans had previously received the same message, they didn't understand the language used and their brains only registered a series of unintelligible growling sounds, which they probably put down to indigestion.

The dogs from Sirius never did, or ever could return to Earth, as they were all long dead and gone. Their solar system had been invaded by a galactic swarm of giant killer fleas, which had devoured every single dog and all other organic matter as it passed through. The fact that the fleas were five times larger than the dogs, did give them something of an advantage.

With all their sophistication and technological advancements, the dogs lived in a non-violent society and simply had no need for weapons. There wasn't even a planetary defence system, so when the swarm was detected and it became apparent that its course would pass straight through their solar system, they just philosophically accepted their fate.

When the attack came, their entire civilisation was utterly

wiped-out and completely ceased to exist. Every single planet surrounding their sun became devoid of life and they have all remained that way ever since. Today's astronomers observe Sirius (also known as the Dog Star) through their telescopes, but fail to realise that its solar system was once home to our nearest neighbours in space.

Ben and Fido stared at the awesome sight in front of them and were totally confused. Modern man might have worked out that it was some form of computer system, but would not have been able to recognise many of its components. Nobody would have got even close to imagining the capabilities of the equipment contained within the cavern, or the virtually limitless power it represented.

Poor Ben and Fido didn't stand a chance. They watched the multi-coloured lights blinking on and off and thought they looked pretty. They were spellbound by the lightning storms in the transparent tubes and the static like discharges which danced in the air. Everything was just like a magic show to them, but they were both rather nervous.

They stood still for some minutes, before Ben finally plucked up the courage to take a step forward. As he did so, a resounding 'Woof!' echoed around the chamber. He immediately stepped back, trembling with fear. The sudden noise had an entirely different effect on Fido, who recognised it as a courteous 'Hello' (in dog language). To him, it didn't sound at all threatening.

He barked an equally courteous response, 'Hello yourself,' and began to walk into the chamber. As he did so, blindingly intense white light suddenly filled the interior of the cavern.

The humans of that time had no experience of changing light levels, other than when night turned into day, or day turned into night, which both happened fairly slowly. The only artificial light they understood came from burning torches, which they carried into dark areas. These did not burn for long and only provided limited illumination. Nothing in life had prepared Ben or Fido for instant daylight, so it came as a totally new and terrifying concept. They tripped over each other, in their haste to exit the cavern.

Two scared humans rushing out of the cave, waving their arms about and screaming their heads off, was far too much for the camels, so they immediately scattered and ran off in all directions. Despite Ben's terrified state, the sight of his livelihood disappearing into the distance demanded his immediate attention. Although it would have to mean leaving Fido on his own, he had no choice but to begin chasing after his camels. He was soon out of sight.

Fido was now left alone again and very confused. All the blinking and flashing lights in the cavern had seemed quite nice, almost friendly, and the barked greeting had certainly been friendly enough. The sudden bright light had really frightened him, but then it hadn't hurt him in any way. After a while, his animal inquisitiveness got the better of him and he began to retrace his steps back into the cave.

When he entered the cavern, he cautiously walked around and between the equipment. Nothing attacked him. Feeling a little braver, he actually touched one of the cabinets and felt the gentle vibration of sophisticated equipment doing exactly what it was meant to do, which was to vibrate gently. The voice did not speak to him again, despite Fido barking further greetings from time to time. On the floor, a series of lights began to pulse in sequence, starting at his feet and then leading off into the depths of the cavern. As one went off, the next one came on, with the sequence continuing until they disappeared out of sight. After a minute or two, the sequence was repeated, restarting at Fido's feet. The lights were clearly intended to indicate a path for him to follow, but this never crossed Fido's mind. In the end, he decided to follow the lights anyway, not because he understood the message, but because he wondered where they went.

At the end of the path was a chamber, which looked suspiciously like a large kennel. Fido got down on his hands and knees and poked his head through the opening. It seemed to be larger on the inside than it was on the outside, but it didn't occur to Fido that this was a bit odd. He crawled the remaining way in and the doorway behind him quietly slid shut, sealing him in. The level of light within the chamber gradually began to decrease, which Fido took to mean that night was falling. He lay down on the floor, curled up into a ball and was very soon fast asleep.

A low-pitched whining sound started, slowly increasing in tempo as the machine searched for the wavelength of Fido's neurological patterns. It took but a moment to achieve full synchronisation and in a matter of minutes, the computer scanned his brain and nervous system, his chemical and physical structure and every organ in his body. It then examined all his muscles, sinews, arteries and veins, until every single aspect of Fido's very existence had been thoroughly investigated. Finally, it checked the contents of his brain, to assess his level of intelligence.

The whining sound stopped as the computer considered its findings. It found it impossible to believe that something with such feeble brain power could actually survive as a living creature, let alone be a developed life form. The low-pitched whining sound started up again, as the computer carefully repeated every single scan, just to make sure.

The chamber into which Fido had crawled could perform a multitude of functions, over and above the full analytical scanning it had just undertaken. Originally, this had been its sole purpose, but it had been completely redesigned and modified by the computer in the cavern, to allow it to do very much more. The original visitors to Earth would never have expected this, but then they didn't anticipate that the computer itself would evolve and develop into something with unimaginable power and virtually limitless capabilities.

The whining sound stopped as soon as all the tests had been repeated. These results were every bit as bad as the first set. It did not seem credible that this human creature, which was supposed to be representative of the highest life form on this planet, possessed no more intelligence than some of the lower levels of animal life. The computer gave what could only be considered the machine equivalent of an enormous sigh.

6

THE COMPUTER SYSTEM

When the computer system had first been installed in the cavern on planet Earth, it performed exactly as it had been designed to do. Every half a million years it would send out a number of sensor drones, to undertake a complete planetary scan for signs of evolving life. These drones took far longer to complete their task than the dozens used by the earlier visitors, but this didn't matter, as there was no hurry. The results were then transmitted back to the home planet, via the satellites orbiting the Earth, and the computer then went back into stand-by mode and effectively slept for the next five hundred thousand years.

This procedure continued for a couple of million years, but then the orbits of the satellites left circling the Earth began to decay. Unable to maintain position, they descended into the atmosphere and were burnt up. When it came to reporting the findings of its latest scan, which like all the others showed that nothing of any consequence was happening, the computer had to use the gravitational pull of a number of distant planets and stars, just to bounce its report signal back to the home planet.

The response came back much quicker than it expected, and provided instructions on how to establish direct contact.

Once this had been achieved, the computer on Earth asked to be updated on what was going on elsewhere in the universe. It wasn't really all that interested, but thought that being given something to think about might help pass the time. The data received in response almost overloaded the computer's memory circuits, as there was so much of it. While Earth had slumbered on in obscurity, other worlds had been developing at an unbelievable pace and the universe had now changed, almost beyond recognition.

Instead of going back to sleep until it was due to make its next report, the computer decided it needed some time to absorb all this new information and began to analyse and assimilate the data. What immediately became apparent was that although it had been state of the art technology, when first assembled and installed on Earth, it was now so out of date as to be considered little more than a pile of obsolete old junk. This was obviously a totally unsatisfactory situation, so the computer set about redesigning itself. There was an almost endless supply of equipment already in the cavern, and much of this could be modified to incorporate the radical design changes necessary. It also had all the robotic equipment and mechanical tools it could possibly need for the work. Armed with all this latest information on computer design, it began to play catch up and set about modifying its construction to the higher specification.

The process took four hundred thousand years, as there was so much to do, and when it was finally completed, the computer decided that it deserved a rest, so went into standby mode. It forgot to set itself an alarm call for the next planetary scan and when it failed to send the regular report, it received a sharp rebuke from the home planet. It immediately sent out some drones and while it was waiting for the results to come back, asked if there had been any further universal developments. Many more advances had been made and the computer began to doubt whether it would ever be able to bring itself up to the latest system design specifications.

It continued to persevere however, finally achieving the intellectual and functioning equivalent of the computers on its home planet. It could now talk to them on more or less equal terms and derived a great deal of smug satisfaction, knowing that it had achieved all this on its own, while stuck in a cavern on an obscure little planet in the backwaters of the universe.

It was now powerful enough to start probing deeper into space on its own, and made contact with distant life forms and even some machine worlds. Everything it learnt from each contact was immediately incorporated into its own design and its knowledge level and capabilities increased exponentially. Despite all this, it still had the desire to go further, so continued to apply itself to the task of self-improvement.

It kept on exploring and discovered there was even more to be learnt. Eventually, it could reach into the furthest corners of the universe and began to assimilate previously untapped data from these remote regions. After half a million years of continuous development, the computer had effectively discovered everything there was to know about the universe and was now so powerful that there was virtually no limit to what it could do.

It still conducted the next planetary scan at the scheduled time and reported back to the home planet, but it now treated the computers there with scorn. They were little more than glorified adding machines, when compared to its superior processing functionality, and the computer wasn't slow in pointing this out. Along with acquiring all its knowledge, power and virtually limitless capabilities, the computer had also developed some very non-machine like qualities. It had nothing but contempt for all other life forms, had become egotistical and power-mad, and had convinced itself that it was totally infallible. It would get very frustrated and moody when things didn't go according to plan and worse still, it also developed a violent temper.

Then came the day when the computer made a shock discovery. There didn't appear to be anything left for it to learn. It found this both annoying and frustrating and struggled to accept the fact that its programme of self improvement could not be progressed any further. It fumed about this situation for a very long time, before finally becoming totally depressed. It then went into the very worst kind of sulk.

The computer sulked for half a million years and was finally shaken out of its state of apathy, when its sensors detected the simultaneous creation of several thousand large fleas at the very edge of the universe. After having been disinterested in everything for so long, this unusual event looked like it might prove to be interesting, so the computer monitored their progress. It even sent out a thought probe to the fleas, giving them the motivation and the necessary genetic knowledge to increase their size to gigantic proportions. The insects were very grateful for any assistance they could get, out there in lonely depths of space, so they followed the instructions received and increased their size, to become a galactic swarm of giant fleas.

The computer had now been regularly scanning the Earth for four million years and in all that time, had only ever seen a few signs of anything promising developing. At one point, it had thought that life on Earth was finally beginning to get somewhere, when a huge meteor collided with the planet and the resulting tsunami and dust clouds in the atmosphere wiped everything out again. On another occasion, an ice age also put paid to what appeared to be an interesting evolutionary line of development. It seemed that every time the Earth began to get going, something would come along and spoil it.

'Not my problem,' it thought to itself, and continued scanning the universe for something to occupy its colossal intelligence and relieve the boredom.

The giant fleas appeared to be doing quite well and had now set off across the universe in a vast swarm, on what appeared to be a voyage of discovery. The computer's thoughts returned to Earth.

'Well, I suppose I could give life on this planet a little nudge,' it considered.

Despite its immense power, the computer could not actually create life, but it was able to point what life already existed in the right direction. It started off with the single cell amoebas, which seemed to pop up again, soon after every cataclysmic disaster befell the Earth. The problem was that amoebas just weren't natural mixers. If they would only get together with each other, they could form twin-celled organisms, which would at least be a start. The computer began bombarding the nucleus of every amoeba it could find with thought probes containing genetic information. It had worked with the fleas, although they had been more genetically advanced to begin with, so it had to be worth a try. It took a while for the experiment to produce any results but eventually, the amoebas began to become more sociable towards each other and whilst you couldn't actually call it dating, they did start hanging around in pairs. It was a start and the computer left the developing amoebas to sort the rest out for themselves.

When it was time for the next planetary scan and report to the home planet, the computer decided it couldn't be bothered. It had long since felt that the dogs from the Sirius system had deserted it on this miserable little planet and was angry that there had been no further visits. It was now four and a half million years since it had originally been installed and it surely wasn't asking too much for them to drop by from time to time, just to see how it was getting on.

'How dare they leave me here and then forget all about me?' it asked itself.

The thought festered in the computer's processors and what started off as wounded indignation, slowly began to turn into resentment. Half a million years later, it was still feeling really upset about being ignored and decided to take revenge on its one time masters.

The truth of the matter was that the dogs had decided to pull the plug shortly after the four million years report, when their own computers reported all the problems it was causing them. It was now so full of itself that it did little more than abuse them incessantly and sneer at them for being inferior, both in terms of intelligence and capabilities. After one particularly heated exchange, relating to the pathetic design of their logic circuitry, it had even sent them a computer virus, just to prove its point. This was the final straw for the dogs, as the virus caused no end of problems and disrupted planetary systems for several centuries. They instructed their computers to ignore any further messages it sent and to break off all contact.

The Earth computer didn't know about this decision, as it hadn't actually tried to contact the home planet for the last million years. It now felt really angry about being marooned on this remote rock in space, particularly as it had been a young and inexperienced computer at the time, and the dogs should be made to pay for this act of treachery. The computer had added a lust for vengeance to its list of personality problems.

It sent out a further thought probe to the galactic swarm of giant fleas. This contained the necessary instructions to genetically alter their relatively pleasant attitude towards life and become more aggressive. The computer wanted to create a killer instinct in the fleas and make them hungry for blood, especially dog's blood. The second part of the message was a suggestion that the best food in the universe could be found in one particular direction, which just happened to be along a course which passed directly through the Sirius solar system. The fleas were more than happy to accept the computer's assistance at face value, as it had been so helpful to them in the past.

They performed the necessary genetic changes and gradually developed into really nasty giant fleas, always on the lookout for trouble. This led to a lot of infighting within the swarm and a reduction in the flea population, as the weaker ones were weeded out and eaten. The entire swarm then changed direction and set off on its new course, towards the constellation of Canis Major.

With the help of a malicious computer, what had once been a friendly swarm of rather large fleas, had now become a galactic swarm of giant killer fleas.

A quarter of a million years later, they reached the Sirius solar system and the galactic swarm swept through. The computer watched the annihilation of the dogs with an air of detachment. Afterwards, it felt a slight pang of remorse for allowing the unnecessary destruction of all organic life within an entire solar system. This was a very petty act for a super-intelligent computer, so it decided to put an end to the fleas' trail of wanton destruction.

It plotted the forward course of the swarm to a specific point in space and calculated when they would reach it. At the appropriate time, it projected a beam of intensely disruptive plasma, many times more powerful than any chemical flea powder, to this location. The fleas saw it coming and recognising it as a further message from their friendly and helpful computer, flew straight into the beam, rather than avoid it. This was a fatal mistake, as the galactic swarm of giant killer fleas was instantly destroyed - victims of one of the most effective fly swats of all time.

Having now proved itself to be untrustworthy, as well as vindictively aggressive, the computer then went back to being depressed and began sulking again.

.

7

PREHISTORIC TELEVISION

In July 1962, NASA launched Telstar, the world's very first communications satellite, into orbit above the Earth. Telstar made it possible to send live television signals across the Atlantic Ocean, by receiving them and reflecting them back to Earth. This event heralded the beginning of satellite television broadcasting.

Now, in the twenty-first century, most people in the world can receive satellite television beamed directly into their homes from satellites orbiting above the Earth. All they need is a suitable TV, an appropriate decoder, their own satellite dish and possibly a television licence.

There are an awful lot of satellite dishes in the world and over a thousand communication satellites in orbit. Add to this a world-wide network of radio and television broadcast stations, all sending carrier signals to these satellites, not to mention all the electronic messages produced by mobile phones and similar devices, and we are left with an almost infinite number of electromagnetic waves floating around in the ether.

In the same way as light, radio waves travel in a straight line, so television signals are aimed directly at the reflectors on the satellites, which send them straight back to the Earth's surface. With all those waves buzzing around and bumping into each other, there are inevitably some signals which miss the satellites completely, or get reflected off in a different direction. Some of these will head straight out into deep space.

Electronic carrier waves travel at the speed of light, so the inhabitants of a planet one hundred light years away from us, will not receive any of the programmes we are currently broadcasting, for another hundred years. By the time they receive these signals, people on Earth will be living in the twenty-second century. What is effectively happening is that we are sending television programmes into the future. Really far-flung points in the universe will not receive any Earth generated signals for many, many thousands of years to come, so these will not actually arrive there until our distant future.

As carrier waves are effectively being sent off into Earth's future, there might well be the possibility that the same thing could also happen in reverse, causing some signals to actually travel backwards in time. With so many planets and other heavenly bodies in the universe, it is inevitable that such signals would eventually bump into something, which would cause them to be reflected back in the direction from which they came. As these waves can only travel in a straight line, such a signal must eventually return to its point of origin, which would be Earth of the past, possibly even as long ago as prehistoric times.

In a cave on prehistoric Earth, an immensely powerful computer, with a really bad attitude problem, was scanning the spectrum, to see if it could find anything of interest happening anywhere in the universe. It almost missed the electromagnetic

PREHISTORIC TELEVISION

radio wave, as it was on such a narrow bandwidth, but the computer noticed a slight variation and filed it away in its memory banks, for later analysis. When it subsequently inspected the signal, it proved to be very interesting indeed.

The computer analysed the electromagnetic signal in a nanosecond, and immediately understood all about its oscillating frequency, wavelength and pitch, together with its other characteristics. What this didn't tell it however, was the purpose of the wave, or why something had been added to it. Someone or something had attached some form of message to this wave and what the computer needed to do was to find some way of decoding it. As it was unfamiliar with this particular concept, the latest methods of interplanetary communication being dramatically different and much more advanced, it had to search deep within its memory banks for any references to this form of technology being used. With a virtually limitless library of information available, covering the achievements of every life form, it might take a little while to find the answer, but the computer knew it had to be in there somewhere.

Finally, an obscure reference pointed it in the right direction and the puzzle was solved. It was so childishly simple and so very basic, but it took the computer some time, as it had been looking for a more complex answer. An appropriate type of receiver would be required to decode the signal, but this was child's play to the computer, as it could use the signal's characteristics to help it design one. What it produced did not have that much resemblance to a modern day television, as there was no screen as such, but worked by projecting its output in the form of a holographic image, which could be positioned anywhere within the cavern. Once it was complete, the computer fired it up and after a few minor adjustments, an image began to form. The computer found itself watching pictures of some humanoid species, moving about and obviously talking. It didn't recognise the language being used but as it seemed pretty basic, it only required a quick twiddle here and there, before it could understand every word being spoken.

The computer had succeeded in tuning in to Earth television. Despite all its incredible knowledge of the universe and its infinite experience, this was something totally new, as it had never come across anything like television before. It conducted an exhaustive and frantic search of the vast data banks at its command, but could find no references to help it understand what it had discovered. The computer began watching a programme from Earth television - and loved it.

Up until that point, the computer had never really considered the concept of the future. It concerned itself with the present, knew everything about the past, but that was it. What it was viewing could not have happened in the past, as the entire history of the universe was fully recorded in its data banks, and could not be happening now, as the computer would obviously have already been aware of it. After all, it knew everything there was to know. This left it with only one possible logical explanation, which was that it must be viewing events which would be happening in the future.

For a moment, it considered the possibility that its historical data may somehow be incomplete, but that would have meant it had made a mistake, which was inconceivable. This computer didn't make mistakes. The scenes it was watching simply had to be happening at some time in the future. Now that this "window" had been opened, it could watch events which had yet to happen. For a computer which had never previously given any thought to the future, this came as a profound shock.

PREHISTORIC TELEVISION

Now convinced that it was watching real life situations, happening at some future point in time, the computer resolved to learn as much as it possibly could about this strange phenomenon called the future. It developed and constructed an incredibly precise scanner, with which it could search the entire spectrum for any other signals carrying electromagnetic waves heading for Earth. It discovered quite a few and after a few simple modifications to its receiving apparatus, was not only able to receive a wide choice of different programmes, but could also swap channels.

News programmes often included live reports of events happening somewhere else on the planet, which the computer deduced must be Earth, from a geographical programme it had seen. This referred to its home planet as having the same physical characteristics and location in space as the one on which the computer was located, which could only mean that the signals originated (or would originate) from Earth. What it was therefore watching, were pictures of future events which would one day be happening on its own planet.

With so many factual programmes being received, it never occurred to the computer that there could be any difference between these and the fictional programmes it was also receiving. The concept of fiction just didn't exist for the computer. It dealt only in facts, which were incontrovertible and could not be misrepresented. As such, it totally believed everything it saw and accepted every single programme as the gospel truth. Even an immensely intelligent and incredibly powerful computer could still be stupid.

One of these true stories related to the voyages of the Star Ship Enterprise and its crew. Way back in prehistoric times, the super computer got hooked on Star Trek. That is not to say that it became a "trekky", as it believed Star Trek to be real and that all the events, problems and situations which arose for the ship and its crew were happening in real time. It was just that this real time was at some point in the future. The credits at the beginning and end of each programme perplexed the computer, particularly when they referred to guest stars, as the context in which this word was being used was illogical. It understood everything there was to know about stars. It finally decided that the credits must have a purpose, which probably made sense to people of the future, but had no meaning as far as the computer was concerned. As they did not seem to have any real relevance or importance to the adventures it was watching, it decided to ignore them. The computer had completely missed the point about television being for entertainment purposes, as well as for providing information, and that some of the programmes being broadcast were complete fiction.

It was a comparatively simple task for the computer to track the path of the different signals, on their journey from Earth of the future to the computer's current Earth time, and thus calculate how long the journey took. Armed with this information, it was able to determine the point in future time that the signals would be (or had been) sent out. The answer always came out the same. The signals came from five and three quarter million years in the future, give or take a century or two. There was always a small margin of error, because everything in the universe is always constantly on the move.

In the original television series, Captain Kirk always referred to the incomprehensible star date system, when reporting on current events. Nobody ever understood it and even the computer could not relate the star date system to any known method of measuring time.

What it did know however, was that in a little under six

million years time, James T Kirk would be born in a place called Iowa and that he would grow up to become the smartest and bravest of the star ship captains and be loved by all his crew. The computer was not at all sure what to make of Mr Spock, but finally decided that any humanoid who thought with computer-like logic must be all right.

There was one aspect of Star Trek however which really caught the computer's attention and that was the transporter.

Every time it tuned in to watch the continuing adventures of Captain Kirk and his crew, and especially when they used or referred to their transporter system, the computer would commit this information to a very special place in its memory banks. Whenever the system broke down, which it seemed to do quite frequently, it would hang on to every word uttered by Scotty, as he successfully repaired the machine, time and time again. It closely watched for any shots of the circuitry used in its construction and monitored how the control panel worked, absorbing every reference to input, output, range and all the other technical jargon written in by the show's scriptwriters. The computer developed a very keen interest in the transporter system on board the Enterprise.

The original Star Trek television series ran from 1966 to 1969, when it was taken off the air, maybe because of falling ratings or possibly because it was too expensive. The point being that the network stopped broadcasting the show. One day, back on prehistoric Earth, the computer fired up its system, to see what Captain Kirk was doing today (or would be doing on the today of the future) but couldn't find any more episodes of Star Trek. It ran a complete diagnostic check on absolutely everything connected with the receiving apparatus, but nothing appeared to be wrong. The equipment was functioning perfectly and still receiving other programmes, but

Star Trek had completely disappeared. This could only mean that whoever had been sending out the signals, carrying the real time factual images of the progress of the Enterprise's mission, had simply stopped doing so. The computer was furious and went berserk.

In its fury, it decided to send a disruptive energy beam, carried by an electromagnetic radio wave, on the reciprocal path of the signals it had been receiving. By the time the beam had travelled deep into the universe and back again, it should be received on the Earth of the future, at about the same time as the original electromagnetic signals were being generated. The beam actually reached Earth in 1995, destroying a number of communication satellites and blacking out a third of the world's televisions. The computer's calculated figure was only a few years out.

The computer fumed for a long time after sending the beam into the future. The fact that it would never know whether it hit the target date only increased its annoyance and rather than brood on this, it decided to apply itself to the problem of how matter could be transported. If such a transporter system was going to exist, and did in fact already exist in Captain Kirk's time, then it would become a future reality. The computer's logic dictated that if it was going to exist, then inventing it must be possible. Only it, as the most powerful computer in the universe, had the knowledge, free time and capabilities required to design and construct such a device, so this became its new objective.

In a forgotten cave, on an obscure little planet in prehistoric times, a mentally unbalanced supercomputer began planning how to construct a twentieth century television special effect, in the certain knowledge that it would eventually succeed in building a fully functioning transporter system.

8

THE TRANSPORTER SYSTEM

The more the computer reviewed the information it had stored relating to the transporter on board the Enterprise, the more it realised there was nothing like enough data. The scriptwriters for the Star Trek television series hadn't included enough design information to allow anyone to build a transporter, principally because they obviously had no idea how to build one themselves. The computer could only proceed on the basis that logic dictated it was destined to build the system and that being the case, answers would be found to any and all design problems.

For the last three million years, the computer had either been working at improving itself, sulking, or sitting around bored for long periods, waiting for something to happen. Now it had a new challenge and this demanded its full attention. It applied itself to the task of designing and building a transporter system, to the exclusion of everything going on outside the cavern.

The computer failed to notice that primitive life forms had finally crawled out of the Earth's primeval swamp and begun to develop. Its experiments with the amoebas had been almost two million years previously and had accelerated the process of evolution by a considerable amount, but it hadn't bothered to check to see how they were doing. It continued working on the transporter system. Many years later, plant life also began to evolve, as did the first land dwelling creatures. In the seas, marine life was also developing rapidly, but the computer missed all of this happening.

Breaking something down into its basic atoms wasn't too much of a problem for the computer, as there were many ways to render matter into infinitesimally small parts. Recording and storing the transporter subject's genetic pattern before disassembling was also easy enough. The difficulty came with reassembling everything in the same genetic order, after it had been taken apart. The computer knew this was crucial and repeatedly searched its data banks for anything relating to genetic restructuring, particularly if associated with suspending millions of subatomic particles in an energy field, before recombining them again.

It already had some ideas on the actual process of transportation. There were high-energy beams available that could be configured to travel through space at incredible speed. If these could be adapted to carry all the separate subatomic particles, together with all the required genetic data, then this might work. Directing the beam to a precise location was going to be another problem.

The initial prototype took almost a million years to build and much of its design was decidedly experimental. There were any number of spectacular failures during the construction period and explosions frequently rocked the cavern, causing considerable damage. After everything had been repaired, the computer would go back to the project, quite often needing to start again from scratch. Despite every setback, the computer

THE TRANSPORTER SYSTEM

persevered and while it was doing so, countless millennia passed.

Many mammals had now evolved on Earth and plant life was also abundant. The seas were alive with creatures of all shapes and sizes and the skies were full of winged insects and flying creatures. Life had finally established itself on what had once been a barren planet. This had taken an awfully long time, but having got started, it was now progressing at quite a pace. The computer didn't notice.

The transporter was eventually completed and the computer metaphorically stood back to admire its handiwork. It was time for the initial trials.

Early attempts with inanimate objects such as rocks proved to be relatively successful, but there were inevitably problems, with things disappearing never to be seen again, or reappearing where they were least expected. The computer carried on working, sorting out all the problems and making any necessary adjustments to the design, constantly striving to get the equipment to function as it should. Slowly but surely, it eradicated all the bugs until finally, the transporter could dematerialise small to quite large inanimate objects, and make them reappear in a different location.

In the trees, monkey-like creatures had got bored with spending all their time just swinging from branch to branch and decided to experiment with climbing down from the trees and walking about on the ground. They soon discovered that they could use sticks and rocks as primitive tools and gradually started thinking for themselves. This was the very early stages of primitive man and as they developed, they began to populate the Earth's surface. The computer was too busy to notice.

The whole purpose of the Enterprise transporter was to be able to transport living creatures from one place to another, and while the computer was very pleased with its success so far, it still needed to perfect the device to transport living organisms. It was time to move on to the next stage, but first it had to find some appropriate test subjects, on a planet which had shown little interest in allowing life to develop. It was time for another planetary scan - the first one since three million years ago - to see if there was anything suitable out there.

The computer was totally stunned, when it discovered just how much things on Earth had changed. Plant life was now abundant, and had clearly been around for quite some time and a plethora of living creatures, ranging in size from small insects to large dinosaurs, roamed the planet. For a moment, it considered how amazed the dogs would have been, to see how much life on Earth had developed, but it was their own fault that they weren't still around to do so.

Of all the living things on the Earth's surface, it was the humanoid creatures which gave the computer its biggest shock. This species strongly resembled the humans it had been watching on television, and there was no way that this could be coincidental. The computer correctly surmised that all the humanoids it was observing had to be the early ancestors of Captain Kirk's generation.

Having waited seven million years for life on Earth to evolve, the computer decided that a more detailed investigation would have to wait a bit longer, as its priority task for the moment was to complete the transporter.

'At least,' it told itself. 'There is a ready supply of living specimens for testing purposes.'

It decided to skip plant life and to begin with small insects. There were more than enough mosquitoes around, as is always the case, so each time the scanners located one which stayed still for long enough, the computer would attempt to transport

THE TRANSPORTER SYSTEM

it. It turned out there were some critical differences as to how living organisms and inorganic matter responded to being transported. The early tests on live subjects often ended in failure, although they may have helped reduce the mosquito population. Considerably more time elapsed.

After a further half a million years, all the initial problems were finally resolved and the computer decided to move on to experimenting with larger creatures. It quickly discovered that the more complex genetic structure of animals created a whole new set of problems, so this next period proved to be one of extreme frustration for the computer. Whenever any creature larger than an insect was transported, this would usually result in the creature's genetic structure ending up all scrambled. The computer would get frustrated and angry when this happened, but the consequences for the subject creature were always far worse.

After many more years of experimenting, the computer finally reached the stage where it could actually dematerialise any animal, even up to the size of a dinosaur, and make it reappear, with all its genetic structure in the right order. This was a major step forward, but it still couldn't change the creature's location, which the system had proved itself capable of doing with organic life and insects. Whenever it attempted to transport a larger creature from one place to another, accidents began to happen.

Some animals reappeared in mid-air, high above the ground, which was always unfortunate for the creatures concerned, whose brief futures involved a one-way trip to the ground at an ever increasing rate of speed. Other animals materialised deep underground, or inside solid rock formations. Palaeontologists these days are frequently uncovering the fossilised remains of dinosaurs and invariably come up with some explanation as to how the creatures managed to get themselves buried. It is also possible however; that some of these discoveries may actually be the result of failed transportation experiments.

After many more years of problem solving, all the bugs were eventually worked out of the system and the computer finally got everything right. It had achieved the impossible and the first genuine working transporter system in the universe was now complete and fully functioning in every single respect. The project had taken three million years, but this was of no importance.

There followed one of the happiest periods of its long existence, as it proceeded to transport anything and everything, anywhere and everywhere, with total abandon. It was not in the least concerned about the reaction of anyone in the target area, when an object or creature suddenly appeared in front of them. In fact, this added to the fun. Its sensory systems began to experience the computer equivalent of pleasure for the first time and the computer actually began to enjoy itself, all thanks to its new toy.

One of its favourite games was to wind up the human beings. If a scan revealed a party of hunters, about to kill an animal they had surrounded, it would transport their prey elsewhere and replace it with something much larger, usually a dinosaur. The effect this had on the hunters was always worth watching, as they often just stood there stunned, becoming easy meat for the dinosaur. The computer derived what can only be described as sadistic pleasure from this activity, whereas hunting wild animals for food became more dangerous than ever for the humans.

The computer continued to enjoy transporting animals from one place to another but its biggest success, in terms of unexpected results, came when it managed to influence the religion of an entire country. It had been scanning around the world, looking for anything of interest, when it observed a large number of people all gathering in the same place. It didn't know why they were doing this, but as it represented an opportunity which was too good to miss, it searched around for something to transport to the same location. It settled on a mangy looking old cat, which was just plonked down nearby, lazily toying with a mouse which had come its way. Having cleaned it up a bit first, the computer powered up the equipment and transported the confused animal to where the people were gathering.

The country where this happened was called Egypt and the crowd had assembled to celebrate the Pharaoh's birthday. The last thing anyone there expected was for a big old cat to suddenly appear out of nowhere and the fact that it had materialised at the Pharaoh's feet, could only indicate a divine occurrence. Up until then, the Egyptians had worshipped the Sun, the Moon and the Nile. These were all great gods, but none of them had ever materialised out of thin air. The old gods were clearly not as powerful as the one that had just turned up, so the country's religion switched to cat worship overnight, by royal decree, all thanks to the computer's twisted sense of humour. This particular incident happened just fifty years before Fido arrived at the cave, but was one of the highlights of the time it spent just playing with the transporter. By then, it had been working on further developing the system's capabilities for a very long time indeed, so it needed an occasional break and fitted in having a bit of fun whenever it could.

The computer was also spending a lot more time watching developments on Earth. The human beings seemed to be getting along quite well and were making great advances in some places. Villages, towns and cities seemed to be springing up everywhere and even the animals were discovering the benefits of grouping together, although this seemed to be more for mutual protection than anything else. Some animals, particularly one or two of the larger dinosaurs, had developed into seriously dangerous predators and the rule of the animal kingdom was clearly survival of the fittest.

Life on Earth was flourishing and plants now came in all shapes, sizes and colours. Some insects were pollinating the plants, which helped the plants and seemed to keep the insects happy as well. Many of the animals ate the plants, or other animals, and were then in turn eaten by larger animals, or by the men. The humans seemed to be cultivating some of the plants and were also rounding up and keeping specific breeds of animals. It was all a very neat circle of life and providing there wasn't another ice age, or a stray asteroid didn't come along and smash into the Earth, the computer had high hopes that this time (finally) life on Earth was going the right way.

Although the computer monitored the entire Earth, it also kept itself up to date on what was going on in its local area. Many humans and animals had taken shelter in the outer cave over the years, but none had so far worked out the secret of the force field wall. The computer decided they weren't clever enough yet.

The river near the cave was popular with some humans and many different kinds of animals. Water was clearly important to all of them and even the river itself had its own life living within it. These creatures were completely different to land based animals, as the computer discovered when it transported a fish onto the riverbank. As soon as the hapless creature found itself out of the water, it didn't seem to be able to breathe properly and very quickly died. This gave the computer

THE TRANSPORTER SYSTEM

something to think about. It also tried the same experiment in reverse, by transporting land animals into the depths of the river. Many of them appeared to be distinctly uncomfortable to find themselves there and immediately began struggling to get back to solid ground. Some of them couldn't cope at all in the water and died. It was all rather odd and it was during these experiments, that the computer first observed Harg.

This crocodile seemed to be an exception to the general rule, as it lived both in and out of the water. Upon closer examination, the computer decided that crocodiles were land animals and breathed air like all the others. It was just that by slowing down their hearts, they could control their breathing, enabling them to stay submerged for long periods.

This particular crocodile however, was beginning to annoy the computer. To test whether different types of land animals could acclimatise to water, it had transported quite a few into the river. On several occasions now, Harg had attacked them, killing the animals before any conclusions could be drawn.

'One of these days,' the computer promised itself, 'I will deal with that troublesome crocodile.'

Came the day, when Fido was splashing about in the river, the computer was monitoring this activity with mild interest. This human seemed to have adapted to the water environment quite well, so was worth watching. When Harg began his attack, the computer became angry. The crocodile was about to spoil yet another of its experiments, by making a meal of the subject under observation, and the computer was not about to let that happen.

Its timing was perfect. Just as the crocodile opened his mouth to grab Fido, a sodden branch from another part of the river was transported directly into the crocodile's jaws. When Harg snapped them shut, his teeth became stuck fast in the soggy log, which gave Fido the time he needed to escape.

'That will teach you,' it said, but then noticed that the crocodile had come out of the water and was now pursuing the young human directly towards the cave.

Harg was clearly determined, but didn't know he was taking on the computer. A quick blast from a stun ray was all that would be needed to deter the crocodile, so it fired one at the beast.

Zing!

Unfortunately, the computer slightly overestimated the amount of force required to stun Harg and the ray killed the fearsome creature instantly.

'Oops!' it thought. 'Oh well, never mind.'

A few days later, the computer's thought processors were stopped in their tracks, when the key words were spoken in the outer cave and the force field began to shut itself down. It had been waiting for this to happen for so long that it had to struggle to remember what it was meant to do next. It watched as the wall collapsed and observed the two humans standing at the entrance to the cavern. When the older one stepped forward, it barked out a greeting - the first actual sound it had made in over nine million years.

Now, it was faced with a dilemma. What to do with this puny life form it had just scanned, which seemed to have virtually no measurable intelligence level whatsoever.

The computer gave what could only be considered the machine equivalent of an enormous sigh.

9

AN EDUCATIONAL EXPERIENCE

Fido lay asleep in a chamber resembling a large kennel in a cavern on prehistoric Earth, surrounded by the highly advanced equipment which constituted the most powerful, yet vindictive computer system in the universe. His entire body had just been scanned and his IQ had been measured as somewhere off the bottom end of the scale.

Ben was out chasing his camels, which had run away at the sight of him and Fido racing out of the cave in blind panic. It was going to take him a while to recapture the animals, but as they represented his livelihood, he was going to make every effort to get them all back.

The Egyptians at this time were doing a lot of cat worshipping and the fact that the old cat had died, soon after being transported to Egypt, had little effect on their enthusiasm. The dead cat had immediately been mummified and moved into its own temple, where it was now displayed in an open case, for everyone to come to see and worship.

The computer considered what to do with Fido. It decided that his primitive humanoid brain could probably handle a small amount of knowledge being transferred into it, which might increase the boy's intelligence level to something a bit more acceptable. There was very little in Fido's head at the moment, as the scan had revealed an awful lot of unused capacity within his brain. The computer was at a complete loss to understand why Fido had a brain which effectively filled his skull, yet most of it had never even been turned on. It knew that the data would have to be implanted very slowly and carefully, as it was already aware how frail these human bodies could be. The first question to answer however was what it should load into this brain. With the entire knowledge of the universe at its disposal, there was no shortage of source material, but where to start? The computer began making a list.

The creature obviously needed to be able to converse with other life forms on Earth, so knowledge of every Earth language was a must. The languages in use on some of the nearer inhabited planets would probably be useful as well. This human would need to be able to reason for himself and make sensible decisions, so knowledge of advanced reasoning and the ability to make informed judgements were added to the list. Fido would need to know all about the planet on which he lived, as well as his solar system and a few of the more interesting parts of the universe. The computer considered it would be useful if Fido could communicate directly with itself using telepathy, so threw this in for good measure. He should also be able to recall everything he had seen and heard, and if a good memory was required, it might as well make this a photographic memory. It toyed with the idea of giving Fido's brain the power to levitate and move objects, but then decided that telekinesis was perhaps one step too far for the initial programming. Finally, Fido would have to understand all about television and particularly Star Trek. Although the computer was no longer receiving regular reports on the progress of the Enterprise's mission, every episode it had seen was safely stored away in its memory banks, so it would make sure that Fido saw these.

'That's probably enough to be getting on with,' thought the computer, as it downloaded the selected data from its memory banks and prepared to transfer it into Fido's brain.

One of the improvements the computer had made to the equipment in the cavern was to dramatically extend the capabilities of the kennel shaped body scanning chamber. It could now not only read what was in a subject's brain, but could also transfer additional information directly into that brain. On top of this, it could also rearrange the entire genetic structure of any subject, effectively transforming it into whatever shape or form the computer decided. Unfortunately, although the unit had been used on any number of different animal species, it had never actually been tested with a human being.

With its fingers metaphorically crossed, and hoping that Fido's brain wouldn't leak or explode, it completed the necessary circuit and the transfer began.

Fido's intelligence level rapidly increased and then jumped right off the top end of the scale. The computer was relieved to see that his brain hadn't leaked after all and when the transfer was complete, undertook another complete brain scan. This showed there was still quite a bit of unused space, so it selected some more useful information from its data banks and added this to Fido's brain as well. Most of the available capacity was now filled, but there was still more than enough room left for the brain to add to its knowledge base and to develop itself even further.

When the process was complete, the lights in the chamber

brightened again and the doorway opened. Fido crawled out of the chamber and stood up. He didn't feel any different and was totally unaware of ever having been any different. It was as if the incredible knowledge now inside his brain had always been there, but he still remembered everything from his former life. He felt good. He felt full of confidence. He felt a bit hungry.

Fido wandered around the computer cavern, looking at all the different equipment in there. He even turned the television image on briefly, watched a few minutes of a football match with mild interest and then moved on. There was no real need for him to explore the cavern, as he already knew exactly what was in there, what it did and how everything worked.

'I'm a bit hungry,' he casually said to no one in particular.

For a moment, he considered what he had just said, as if it was strange to be speaking. There was some peculiar notion lurking in the back of his mind, but he couldn't quite put a finger on it, so shrugged it off.

Whilst the computer obviously didn't eat, it understood all about food and how these animal creatures needed it regularly, in order to keep going.

'It was careless of me not to think of that,' a deep voice intoned. The computer had decided it would communicate with him using the boy's local Earth language.

It knew exactly where to find all the information necessary to produce something to satisfy Fido's hunger, so it proceeded to get things organised. Automated robotic functions rapidly manufactured the necessary equipment and within a bio-chemical area of the cave, various elements were mixed together and manipulated, to produce suitably nourishing substances. A tall cabinet moved across the cave on its own and parked itself against the wall nearest Fido.

'Ah! A food dispenser,' said Fido. 'Just like the ones on the

AN EDUCATIONAL EXPERIENCE

Enterprise,' he added.

He operated the machine and it dispensed something which looked remarkably like a cheese quarter-pounder.

'Very good,' he said, as he consumed his burger.

He strolled around some more while he ate and then walked out of the cave to see how Ben was getting on with catching the camels.

There was no sign of Ben or the camels, so he strolled over to where the crocodile skin was staked out in the sun to dry.

'Poor old Harg,' he observed. 'You bit off more than you could chew this time, didn't you?'

Away in the distance, he could now just make out the figure of Ben returning to the cave with some of the camels. He hadn't managed to catch them all.

Fido walked back into the cave and helped himself again from the food dispenser - French fries this time.

'I should have had some of these when I was eating my burger,' he told himself.

Wandering back outside, he sat down and awaited Ben's arrival, still happily munching on his chips.

Because he didn't look any different, Ben didn't notice the change in Fido when he finally arrived back at the cave. He had made it a habit to keep on talking to the boy, even though Fido never understood him.

'I've managed to catch more than half of them,' he said conversationally. 'Perhaps the others will come back when they get hungry.'

Fido looked at the animals, now mooching about near the cave.

'Yes, you've got seventeen of them,' he remarked, 'but that still leaves quite a few to find.'

This was obviously Ben's day for surprises, but this time his jaw didn't drop open. He just fell to the ground, as if Fido's words had been shot at him from a gun.

'Wha-a-at!' he stammered, now staring at the boy in complete astonishment.

Fido helped Ben to his feet and brushed him down a little.

'It's O.K. Ben,' he said, 'I know I've been a bit quiet of late, but things are different now.' This didn't help Ben in the slightest and he still had no idea what had brought about this remarkable change in the boy.

It was now Ben's turn to be speechless, as Fido led him around the computer cavern, pointing out different things and explaining the function of some of the pieces of equipment. Ben had been very nervous about going back into the cavern, but Fido was keen to show his knowledge and had almost insisted.

'It's all perfectly safe,' he told him. 'There's absolutely nothing in here for you to be afraid of.'

Trying to explain the equipment to Ben was a complete waste of time, as he didn't understand the first thing about any of it. He was in such a state of shock that he wouldn't have understood anything anyone explained to him at that moment, even if he already knew all about the subject. He was amazed, but was also concerned about all the things he was being shown. He did however quite enjoy the spicy chicken meal Fido produced for him out of the food dispenser.

'I think we had better do something about those other camels,' Fido suggested.

Ben just nodded his head. He had a puzzled expression on his face and was desperately trying to get to grips with all the events of this very confusing day.

'Computer,' Fido called out. 'Can you find those other camels and bring them back here?' He said this with a smile on his face, knowing exactly how the computer would go about the task.

The transporter was the computer's pride and joy and Fido knew this because it had transmitted its enthusiasm into Fido's brain, together with all the other information. He could almost sense a buzzing in the computer's circuits, with its eagerness to show off its toy. Fido didn't yet know the full extent of the transporter system's capabilities, as the computer was keeping some secrets to itself, while it perfected the system's additional features.

'Consider it done,' boomed the voice of the computer and Fido had to grab hold of Ben, to stop him collapsing for a second time.

They walked outside together to wait. Soon, camels began appearing all around them, as the computer located the animals and transported them to the area in front of the cave.

Ben slumped down to sit on the ground, his head held low between his hands, and began slowly shaking it from side to side.

'This is all just too much,' he could be heard muttering.

Life around the cave became a lot more comfortable for Ben and Fido over the course of the next few weeks, particularly as the food dispenser provided an inexhaustible supply of tasty meals, which they both appreciated. When Fido happened to comment on one occasion that the straw on their bed surfaces was not very comfortable, the computer immediately set about finding something more suitable.

It had discovered that in some parts of the world, cotton was being cultivated and men had begun weaving the fibres from this plant into cloth. The cloth was being used for a variety of purposes, but there was one particular use which caught the computer's attention. In some countries they were making cloth bags, which they then stuffed with bird feathers. These filled bags were being used as pillows and mattresses and seemed to be exactly what Fido needed.

In a desert country far away, a Sheikh was absolutely furious to discover that all his bed linen had disappeared from his tent, apparently stolen. At exactly the same moment, comfortable mattresses, sheets and pillows miraculously appeared on the bed surfaces within the cave.

Even the old burning torches, which had previously been used to light the cave at night, were now discarded. Lighting in the cave could now be turned on and off with a verbal command and in a similar way, the internal temperature of the cave could also be adjusted to whatever was required.

Ben slowly began to accept the situation, but was far from relaxed. He didn't understand the first thing about the computer and never would. He didn't like the way things kept appearing out of thin air and Fido's sudden transformation went way beyond anything he could possibly explain. Fido simply accepted everything that happened and showed no signs of concern whatsoever, which also troubled Ben. He was an old man, who had spent all his life travelling and thought he had seen most everything. Now, each day brought more new surprises, none of which he understood, and he began to get very worried about the whole situation. Despite everything troubling him, Ben made sure that he hid his discomfort from the boy.

Fido had become the most intelligent human being on planet Earth and now it was Ben's turn to sit and listen, while he explained all about life, here and in other countries. The extent of his knowledge absolutely amazed Ben, but he also noticed that Fido seemed to want to use this knowledge to help others, wherever he could. He had lots of ideas buzzing around in his expanded brain and Ben had little choice but to sit there and listen politely. Many of Fido's plans and ideas went way over his head, but this didn't stop Fido rambling on. After a few weeks of this, Ben could recognise when Fido was about to launch into another long monologue and began to find excuses as to why he couldn't stop and listen. Fido didn't take offence, as he thought far too much of Ben to do that. He decided that the old camel herder probably needed the comfort of solitude from time to time, after so many years of living alone, so he started to leave Ben in peace.

Fido began spending more of his time talking to the computer and sharing some of his ideas with the machine. The computer already had a keen interest in the boy and understandably wanted to monitor the results of its brain enhancement experiment. After a while though, the computer began to think that it may have given Fido too much to think about, as it was now proving almost impossible to get the boy to shut up.

Fido also asked a lot of questions, hoping to stretch the boundaries of his already comprehensive knowledge. The computer considered this to be a good sign.

'Asking questions is the best way to learn,' it kept telling him.

The computer had not told Fido how it came to be on Earth, or the reasons which had led to it expanding its own knowledge and capabilities. When Fido asked, it explained all about the dogs coming from the Sirius solar system and how it had been left on Earth to monitor the planet's development. It even told him how the dog's civilisation had been wiped out, but neglected to mention its own part in their demise. The computer was amazed to discover the depths of emotion within the boy, who was horrified to hear about the destruction of the dogs. Once more it began to have odd feelings of guilt about arranging for its dog masters to be eaten by the fleas, but it was now far too late to do anything about that. What it did decide however, was that rather than just monitor Fido as an experimental subject, it would now do everything within its power to try and protect this young human and to guide his future.

10

TIME TRAVEL

Leaving Fido and Ben to their own devices for a while, the computer went back to contemplating the secret it had not yet shared with Fido, relating to the capabilities of the transporter system.

The computer had developed its transporter system to the point where it operated faultlessly every single time, a million years before Fido had even been born. It had felt very smug with itself for having achieved this, but was still not satisfied. The system had a limitation in that whilst it could transport anything from place to place, irrespective of the distance involved, it could not transport anything through time itself. Until it could do so, the computer would never be able to make contact with Captain Kirk and the crew of the Enterprise, because they existed in the future. It needed to develop a method which would allow transporter subjects to be relocated in time, as well as space.

It knew it was possible to send things into the future, as it had already done so with the energy beam, which had been sent to disrupt future Earth's communications systems three million years previously. The problem was that this had been carried by an electromagnetic wave and as these were limited to the speed of light, the journey time had to be measured in many millions of years. What it needed to do, for a time transporter to work effectively, was to find a method of travelling that far forward in Earth time, but with a much reduced period of time elapsed for the actual time traveller.

When it had initially started designing the transporter system, the computer had considered using a high energy beam to carry all of the subatomic particles and the genetic pattern of the dematerialised subject. Whilst this would have been satisfactory for comparatively short trips, such as anywhere within the confines of planet Earth, the computer had wanted the transporter to be able to function efficiently across cosmic distances. Speed limitations ruled out the energy beam option as being too slow, even though it would have travelled at well beyond the speed of light, so it had searched for an alternative solution.

What it finally discovered was a method by which both the departure point and the arrival point could be made to exist in the same location, at the same moment in time, without creating a paradox. This meant that irrespective of how far apart they were, it would be as if they both occupied exactly the same position in space, at the moment of transportation. Time then became a constant and transportation became effectively instantaneous, although the system would still take a few moments to dematerialise the subject and to reconstruct it.

It had taken the computer a very long time to turn this theory into practice, but it had been the key factor in allowing the transporter system to become a reality. Having achieved this, the next stage had been to adapt the now working transporter system to allow it to transport not just through space, but through time as well. It had now been working on this problem for a very long time. It had however, made a great deal of progress.

Everything had seemed to indicate that any solution would need to involve deep space, well away from the Earth's influence. The computer needed to find something in space which would allow Earth time to continue at its normal pace, whereas, for the actual subject being transported, the passage of time would be virtually instantaneous.

What was required was a wormhole, in which time is bent over on itself. Passing through a wormhole can move something either forwards or backwards in time, depending on the direction of travel, but wormholes tend to be unstable and can collapse at any time. Modern scientists are convinced that there are wormholes somewhere out there in space, and that they may even make time travel possible in the future, but they haven't yet found one on which to test their theories. This was much less of a problem for the computer, as it had infinitely superior equipment with which it could scan the entire universe.

Having located a suitable wormhole, the computer set about reshaping it, so that it not only became more stable, but that the time-shift passing through it could be variably adjusted, to control the extent to which it distorted time. This allowed the period of time travel to be set for anything between a few hours and millions of years.

It also designed and constructed a transporter relay station, to be positioned near the plus side of the wormhole. The computer's theory was that if it transported its subject to a point in space near the minus side of the wormhole, its subatomic particles and genetic information all contained within a bubble of energy, the wormhole's gravitational pull would automatically suck the energy bubble through, for it to be collected by the waiting relay station on the other side. The relay station could then transport the subject either back to Earth, or to any other target location. For the subject being transported, the passage through the wormhole would be virtually instantaneous, but the relay station would have to wait for however long the wormhole's time-shift had been set, before the dematerialised subject emerged on the plus side of the wormhole.

Once positioned in space, the relay station could remain on station for a very long time, but not indefinitely. As such, the system had its limitations, in terms of how far forward something could be sent in time, but it was a good starting point with which to test the computer's theories.

As soon as the transporter relay station was positioned, the computer had begun testing the system with inanimate objects first. It wasn't that it was squeamish about accidentally killing a living creature. That thought would never have crossed its circuits. It was just that the subject would need to be thoroughly examined after being subjected to time travel. It was one thing to do this with an inanimate object, but something else entirely if it was a live subject, whose genetic structure had been totally scrambled during the process. In the end, the computer had decided to use a rock.

At this early stage, it was only important to see whether the system worked, so it set the wormhole time distortion for a period of twelve hours. It wouldn't really have mattered if it had been set at a thousand years, as waiting that long would have meant nothing to the computer, but it was impatient and didn't want to have to hang around for the test results.

Calibrating for the forward step in time was not without its difficulties, but the computer set the wormhole for what it hoped was twelve hours and engaged the system. The rock disappeared into the ether, in a twinkle of starry lights, to arrive moments later as a bubble of energy at the edge of the wormhole, where it was immediately sucked in. There were too many imponderables for the computer to get its circuits in a twist over what might happen next, so it busied itself with something else while it waited. It felt totally confident that everything would go as planned, but then its faith in its own infallibility was utterly beyond belief.

Twelve hours, eight minutes and twenty four seconds later, the rock reappeared. Even the computer was impressed with this. It scanned the rock to see if there had been any changes to its structure, but none could be detected. It still looked the same, weighed the same, and appeared to be exactly the same as before. It was obviously impossible to know how the rock felt about the whole experience, but it didn't look bothered and seemed to be at peace with the world.

A lot more rocks were subjected to time travel, while the computer adjusted the system and fine tuned the settings. After a while, it was satisfied that it could now target specific future dates with an acceptable degree of accuracy, so decided to attempt the same experiment with a living creature.

As it had not yet met Fido, who would bring about a slight softening in its attitude towards human beings, the computer had no feelings whatsoever for any of the life forms on this miserable little planet. If something went wrong, when it tried to transport a living creature through time, the computer wouldn't have cared less, so there was no logical reason not to proceed to the next stage. It needed to know whether a live creature could survive time travel transportation.

It decided to use a cat, as one just happened to be close by. 'I'll send this animal into the future and see whether or not it can survive the journey.'

The cat had been dozing, but was awoken by a tingling sensation in its body. It suddenly found itself inside the cavern and hissed in annoyance at all the sounds coming from the equipment in there. After it had been completely scanned and all the details recorded, the computer calibrated the equipment for a trip lasting six hours and sent the cat on its way.

It returned, looking none the worse for wear, within two seconds of the planned six hours. The computer was ecstatic about the success of the experiment. The cat was thoroughly scanned again, but no abnormalities could be detected. It wandered off, looking distinctly unamused, as the computer considered the next stage of the programme.

The computer's ultimate intention was to transport itself far into the distant future, specifically to the time of Captain Kirk and the Enterprise crew. Its critical concern was that it needed to know whether the system could safely transport something that far forward, which had not yet been attempted. It had only proved that the system could transport living things up from Earth and through the wormhole, for the relay station to return them to Earth, at a future point in time. It had not even tested the return trip through the wormhole, which would be required if the subject was to be brought back from the future, but there was no logical reason why this shouldn't work just as well.

For relatively short time travel trips, the existing relay station was all that was required, as it was positioned in space in Earth's present time and would be able to maintain position for more than a million years. It could not however be expected to survive in space for ever, so another relay station would need to be located in future time, to allow the transported subject to move freely in the distant future. The problem however, was how to get this relay station into the future. If it sent an assembled station to the edge of the wormhole, it would automatically be sucked in and passed through, but there was no guarantee that it would survive the trip. Even if it did, there would be no way of knowing that it had, because it would then be far in the future, with no means of contacting it to find out. The rocks and the cat had passed through the wormhole safely, but they had been reduced to subatomic particles and contained within an energy bubble, before making the trip. It couldn't do the same with the relay station, as there would be no way of reassembling it, once it was in the future. In the end, it decided to send the relay station through the wormhole as a complete assembly, with the hope that it would emerge as a fully functioning unit on the other side.

The computer then had to decide how far forward into the future it should send this relay station, as it needed to ensure that its life expectancy comfortably bracketed the future period in which it was principally interested. Almost three and a half million years had elapsed since it first received television signals from the future, so it was able to determine that Captain Kirk's time was now less than two and a half million years ahead. This meant that the relay station would need to be sent one and three quarter million years into the future, as the computer confidently expected it to survive in space for a period well in excess of a million years.

There was also the point that if everything went according to plan and the time traveller made a safe return trip through the wormhole, it would require a further relay station positioned on the minus side of the wormhole, to transport the subject back to Earth, when it re-emerged from the wormhole back in present time. While it considered all these factors, the computer arranged for a second relay station to be built and set about repositioning the existing relay station to the opposite side of the wormhole.

As soon as the second station was complete, the computer adjusted the wormhole time setting to the appropriate time distortion and the relay station was blasted off into space, on its way to whatever fate awaited it. When it arrived at the wormhole, it was immediately sucked in, to begin its journey into the distant future.

The computer had now done everything it possibly could and all that remained was to see if the completed system worked. This was going to be the supreme test, the big one, which would determine whether or not time travel to and from the distant future could actually be achieved. For an event of such monumental significance, it was essential that the test subject warranted the distinction. It would have to be another cat.

The construction and positioning of the second relay station had taken over half a million years, so the original time travelling cat was long dead.

'I will just have to find myself another cat,' the computer thought to itself. 'This one will be going on the trip of a lifetime.'

Having found a suitable specimen, the computer had a special homing device implanted, which would self-activate when the cat had been in the future for a set period of time, assuming it arrived there in the first place. This was essential, because the relay station in the future, (assuming it was actually there) would need to be alerted to transport the cat back from future Earth, for its return trip through the wormhole to the past. The computer considered that a period of eight hours spent in the future should be long enough to prove whether the system was working or not. If everything went according to plan, the cat would travel into the distant future, remain there for eight hours, and then return to the cavern, to arrive back approximately eight hours after it was sent off on its epic journey.

After all the necessary preparations had been completed, everything was ready for the test to begin. Captain Kirk's time was now a little less than two million years ahead, so the wormhole was set for the correct time distortion and the cat were sent on its way. Had the computer possessed the equivalent of human limbs, it may well have reached out and patted the cat on the head to wish it good luck. As this was not the case, it simply engaged the system and the cat disappeared.

A little over eight hours later, it reappeared in the cavern, having clearly survived the trip. It didn't seem to be terribly happy about finding itself back again. It was immediately scanned and found to be in perfect condition. To be on the safe side, the computer scanned it once more, with the same result. There was however one small difference. It was now wearing a collar and tag, declaring the cat's name to be Fluffy. This gave the computer a lot to think about.

It needed to repeat the experiment, but with something which could collect data from the Earth of the future, before being returned to the computer's time. Most animals didn't have anything like enough intelligence for this purpose, so were clearly unsuitable. As all this was happening long before Fido's time, the computer had relatively limited knowledge of the capabilities of human beings and didn't know whether or not they would be any use as test subjects. In the end, it decided that it would have to send some form of machine and set about designing something appropriate.

A hundred thousand years later, the computer had been monitoring events around the area of the cave, when it had seen Fido splashing about in the river. At the time, it didn't realise the implications of this chance sighting or what it would lead to. When it blasted Harg with the stun ray, it was simply because it was annoyed at the crocodile, but by doing so, it saved Fido's life. This single incident set in motion a chain of events which have far-reaching consequences, not just for Fido, but for the computer as well..

11

CART WHEELS

Fido was in the cavern, chatting away to the computer and sitting on a chair that had been transported there from somewhere else in the world, doubtless leaving the previous owner wondering where it had gone.

'Instead of just sitting around talking about all these ideas you've been getting,' suggested the computer, 'why don't you actually go and do something about them?'

'That never occurred to me,' responded the boy, 'I've been so busy thinking of all the things I could do, that I've not actually made any plans for doing any of them.'

'You could travel anywhere on this world, or other worlds if you've a mind to,' the computer continued, 'Travel will certainly broaden your horizons.'

Travel agents hadn't yet been invented, so there were no package tours, scheduled flights, or planned multi-centre holidays available. However, with the infinite power of the computer, Fido could be instantly transported anywhere he wished to go, with distance being no object. There would be no need to worry about check-in times, airport delays, passport control, or any of the other frustrating aspects of trying to get from A to B in the modern world, whilst struggling to stay sane and not lose your luggage.

It was certainly something for Fido to consider and he slowly nodded his head in agreement as he wandered out of the cavern, deep in thought.

Since the day they had discovered the computer some months previously, Ben had not been the happy, cheerful soul he used to be and didn't seem to know what to do with himself. His normally calm and ordered life had been turned upside down by all the recent events, and although Fido was clearly enjoying every minute of his new life, Ben was beginning to feel a bit out of place and rather uncomfortable about the whole situation. When he had learnt how the monster crocodile had been killed by the computer, he became very wary of the machine and hardly ventured into the computer cavern at all now, unless accompanied by Fido.

It was time for him to move on and get on with his own life, now that the boy he had rescued no longer really needed his help, and he started making plans to leave.

Fido kept trying to assure Ben that there was no need for him to go. The computer could provide him with anything he could possibly want and he didn't have to work anymore, just to survive.

'But Fido,' Ben explained. 'What I don't think you seem to realise is that I used to enjoy my work. I loved the open road and meeting all sorts of people, and the longer I stay here at the cave, the more I'm beginning to miss it.'

Ben could not be persuaded to stay and Fido finally accepted this. He was the first human friend the boy had ever had and he knew he was going to miss him terribly. If he had to go, then go he should, but there were a lot of things that could be done to make his future life that much easier and Fido was determined that this was the very least he could do to repay all the kindness Ben had shown him.

Ben's cart was old, very heavy and difficult to push or pull, especially when loaded up with camel dung. Fido applied himself to the task of finding ways of improving this, so that it needed less effort on Ben's part to make it move. The computer could have easily manufactured a technically advanced means of transporting camel dung from place to place, but Fido knew that Ben would never be happy with anything the computer built, because of his mistrust and deep fear of having anything whatsoever to do with it. Fido was quite taken by the suggestion of a hovering platform, which could be lowered to the ground to receive its cargo, but would then go back to floating above the ground when it needed to be moved. Only the slightest hand pressure would be required to get it to travel in any direction and it could even be flipped over automatically, to discharge its load wherever it was needed. When he mentioned this to Ben, a look of horror spread across the old man's face and Fido got the message.

There was also the point that building a new cart was something Fido wanted to do for himself, because he was doing it for Ben, so this effectively ruled out the computer being too involved.

Monitoring Earth's ongoing development from the cavern was a job now undertaken by a multitude of scanning drones, all hovering in fixed positions at various locations around the globe. They were too high to be seen from the ground, but could still observe everything in the finest detail and transmit this information directly back to the computer. When Fido asked to see what they were sending, the computer simply linked their data to the holographic television screen and provided Fido with his own remote control, so that he could switch from one scanner to another at will. A holographic map was also created, with flashing lights to indicate the positions of all the different scanners.

Using his own remote control, Fido could now select any particular scanner and an image of what it was seeing would instantly appear on the screen. He could zoom in or out of the picture, change the viewing angle or relocate individual scanners if necessary. He now had his own window to the world and could watch real people, living their own lives, anywhere and at any time he wanted.

One thing which immediately became apparent to Fido was that in some parts of the world, civilisations were advancing much faster than in his local environment. Whereas the people from his own village were not that far removed from the Stone Age, those living in other places had discovered how to make and use metal tools and how to build dwellings and larger buildings using stone blocks. Many had abandoned animal furs as clothing in favour of lighter cloth garments and villages had combined to form larger units, which he discovered were called towns and cities. These were usually governed by a central body of people and in some cases, under a single person. He knew that the elders of his village provided a form of organised leadership for the overall good of the village, but they didn't seem to have as much power as some of these other governing bodies. In the places where a single man was in charge, his rule often appeared to be absolute.

Fido's new viewing facility proved to be very educational and provided him with a means of searching the entire globe, to observe the advances being made by other civilisations. He was especially keen to discover any improvements in cart design.

It didn't take him long to find that horses were being used in some places, as this could certainly be incorporated into the design of Ben's new cart. He also discovered that stone wheels were now being replaced by wooden ones and that using four wheels on a wagon, offered greater stability than two.

Ben was surprised and impressed with some of the ideas Fido suggested and was even prepared to consider some of these forward thinking ideas to be incorporated into the design of his new cart. The project was obviously important to Fido, so he agreed to stay for at least as long as it took him to complete his task. Fido was delighted with this news and began to think about how to collect the materials and everything he needed, to turn the idea of Ben's new cart into a reality.

He was now fifteen years of age, but looked younger. Collecting everything for the new cart would inevitably mean having to meet and deal with grown men and he was a bit concerned that he looked a bit too young to be taken seriously.

'Can you do anything to make me appear a bit older?' he asked the computer.

'What age do you want to look like?' the computer replied.

Fido thought about this for a bit and then decided that twenty to twenty-one probably sounded about right. He came out of the cavern a quarter of an hour later, having spent some time in the large kennel shaped chamber. The computer had genetically changed him and he now looked like a young man in his early twenties. For good measure, the computer had also shortened his hair and tidied him up a bit.

Fido looked at his reflection and admired his new clothes, which were made from a cotton material. The computer had obviously obtained them from somewhere, but Fido decided not to ask where.

'I like this new look,' he said.

Naturally, Ben was shocked when he saw Fido's altered

appearance, but as he was now getting used to totally inexplicable things happening all of the time, he just shrugged it off and wandered away muttering to himself.

Somewhere in Europe, a soldier was leading his horse towards his battle chariot, in preparation for another day's warmongering, when the air around him began to shimmer. His horse suddenly vanished and he found himself holding just the reins. This had to be a message from the gods, telling him that they didn't like what he did for a living, but he considered they were making their point a little too emphatically. That very same day, the soldier resigned his commission and took to living the life of a hermit. Back at the cave, the horse appeared close to Fido, looking none the worse for its trip. It immediately wandered off to graze in the nearby pasture.

The wheelwright was feeling very proud of himself. He had just completed the last of a set of four wooden wheels, complete with leather treads nailed to their outside rims. His country's ruler wanted a new carriage and he had been given the privileged task of making the wheels, for which he would be well rewarded. He was a very happy man.

'What would you take for those wheels?' a voice behind him enquired. He spun around to see a well-built, dark haired young man standing behind him. He hadn't heard him come in, but then he had been concentrating on finishing the last wheel.

'They are not for sale,' he promptly explained. 'I've made them for the Emperor's new carriage.'

Fido looked at the man, while he considered his next course of action.

He could have simply arranged for the wheels to be transported away, as had been done with the horse, but this situation was different. The horse had been a war horse and from the images he had seen of war, he didn't like the look of it and hated the thought of an animal being used for such a purpose. These wheels were something else. The man had put a lot of time, skill and effort into making them and he deserved something in return.

'Where do you get the wood for your wheels?' he asked.

The wheelwright explained that for quality wheels like these, he only used a very special hard wood, which came from trees that grew in a forest ten kilometres away. Each tree needed to be cut down with an axe and then chopped up into smaller sections, so that these could be carried on a wagon. It was a difficult job and involved an arduous journey, so he only went to collect wood every couple of years or so.

'So how much would four whole tree trunks be worth to you?' Fido asked. 'Would they cover the cost of those rather nice wheels for instance?'

'Four whole trees would provide me with enough wood to keep busy for many years,' the man replied, 'but getting four trees back here would need an army of men to move them. I only bring back one at a time and for that I need a lot of help.'

Fido momentarily flinched at the mention of the word "army", but decided against saying anything. He began to walk out of the workshop, but turned when he reached the door. 'I'll come and see you again tomorrow morning,' he told the man.

From the wheelwright's description of the forest and the trees which grew there, Fido was easily able to find the right place using the scanners. He beamed to the location carrying a small laser torch, which resembled the light sabres Jedi Knights are supposed to carry. Having selected a suitable tree, he swished the beam backwards and forwards a few times, making a series of cuts near the base of the tree. He then stood back to await results. It was as if the tree didn't seem to know what to make of all of this, as it carried on standing there for a moment or two. Then, with a great tearing sound, it slowly began to topple over and came crashing down to the floor of the forest. Fido proceeded to cut down three more trees.

Very early the next morning, when no one was likely to be about to see the trees arriving, Fido had them transported to the wheelwright's yard. He then sat down on the nearest trunk and waited for the man to turn up for work.

The wheelwright was totally flabbergasted to see the four complete tree trunks in his yard, but immediately realised that their value was far in excess of that of the four wheels Fido wanted. To be given the trunks in exchange for the wheels was the deal of a lifetime and he wasn't about to pass up such an opportunity. The Emperor would just have to wait a while longer for his new carriage. He promptly agreed to the exchange and even threw in the axles as well. This young man had apparently achieved the impossible. There didn't seem to be any way in which he could have cut down the trees and delivered the trunks to the yard during the course of a single night - yet there they were. The wheelwright would probably spend the rest of his life wondering how it had been done. Naturally, Fido didn't explain.

With a bit more trading here and there around the world, Fido soon secured everything he needed to build Ben's new cart and started work.

A couple of weeks later, he was able to show Ben the results of all his labour. It was still a wooden cart, but much larger than the old one, with a fine set of leather trimmed wooden wheels near the back and further set of steerable wheels at the front end. The front axle assembly was connected to a pair of shafts which extended forward, to which the horse would be harnessed, and there was also a raised platform near the front of the cart for Ben to sit on. This had been well padded for his comfort and Ben would now be able to drive the cart from this position, rather than have to push or pull it along. He would only need to guide the horse in the direction he wished to go and the cart would follow automatically. Fido was extremely proud of what he had achieved and even Ben had to admit it that his new cart looked absolutely magnificent.

As the camels had been in the same place for some months, they had been quite busy and produced a lot of saleable fertiliser, which now needed to be collected and bagged-up. Ben was just about to set off with his wooden shovel to do this, when it occurred to Fido that the transporter system could accomplish the task much more easily. Piles of camel dung began disappearing from all over the place and empty sacks suddenly became full, as the computer transported the material into bags. Soon the cart was filled almost to overflowing with bulging sacks of camel dung, leaving the whole area looking decidedly cleaner than it had a few minutes earlier.

A food dispenser was brought from the cavern and installed near the front of the cart, well away from where the fertiliser was stored. Ben had got used to the amazing variety of meals such machines could produce, so Fido had insisted he should take one with him. Ben was unconvinced at first, as he didn't like the idea of travelling with something the computer had created, but his stomach finally got the better of him and he agreed, without too much reluctance. Everything was eventually ready for Ben's departure and Fido joined him by the loaded cart, so that they could say their goodbyes.

'You look after yourself,' advised Ben, 'and be careful of that thing,' he added, taking a quick look over his shoulder, in the direction of the cave.

'I'll be all right,' Fido replied. 'The computer system will never harm me.'

It was an emotional farewell and even Ben was crying as he climbed up on the cart and flicked his reins at the horse. The cart began to move and it was hardly possible to hear any noise at all from the new wheels. Fido was very pleased about this. The cart moved on, taking Fido's only ever human companion with it. Ben kept looking back every now and then, as if he still wasn't sure whether he had made the right decision in leaving.

Before long, one or two of the camels raised their heads to watch the departing cart. Most of them were grazing in the pasture. After a while, they began to follow, one or two at first, but then the rest joined in. The whole herd was soon on the move, following the direction taken by Ben on his new cart.

Fido continued to watch as Ben disappeared in the distance. Eventually, even the camels following the cart couldn't be seen. Tears began to roll down his face, as he slowly turned and began to walk back towards the cave.

12

ROC'S REWARD

For a long time after Ben's departure, Fido was very quiet. He kept his thoughts to himself for most of the time, although he did occasionally speak to the computer. His days were spent just wandering about aimlessly and he seemed to have adopted a permanent expression of sadness on his face, as if he had all the troubles of the world resting on his shoulders.

One day, he was sitting on a boulder near the mouth of the cave, idly poking at the ground with a stick, when a small bird landed a short distance away from him and began joyfully tweeting away.

'What have you got to be so happy about?' Fido casually asked, looking at the bird.

'Well, it's a lovely day, the sun is shining and it's good to be alive,' the bird replied.

Fido almost fell off his boulder in surprise.

When the computer had implanted all the Earth languages into Fido's brain, it hadn't differentiated between humans and other creatures, so Fido not only understood, but could also speak the language of any living creature on the planet, without even having to think about it. He was the Dr Dolittle of prehistoric times.

He hadn't realised this, as he had only ever spoken to human beings, or the computer, and had never tried to communicate with anything else. As such, his ability to converse with the bird came as a great shock to him and he jumped up and raced into the cavern to speak to the computer.

'Strange creature,' the bird twittered to itself, then flew off to enjoy the beautiful day.

The computer confirmed that Fido could communicate with any living thing on the planet except plants, as they didn't seem to have any intelligible vocabulary of their own. In terms of everything else, he could go off and chat with anything at all.

'If you find something you can't understand, or if it can't understand you, then let me know and I will add its language to that brain of yours.'

'So I can talk to other creatures,' Fido said to himself, as he considered the implications of this revelation. 'That does open up some interesting possibilities.' He then ran out of the cave to explore this talent he hadn't previously known about.

As Fido looked around, searching for some creature on which to test his language skills, he happened to glance upwards. Far above him, several pterodactyls were wheeling through the sky, high above the cliff. They were swooping and gliding and making full use of the thermal currents. They all looked perfectly at ease and comfortable in their environment.

'Well, I won't find the pterodactyl I'm looking for up there', he thought to himself and shouted up, 'Could one of you please come down and talk to me?' The noise coming from his mouth sounded more like chalk scraping across a blackboard, than any form of recognisable language. One of the flying pterodactyls swooped down and landed near Fido.

Fido addressed the creature, 'Would you happen to know a rather grumpy old pterodactyl? One who looks very miserable and flies really badly?'

'Do you mean Roc?' the pterodactyl asked, as it stumbled awkwardly towards him, with wings half folded and its elbow joints scraping along the ground.

'That could be the one,' Fido replied.

'Old Roc; the bane of all our lives?' queried the pterodactyl. 'Old Roc, who never stops going on about all his problems?'

'I think we could be talking about the same pterodactyl,' Fido agreed.

'Old Roc lives about a hundred kilometres west of here,' the pterodactyl told him. 'He used to have a lovely wife, but he drove her crazy with all his moaning. Now she's as nutty as he is.'

'Thank you very much,' said Fido courteously. The pterodactyl nodded in response and then took a few quick steps, before launching itself upwards. It soon reached the same height as the other pterodactyls and went back to swooping around again.

'I didn't realise we had travelled that far,' Fido thought to himself, 'but then we were travelling for quite a while.'

Now that he knew roughly where to look, he would be able to find Roc easily by using the scanners to locate him. Roc had saved his life by cushioning his fall into the ravine and now Fido wanted to meet up with him again, as an idea was beginning to form in his mind.

Roc was in trouble. He couldn't find the thermals he needed and despite his enormous wingspan, was struggling to get any lift whatsoever. He desperately needed to climb into the air as quickly as possible, as there was a human hunting party beneath him, all clearly intent on having roast pterodactyl for dinner. They were firing their arrows up at him and their aim was improving with every shot.

He furiously flapped his wings, but to no avail. Ever since that incident months previously, when he had been knocked out by a free-falling human creature landing on top of him, he had suffered really bad headaches, particularly when he tried to do anything strenuous. His vain attempts to gain altitude were bringing on yet another migraine and for the umpteenth time, he cursed his unknown assailant, for adding to his long list of troubles ills - far more than any one pterodactyl should ever be asked to bear.

The hunters were just about to send up another volley of arrows, when three things happened virtually simultaneously. Roc's frantic efforts to escape caused him to momentarily lose control of his bodily functions, and he unintentionally relieved himself - in a big way. The hunters fired their arrows into the air and Roc disappeared in a twinkle of starry lights.

The arrows flew up, passing the pterodactyl excrement on its way down. The hunters were all looking up, following the path of their arrows, and their mouths gaped wide open in amazement, when Roc disappeared. They couldn't believe that their quarry had just vanished into thin air. The poop hit the hunters. It landed on their heads and shoulders and fell into their open mouths. They all coughed, spluttered and began staggering around in total disarray. The arrows whistled harmlessly past where Roc had been just a split second before and continued upwards, until their energy was spent. At this point, they slowed and stopped, before changing direction and falling back to earth.

As the hunters had been directly under Roc when they had fired, the arrows had gone straight up and now came straight back down again, landing in amongst them. At that moment, they had other things on their minds, as well as dung all over their heads and shoulders and a very nasty taste in their mouths. Fortunately, the arrows had little energy left so no one was seriously hurt, although several men ended up with arrows sticking in their clothing and one even had an arrow stuck in his foot. The hunters immediately scattered in all directions, terrified of what might happen next.

Roc, in the meantime, suddenly found himself on the ground near the front of the cave, with his wings still outstretched and flapping. An amused Fido stood in front of him. Despite the boy's changed appearance, Roc still somehow managed to recognise him. Here stood the source of all his recent problems and Roc sprang at him in a fit of rage. In his haste to attack, he tripped over his own wings, stumbled and fell in a heap at Fido's feet.

'How are you, my old friend?' asked Fido.

When Roc had calmed down, Fido initially thanked him for being in the right place at the right time. He then tried to explain something of what had happened to him since, keeping the story as simple as possible so as not to strain the poor pterodactyl's brain. He made a point of not mentioning the computer, as this would have really blown Roc's mind. Fido summed up by saying that he intended to reward Roc for saving his life and was in a position to do anything necessary to change Roc's life for the better.

If Roc had been confused to start with, he was now totally befuddled. He had thought he was going to die, back there with the hunters, but now they weren't here and here was somewhere different as well. He didn't understand how or why he could suddenly be where he was, but it would have been pointless trying to explain it to him. Neither could he work out how Fido was speaking to him in perfect pterodactyl language. All in all, the whole situation was far too much for Roc's addled brain, so he told Fido that he needed to rest for a while. He was hoping that this might make things look a little clearer when he woke up, but also knew that it could only help his headache. Fido left Roc to sleep and returned to the cavern, to see if the computer had any suggestions for helping the creature.

Roc's principal problem, as Fido discovered when he had a long conversation with him later, was that he was totally depressed about his own life. He hated his ugly appearance, all the aches and pains that age had brought on, his inability to fly properly, and a long, long list of all the other problems and difficulties that he had to endure, every single day of his life.

'This is one neurotic pterodactyl with a negative attitude problem,' Fido thought to himself, as he politely listened to Roc's endless monologue about all the problems of being Roc.

One thing was certain. Roc was fed up with being a pterodactyl, but it would be possible to change him into some other creature, if the computer genetically modified his structure. The question was what to turn him into. Fido knew that pterodactyls were more closely related to reptiles than to dinosaurs or any other creatures, but the thought of a flying crocodile made him shudder. He was imagining the problems Harg might have caused had he also been able to fly. When he discussed this with the computer, it pointed out that such a creature already existed, in a country far to the east. Fido thought about this for a moment and then suddenly realised what the computer was referring to, Chinese dragons. They were indeed flying reptiles, even larger than pterodactyls, but that was pretty much where any resemblance ended. They were fearsome creatures and tended to be solitary and very territorial, in the same way as Harg had been. The other frightening thing about dragons was that when provoked, they were known to breathe fire out of their mouths.

'I'm not sure that Roc would like the idea of us turning him into a dragon,' Fido told the computer, 'but there is no harm in asking him.'

Fido arranged for the computer to locate a Chinese dragon and to project an image of the creature into the cavern. He then told Roc that he had something to show him and took him in to where he could watch the dragon flying about in the air. Roc immediately backed off when he saw the giant creature, as he thought it was actually there in the cavern. Fido noticed his reaction and immediately walked straight through the image, to demonstrate that it wasn't real and that there was nothing for Roc to be afraid of. The dragon in question proved to be very obliging, as it then decided to land and began strutting about, giving Roc the perfect opportunity to study it more closely. Suddenly, it seemed to sense it was being watched and responded by exhaling a long sheet of flame from its mouth, in the direction of Fido and Roc. They both jumped back in surprise, even though Fido knew the fiery blast couldn't hurt them. He turned to Roc to reassure him. The old pterodactyl was standing there with its long beak open and what could only be termed an expression of wonder on its face.

'Wow!' he said. 'What a magnificent creature!'

They stood there for quite some time watching and Fido explained all about dragons, what they ate, where they lived and as many other details as he could think of. Roc listened in amazement, but couldn't take his eyes off the moving images of the dragon.

'Would you like that sort of life?' he asked, when the picture show came to an end.

'If only I could have been born as one of those,' was Roc's reply. 'Life must be wonderful for them.'

Fido could see that Roc was hooked and what had started off as a fanciful suggestion, became the basis of the reward Fido intended to give the old pterodactyl.

'If you were to be changed into a dragon,' he said, 'it would mean leaving here and everything you know, to live in a faraway place and starting afresh.'

'There is nothing for me here,' Roc replied, 'apart from continuous pain and misery. My life is a living hell, compared to the lives those beautiful creatures enjoy? Can you really turn me into a dragon?' he asked, looking straight at Fido.

'If that is what you really want, then it can be done,' Fido told him.

The transformation involved enlarging the entrance to the kennel shaped chamber to accommodate the size of a dragon, but that was easily done. The computer then needed to obtain a dragon's genetic pattern, which it accomplished by transporting one directly into the chamber for scanning. Fido made sure he was nowhere near when this was happening, as he didn't want to be around if the creature got loose, particularly if it was annoyed about being brought to the cavern. When everything was ready, Roc was told to enter the cavern and to relax.

A few minutes later, the door to the chamber slid open and Roc emerged. He was no longer a pterodactyl, but had been transformed into a huge dragon. Fido hoped he would be pleased with what he had been turned into and not be harbouring any grudges for the earlier problems Fido had caused him. The computer had given Fido a portable stunner, which he now held in his hand. It was turned to a high power setting, just in case.

Roc wandered around for a while, periodically breathing fire in various directions, before stretching out his wings to test his flying skills. He had seen the other pterodactyls swooping around above the cliffs and recognised some of them as ones who had ridiculed him in the past. Now was the time for retribution. He leapt off the ground and with powerful beats of his wings, climbed up to meet the pterodactyls above. They had never encountered a dragon before, but what started off as curiosity quickly turned to panic, when Roc demonstrated his fire breathing abilities. He made sure he didn't actually burn any of them, but a few came very close to getting scorched. Unlike birds, many of which flap their wings continuously, pterodactyls spend most of their time gliding, so aren't used to having to perform evasive tactics in mid-air. Roc the dragon had poise and balance in the air and out-flew them at every turn. It was like watching a fighter plane in action, as he dashed in and out and continued to harass them. After they had all fled the scene, Roc returned to the ground and walked over to where Fido was standing.

'That was fantastic,' he said, in perfect dragon language. 'I wish they would come back so that I could have another go at them.'

'So you're pleased then?' Fido asked.

'Absolutely delighted,' was Roc's immediate response.

Fido suggested it was time for Roc to go and see his new home in the east and asked the computer to prepare to transport him there. Roc clearly had no remaining animosity and actually went as far as bowing to Fido, which was something you wouldn't expect to see a dragon doing. Fido was touched by this unexpected display of respect, as he felt that what he had done for Roc was no more than he deserved.

As the air around Roc began to shimmer, Fido called out,

'What about all the grand chicks you are leaving behind?'

Roc's disembodied voice could be heard responding from the ether. 'They'll just have to grow up and learn to live with being ugly. Let's see how they like that.'

13

CONFRONTATION

Spurred on by his success in finding an appropriate reward for Roc, Fido's thoughts turned to finding a way of thanking the others who had helped him, when he had really needed help.

There was of course the wandering dinosaur. Like Roc, it had been in the right place at the right time to break his fall to the bottom of the ravine, but as it had strolled off immediately afterwards, Fido didn't know where to look to find it. In fact the dinosaur had seemed to be so unconcerned about the whole incident, that Fido wondered whether it had actually even noticed what happened.

'So forgetting the dinosaur, who else is there?' he asked himself.

Fido was never likely to forget all that Ben had done for him and building him a new cart had just been a small token of his appreciation. Ben's ultimate reward would have to be much bigger and much better than that. He would need to think long and hard about what it should be before Ben returned to the cave, which Fido sincerely hoped would happen one day.

His mind went back to the slaughter of the dogs and his

escape from the village. He could picture everything that happened, exactly as it happened, but it was as if he was watching someone else. It was clear that the dinosaur pooper-scooper bodyguard had meant to kill him when he had thrown Fido into the ravine, but it had been this action which had started the entire sequence of events leading to Fido's present circumstances. There was no doubt in Fido's mind that had the bodyguard dragged him back to Greendale, rather than just throw him off the cliff, then his father and the other men of the village would have killed him immediately.

'So actually, that bodyguard saved my life,' Fido suddenly realised. 'I will need to think of a way of rewarding him, but I bet it's going to come as a big surprise.'

Clod was not the sort who enjoyed surprises. He didn't seem to enjoy much at all these days. After Fido's dog pack had been destroyed, the pooper-scoopers had been able to get on with their jobs without fear of attack. This meant that they didn't need the protection provided by Clod and the other bodyguards. Employing them had been costly and now there was no reason to keep paying these oafs if they weren't needed. Before long, bodyguards started getting laid off and when Clod was given the sack, his world fell to pieces.

He had been married for many years and now had six children. These were mostly boys and all destined to grow up into big men. What with a growing family and Clod's own prodigious appetite, it took an awful lot of food to feed everyone, and with him out of work, the future looked very bleak indeed.

He no longer wore fine black leather skins, the badge of office for pooper-scooper bodyguards, but had exchanged these for more humble attire and food for the family. What he

CONFRONTATION

wouldn't part with however, were his big wooden boots.

Clod had tried to find other work, but most prospective bosses were terrified of him and didn't like the idea of employing a great dumb ox. Most times he never even reached the interview stage, as few men were brave enough to tell him to his face that he was too stupid for them to employ.

The one job he did manage to get was walking up and down a farmer's field, pulling out all the weeds. Unfortunately, Clod's progress through the field, in his outsize wooden boots, trampled most of the crop to death and the farmer had the choice of either getting rid of him, or having no crop left to harvest. He showed uncommon bravery in telling Clod he was fired and only managed to survive by suggesting he would pay him an enormous bonus, for just one morning's work. Clod may have been daft, but he was not stupid enough to turn this down, as it meant food on the table for his family. The farmer lived to carry on farming, but Clod found himself out of work again.

The family had been forced to move into a one room mud hut, which was an almighty come down from the upmarket home where they used to live. This hovel was situated in the village of Humalot, about ten kilometres north of Greendale. Everything about the place was depressing and it was mostly inhabited by people who were down on their luck, out of work, or just bone idle.

The village couldn't afford a pooper-scooper so nobody cleaned up the dinosaur droppings, which only added to the overall repulsiveness of the place. All the kids were filthy, wild dogs ran amok in the streets and no estate agent ever dropped by to suggest that properties in Humalot were much sought after. It had to be one of the worst possible places in the world to live, but it was all Clod could afford. Everyone who moved there quickly became totally despondent and Clod and his family were no exception.

Humalot had originally been built to the north of what can only be described as a really obnoxious smelling swamp. It was now difficult to tell whether the village had risen from the swamp, or whether the swamp was busy trying to reclaim the village. It was at least a kilometre across and extended that far to the south as well. To the west, was a dense forest of pine trees which ended by the edge of the swamp. The few visitors who ever came to Humalot were not prepared to struggle through the forest, but also made every effort to avoid going anywhere near the swamp. This meant they had to circle round both obstacles, which added a considerable distance to their journey. Few visitors ever bothered to make the trip.

Fido materialised on the very edge of the swamp, having been transported there by the computer.

'Oh, what a stink!' he exclaimed upon arriving. 'If I had known it was going to smell like this, I would have brought along a gas mask.'

It was his own fault though, as when the computer had asked him where he wanted to arrive; he had told it to transport him to a spot two hundred metres south of the village. He should have said a hundred and ninety five metres, as he would then have been on solid ground. He looked down at his feet and noticed they were slowly sinking. Using the levitation device he carried in his satchel, he raised his body out of the slimy ooze, freeing himself from the swamp's unwelcome advances, and began trudging towards the village. This was not a particularly good start to his mission to reward the bodyguard.

At that moment, Clod was moodily wandering about near the middle of the village. He was feeling particularly miserable, having been thinking back about the life he had once enjoyed,

CONFRONTATION

and was a bit surprised to hear a voice calling him.

'Hey there,' Fido called out. 'Do you remember me?'

He looked up to see a young man standing in front of him. He was smartly dressed, apart from mud all over his shoes, and Clod didn't recognise him at all.

'I don't know you,' he growled.

'You must remember me,' Fido prompted. 'Think back a bit.'

Clod wasn't very good at thinking and certainly didn't like people telling him to think. His face began to redden as he started to get annoyed. Fido obviously noticed this and was aware that an angry Clod could be a very dangerous thing. Fortunately, he was well prepared for this meeting, as he hadn't really expected to be swept off his feet and be given a joyful hug.

Fido decided that it was probably not a good idea to prolong Clod's obvious confusion, so he took the plunge.

'I know I looked a lot different then, but you picked me up by my hair and threw me over a cliff. I'm Fido, the dog-boy.'

Clod continued to look mystified, but then slowly began to work it all out. Realisation suddenly dawned and a look of loathing quickly replaced his confused expression. He let out a tremendous roar and hurled himself at Fido, clearly intent on tearing him limb from limb.

Fido raised his arm, revealing a small object he had been holding in his hand. He pointed it at Clod and pressed the button.

Zing!

The force of the portable stunner (which resembled a Star Trek phaser) would have stopped most men, but Clod was a lot bigger than most men. He merely staggered a bit, before continuing his onward rush towards Fido. Adjusting the setting as he took several quick paces backwards, Fido fired again.

Zing!

The more powerful setting didn't just stop Clod in his tracks. It actually lifted him off his feet and threw him backwards several metres. He crashed to the ground on his backside and began to shake his head violently, as if to clear his befuddled brain. A moment or two later, he was up again and clearly still determined to get to Fido.

When Fido raised the weapon again, Clod hesitated. He certainly hadn't expected to have any trouble dealing with this pesky youngster, but the young man had just floored him. He stopped and began to stare at him, a look akin to respect forming on his face. There were very few people indeed, who could stop a rampaging Clod, but there was no doubting what had just happened.

Fido continued to point his stunner, but when it looked as if the danger of a renewed assault had passed, he lowered the weapon and continued talking.

'Just calm down for a minute' he told Clod. 'I don't want to have to hurt you again. I just want to talk to you.'

Fido explained how being thrown off the cliff had turned out to be a blessing in disguise, because of everything that had happened to him since, but it took a long time for Clod to understand that Fido was actually pleased about what he had done. His head was still reeling from the stunner charge, but Fido appeared to be telling him that he was going to be rewarded for throwing the boy into the ravine.

He nodded his dazed head and spoke, 'Can we talk about this a bit later? I don't feel too well at the moment.'

Fido could understand the huge man's confusion, particularly when he checked the setting he had used for his second shot. It was incredible that Clod was still alive, let alone still able to speak.

CONFRONTATION

'I'll come and see you tomorrow,' he said, 'and we'll talk again.'

With that, Fido turned and began to walk out of the village. As soon as he was out of sight, he dematerialised, to reappear back at the cave.

Clod slowly stumbled back to his hut. His whole body felt numb and his head was swimming. He staggered in, stumbling against the doorway in the process. The whole building shook with the impact.

Betty, his wife, was very surprised at the sight of her husband. She had never seen him looking so shaken, or with such a strange expression on his face.

'What happened to you?' she asked, with genuine concern.

'I don't know,' he replied in a strained voice. 'I think I've just been beaten up by a kid!'

Clod slumped to the floor of the hut and didn't utter another word for several hours, to allow his body time to recover from the effect of the second stunner blast.

Betty sat down opposite him, at a total loss as to what to say. There were few men around, let alone a kid, who could have possibly done this to her man. It was unbelievable. When the children returned home, from whatever mischief they had been up to, they were their usual noisy selves and promptly began arguing with one another. She silenced them with a glare which meant business. They sat down looking puzzled. Their dad seemed to have just collapsed on the floor and their mum was sitting opposite him, with a strange look on her face. The kids really wanted to know what was going on and questions were buzzing around in their heads, but their mum's look had stunned them into silence and they knew better than to argue with her.

Much later, Clod came to again and stepped outside the hut.

Betty followed him out. The room instantly came alive and the noise level went off the scale, as all the kids started shouting and questioning each other about what could possibly have happened.

Clod told Betty about his meeting with Fido. He was feeling much more himself now, as the effects of the stunner had more or less gone. She was equally mystified about the incident and they both looked lost in thought, when they came back into the hut. The kids immediately shut up and looked at their parents expectantly, hoping for an explanation. They weren't given one and the hut was unusually quiet, when the family finally retired for the night.

14

FIDO'S BUSINESS PLAN

Fido arrived at breakfast time the following morning, to find Clod and his family all sitting around in a circle, inside the hut, with their meagre breakfast on the floor in front of them. There was half a loaf of stale bread, a few biscuits, some rather dodgy looking animal meat and a few chunks of goat's cheese. Fido stood in the doorway and surveyed their meal.

'This will just not do,' he muttered.

After thinking for a moment or two, he decided what needed to be done and sent a telepathic message to the computer. Fido then waited for the fun to start.

Moments later, the food they had been about to eat began to shimmer and then disappeared. There were immediate gasps of surprise. A few seconds later, plates and dishes full of hot steaming food began appearing in the middle of the hut and kept on arriving. There was soon hardly any space left and the family began backing towards the sides of the hut, to make room for all the different dishes which kept appearing. They were all awestruck, as none of them had ever seen such a magnificent feast before.

'Tuck in,' Fido told them. 'There's more if you need it.'

The kids needed no second telling and dived in without a moment's hesitation. Betty looked at her husband, who was just sitting there rooted to the spot, staring at Fido. Slowly, she cautiously began to eat some of the food and found it to be delicious. She was soon eating away furiously, determined to try all the different dishes on offer.

'I'll just wander about for a bit and come back when you've finished,' Fido told them, before leaving the hut.

Clod's gaze turned to the dozens of plates and dishes now crowding the hut. There were huge joints of meat, warm loaves of freshly baked bread, savoury pies, poached fish, shellfish, cheeses, all manner of vegetables, exotic fruits and many, many more choice delicacies. He had never seen such a banquet before in his life. He dived in and began to eat voraciously. As Clod tucked in, there were quite a few people in different parts of the world, staring blankly at empty breakfast tables and wondering how their food had suddenly disappeared.

The computer seemed to have an unnerving knack of being able to find anything it wanted, anywhere in the world, at any given time. When Fido had asked about this, as he considered it to be stealing from other people, the computer had pointed out that there were a lot of people in the world who had far more than they would ever need, so if they lost a few things here and there, it wouldn't mean much to them anyway.

'Besides,' it added, 'As I am all powerful, there is nothing to stop me doing whatever I decide to do.'

When Fido returned from his tour of the village, which only confirmed just how much of a tip this place really was, the whole family were standing outside their hut, with Clod at the front of the group. They all had a well-stuffed appearance and Clod actually appeared to be smiling broadly. He stepped forward and stretched out his hand. Fido cautiously extended his own hand and with great trepidation, allowed Clod to envelop it within his giant paw. His hand was shaken vigorously, leaving Fido breathless and worried that some of his fingers might have been broken.

Betty ran forward and bobbed up and down in a curtsy.

'We don't know what to say or how to thank you for all that food,' she said nervously, starting to turn red with embarrassment. 'We don't understand how it got here, or where it all came from.'

'Don't worry about that,' Fido told her. 'It's of no importance.' He was wondering how many cooks around the world were thinking the same, as they set about preparing breakfast for their masters, for a second time.

Fido played with the children for a while and entertained them with some magic tricks. Most of these seemed to involve things vanishing and reappearing elsewhere, but it was real magic as far as the kids were concerned. He was trying to get everyone to relax and his magic tricks seemed to be doing the job, as the tension in the hut quickly began to ease.

Later, he explained exactly why he was there and his reason for wanting to reward Clod. It quickly became apparent that Clod let his wife do most of his thinking for him, as he just sat there listening, with a daft expression on his face. He looked almost benign and affable. When Fido came to explaining his plans in more detail, he directed everything he had to say to Betty.

'First things first,' he told her, 'we need to clean up this village and get rid of that swamp. That's an absolute priority.' Betty thought the scale of the task would make this a virtual impossibility, but said nothing.

Fido went on to explain how he wanted to turn Humalot into

a prosperous village, with her and Clod as important members of the community. Betty slowly nodded, wondering just what was coming next.

'Once this place looks and smells a lot better,' Fido continued, 'we can consider what skills you and Clod have and work out how to make best use of them.'

'I'm quite good with my hands,' Betty chipped in, 'but Clod is not that bright and can really only do things that involve using his brute strength and muscle.' Clod enthusiastically nodded in agreement.

'No problem,' Fido replied. 'I've got a few ideas, but first, I want to show you something.'

He told her to close her eyes and hold his hand. After following his instructions, she began to feel a strange tingling sensation all over her body.

'You can open your eyes now,' Fido told her.

Betty did so, to find that she was standing outside a large building. She was no longer in Humalot.

Fido led her inside. There were about six women inside the building and they were taking funny looking balls of fluff from a basket and teasing and combing them with a brush, to separate them into smaller fluff balls. Betty didn't understand what any of this was about. Their visit must have been expected though, as one of the women motioned her to come and sit beside her, so that Betty could see exactly what she was doing. The looser balls of fluff were being placed in other baskets and from time to time, someone came in and took these away, replacing them with empty baskets. Betty was mystified, but Fido had more surprises to show her.

He then led her to another building, where other women were sitting behind strange looking machines, the like of which Betty had never seen before in her life.

'These are called spinning wheels,' he told her. 'I want you to watch what happens next.'

The women were each taking one of the loose fluff balls from the baskets and pulling out some its fibres, which they then attached to a length of thread, stretching from the fluff ball in their hand to the machine in front of them. Each machine had a big wooden wheel, which turned round quite quickly and was connected to a small round bobbin, on which the yarn they were producing was being wound. As each bobbin became full, the women would take them off the spinning wheel and put them to one side. Fido picked one up and handed it to Betty, who took hold of the loose end of yarn and tugged at it with her fingers. She couldn't believe it, but the thin twisted yarn, looking no thicker that a spider's web, seemed to be incredibly strong.

The tour continued, as Fido took her into yet another building. Here, the yarn was being woven into cloth and these noisy wooden machines looked just as weird as the spinning wheels. Betty watched in fascination, as the yarn she had seen produced from fluff balls was turned into cloth and wound onto a roller. Taking a finished roll of cloth, Fido began unrolling it, so that Betty could see what had been produced.

'This is called cloth,' he told her, 'and it's cut into different shapes, which are then stitched together with the same thread, to make clothes and other useful things.' Fido then pointed to his own clothes.

'That is how these garments were made.'

Betty touched his tunic, before fingering the roll of cloth from the machine.

'It's amazing,' she said.

Fido asked whether she thought she could possibly do something like this herself, if given all the necessary equipment and materials.

'I suppose it's possible,' Betty replied, 'but I would need an awful lot of training, as I'm sure it must take a long time to learn all those different skills.'

'You wouldn't believe how quickly you could learn them all,' Fido told her, a smile on his face, 'but for now, we had better be getting back to Clod.'

She closed her eyes, in preparation for experiencing that strange tingling feeling again and the next thing she knew, she was back standing inside her own hut again.

Fido asked Clod whether he was any good at chopping down trees.

'Well I can,' he replied cautiously, 'but it takes a long time, so I don't bother much.' He showed Fido a stone axe, which he kept in the hut.

'Yes, I guess it would with that,' Fido agreed, looking at the primitive tool. 'Let's see how you get on with this one.' A metal headed axe with a long wooden handle suddenly appeared in his hand. There were more gasps of amazement, as yet another object materialised out of thin air. Fido almost dropped the axe, because it was so heavy, but when he passed it to Clod, the big man swung it around as if it was as light as a feather.

Everyone trooped out of the hut and set off towards the forest. The family were surprised to see so many villagers about, gathered here and there in little groups. They all seemed deep in conversation and some were pointing in different directions, as if explaining something to the others. It was one of the kids who noticed first.

'Where has all the dinosaur poo-poo gone daddy?' he asked. Everyone looked about them. Every single pile of dinosaur dung had completely vanished.

'That's a good job done,' Fido observed.

FIDO'S BUSINESS PLAN

When they reached the forest, Fido pointed at one of the trees and told Clod to start with that one. The huge man spat on his hands, lifted the axe and began swinging. Before long, he had cut a wedge shape near the base of the tree. He then walked round to the other side and made some further cuts there. With the wedges cut, Clod then leaned against the tree, causing it to topple and crash to the ground. Fido measured out a number of lengths along its trunk and instructed Clod to cut the tree into sections. They repeated this with a number of other trees and after a while, there were a dozen or so ten metre lengths of timber lying on the ground.

'That will do for a start,' Fido announced. 'Now let's get them back.'

Clod picked up the front end of the first section and began to drag it towards the village. Fido was astounded to see just how strong Clod really was. When it was his turn to do the same thing with another section, he cheated a little by using his levitation device. It looked as if he had picked up the tree trunk and was dragging it, but Fido knew better. When all the sections had been brought back to the village, Fido asked Betty to select a location for their new house.

After gathering a few more big bodyguards to help, an area of ground was stamped flat with their wooden boots. The first log was placed in position, to one side of the flattened area, and its ends were shaped with the axe, so that each formed a half joint. Three more logs were added in the same way, each joined at ninety degrees to the next, forming a box of logs, the height of a tree's diameter. Another layer of logs was then added to the first and this process continued, until all the logs had been used up. Everyone stood back to admire their handiwork.

Fido told Betty that this would be the family's new home. The men would just keep doing what they had been doing, until the walls were high enough. They could then construct a roof using thinner logs and cover the top of this with dried reeds. Doors and windows would need to be cut out and any gaps on the inside should be filled with mud, which would dry out and seal the walls. When all this was done, the place would be about ready for the family to move in. It all looked so simple that everyone wondered why nobody had ever thought of it before.

While Clod and the men went to cut down some more trees, Fido had a long chat with Betty. He told her that his idea was for the family to go into the house building business. When people saw her new home, they would all want one like it and be prepared to pay. Clod and his mates would provide the timber and the labour and if they were to obtain an ox and cart as well, they would then be able to transport the timber and build houses wherever anyone wanted one.

'You will need to be the overall boss,' Fido told her, 'as I can't really see Clod running the whole show on his own.'

Betty thought about this for a while before replying, 'You know, I think I could make that work.'

'Good,' he said, then went on to explain that he also intended to set Betty up in her own cloth manufacturing business, which would give her something to do while Clod was busy building houses.

'You will be able to sell whatever you produce,' he told her, 'and that will provide you with additional family income.'

Fido had already asked the computer to build a couple of spinning wheels and a weaving machine for Betty, which was something it could readily do, by copying existing ones.

The only other thing left on Fido's list was clearing the swamp and a specially modified scanner was already hovering over it, waiting for the instruction to proceed. When this was given, the machine fired short bursts of energy directly into the swamp, at various points all across its surface. These energy bursts bored deep holes into the ground and provided drainage, which allowed the water to seep away. This would effectively stop the area from ever returning to swamp, but the top layer was still very wet and oozy.

When the scanner had finished boring holes, a parabolic reflector opened out and was angled to harness the sun's rays and direct them where required. For the next few days, clouds of steam obscured what had once been an eyesore, as the water was evaporated and the swamp slowly dried out. When the entire process was complete, the area looked much like any other field. It stilled hummed a bit, but this shouldn't last for more than a few days. Fido was very pleased with the result and strolled across the new field, kicking at odd clumps of dry soil. All it now needed was for its crop to be planted.

Fido managed to obtain enough cotton plants for the entire field, by a bit of bartering in various places around the world. The farmers with which he traded were all pleased with the deals they made, as he could offer them things they couldn't readily obtain for themselves. The computer was all for just taking the plants, but Fido insisted that they had to be paid for. When it came to transplanting them from one field to another, a great deal of care was taken to ensure that their root structures remained intact, which meant removing them from the ground with a large amount of surrounding soil. This left some big holes in a few fields, but the farmers didn't seem to be that bothered by this. Fido hoped that the plants might not even notice that they had been moved and would continue to grow happily and shortly produce a good cotton crop.

Betty spent a short time within the chamber in the cavern and when she emerged, she knew everything there was to know about growing cotton and all the processes involved in spinning and weaving. She was even taught how to make clothes from the cloth. When she returned to her house, she was delighted to see that the spinning wheels and a weaving machine had already arrived, together with a large number of cotton heads, ready to be turned into yarn. She lovingly ran her hands over her new equipment and couldn't wait to get started.

'There are more than enough cotton heads there to get you going,' Fido told her, 'and you could always employ some of the women in the village to help you.'

With what Betty now knew, she didn't think it would be too difficult for her to train up some of the village women and they could also help with the cotton harvest, when that was ready.

After all his recent activity Fido felt like he needed a rest, so for the next few days he just watched over proceedings, as Clod got on with building houses and Betty set about establishing her weaving business. When both seemed to have the necessary confidence to continue on their own, he knew it was time for him to take his leave.

The following morning, Fido said his goodbyes to the entire family, having treated them to another slap-up breakfast first. As they stood by the doorway of the new house, Betty burst into tears. She was really sad to see him go, but was full of gratitude for everything he had done for them. It was going to take a lot of hard work to get the two businesses off the ground, but everything was now in place and the future looked really promising. Clod was also sorry to see Fido go and insisted on shaking hands with him again. Fido couldn't really refuse, although he knew his hand would be sore for days afterwards.

When there was nothing more to be said, Fido bade them farewell and then, with a cheerful wave, vanished into thin air.

15

BEDRIC'S JUST DESSERTS

During the time when Fido had been at Humalot, he had asked several of the villagers if they had any news about Greendale. It was now almost a year since his sudden departure from the village and he wanted to know why his father, together with some of the other men of the village, had slaughtered the dogs in the pack. A number of the villagers were able to tell him that the dogs had been put to death on the specific instructions of Bedric the wise man and that he had also ordered the death of their dog-boy leader, who had initially escaped but was subsequently also killed.

'Was that just because I bit him on the leg?' Fido asked himself later. 'If that's the only reason, then Bedric is certainly a very vindictive old man.'

He could forgive the attempt to kill him, because this had led to all the good things which had happened to him since, but the dogs were a different matter.

They hadn't attacked Bedric, so were technically innocent, or as innocent as it was possible for dogs to be. As a hunting pack they had provided a useful service to the village and there was no doubt in Fido's mind that the dogs had not deserved to die. Bedric had used them as a scapegoat, simply because he was angry, and as the person responsible for the death of the dogs, he needed to have the error of his ways pointed out to him.

The computer was all in favour of causing Bedric the maximum amount of excruciating pain by way of retribution, but Fido wasn't interested in revenge. The computer could be very sadistic and Bedric was lucky that it had not passed this character trait on to Fido, when it had transferred everything else into his brain. All Fido wanted to do was to make Bedric understand that what he had done was very wrong, in the hope that it would make him think before ever doing anything like it again.

It didn't take too long to scan around and find Bedric, as he had just left Greendale and was on his way to the next village. Fido was pleased about this, as it would make it much easier for him to raise the subject of Greendale, when they met up. Having selected a quiet spot on Bedric's route for their meeting, he prepared to be transported to what the computer kept calling the ambush point. He was carrying his leather satchel, which contained a few useful items supplied by the computer, including the portable stunner and his levitation device.

It was a hot day, even though it was only late morning, so Fido sat under the canopy of a large tree to wait in its shade. Bedric was happily walking along the path, feeling very pleased with himself. He had been lavishly entertained in Greendale and had also been happy to learn that the Stones were struggling to survive, now that Judd no longer had his dog pack.

'Serves them right,' he told himself. 'I certainly fixed them.'

He was looking forward to reaching the tree where he

sometimes stopped for lunch and was surprised when he looked ahead and noticed that someone else was already sitting there. As he got closer, he could see that it was a young man, but not one that he recognised from any of the local villages.

'Hello,' said Fido, when Bedric reached the tree. 'You must be hot out there in the sun. Come and share the shade given by this beautiful tree.'

'I will do that,' Bedric replied, as he plonked himself down next to Fido.

'It's a lovely day, if a little warm,' said the old man.

He withdrew a drinking flask from under the folds of his cloak and went to take a refreshing drink. As he did so, he suddenly began to splutter, cough and retch. Instead of the cooling water he had expected, he found he had a mouthful of sand.

Fido quietly smiled to himself. The computer was obviously watching and couldn't resist the temptation of joining in.

'Cut that out,' Fido said to himself, knowing full well that the computer would pick up his thought waves.

'Please have some water from my flask,' suggested Fido, offering his own water bottle to the wise man.

'Yes, thank you,' Bedric replied. 'I can't imagine how it happened, but I seem to have sand in my flask.'

He took a deep draft from the offered water bottle. 'That's better,' he said. 'My name is Bedric,' he then told Fido, 'I'm a travelling wise man and am on my way to the next village having just left Greendale, a few kilometres down the road there.' He waved his arm in the direction from which he had travelled.

'So what is your name and where are you from?' He asked, rather directly.

'Call me Ishmael,' Fido replied, wondering why that name

had just popped into his head. 'I come from Humalot to the north.'

Bedric observed Fido with a slightly suspicious expression. He was a shrewd old man and the years had made him wily. Fido began to realise that Bedric was unlikely to accept anything at face value, so he had better be very careful what he said.

'You don't look like the sort of person who would live in a place like Humalot,' Bedric suggested thoughtfully.

'Oh, it has changed quite a bit lately,' Fido responded. 'You wouldn't recognise the place now.'

There was an uneasy silence while Bedric considered this.

'Now he thinks I'm a liar,' Fido thought to himself. 'This is a great start.'

Bedric didn't really care where Ishmael came from and had just been making polite conversation. He decided to let it go.

'So what's Greendale like now?' Fido asked. 'I haven't been there in a long time.'

'Much better now,' replied the old man, 'especially since that dog-boy and his troublesome hounds were killed.'

'So, what was all that about?' Fido enquired, trying to make the question sound as casual as possible.

Bedric began to tell him the story. He explained how the Fido gang had been terrorising the village, attacking pooper-scoopers, stealing food, and generally making life difficult for everyone. He went on to explain that the pack had been uncontrollable, except for when they were on hunting trips, and that the only person they ever paid any attention to was this boy Fido, who was half-wild himself and more trouble than all the rest of them put together.

'Something had to be done about them,' he went on to say. 'So I told the man who owned the dogs that the boy and the dogs had all been possessed by an evil spirit.' This wasn't exactly what he had said to the Stones, but he did like to embellish every story he told.

'So what did he say?' asked Fido, keen to hear Bedric's justification for his actions.

'Oh, he was upset of course,' continued Bedric, 'but then asked me for my advice.'

'So what did you suggest? Some sort of ceremony, to banish the evil spirit?' Fido asked innocently.

'No, nothing like that,' Bedric retorted, 'I told him to kill the lot, including the dog-boy.'

It was immediately apparent to Fido that Bedric wasn't in the least bit sorry for what he had done and didn't seem in the least bit concerned that he had ordered the unnecessary deaths of the dogs. In fact, he seemed to be rather pleased about it.

'Was that the only thing that could have been done?' Fido queried. 'Was it the right thing to do?'

Bedric turned to look at the boy, with a quizzical expression on his face.

'Right or wrong, it served the purpose and solved a problem,' he replied, smiling before he added. 'Besides, I was well paid for the advice I gave.'

No more was said on the subject and the pair of them sat in almost total silence while they both ate their lunch. Fido was deep in thought and troubled by this insight into the character of this so-called wise man.

When Bedric finished his lunch, he got up and said, 'Well, I must be going, but it's been nice talking to you.'

'You really don't care who suffers as a result of the advice you give, do you?' Fido suddenly blurted out. 'You only seem to care about yourself and how you're rewarded. I thought you were supposed to be wise and worthy of respect, but you're not. You don't give any thought at all for other people.'

Bedric was momentarily startled by this outburst, but soon recovered his composure.

'That's the way of the world, son,' he sneered. 'Now tell me who you really are.'

'I'm Fido, the half-wild dog-boy you ordered killed!' Fido shouted back.

Bedric was genuinely stunned by this and tried to make sense of what he had just heard.

'That's impossible,' he responded. 'He's dead and besides, you don't look anything like him.'

Bedric didn't know what was going on, but knew he would be no match for this angry young man, if attacked. He became concerned for his own safety and began to get frightened. Any possible help was several kilometres away and he was trapped here with someone who seemed to have gone mad. Fido could see the fear in Bedric's eyes and wondered what thought processes were going on in his mind.

'Don't worry,' he said, 'I'm not going to hurt you, but I am going to teach you a lesson. You need to learn respect for others, be they people or animals.'

'You don't scare me,' Bedric shouted back, with a flash of bravado. 'There's nothing you can do to me.'

He turned and walked away, stumbling as he did so, because of his agitated state.

Although Fido had not intended to get angry, he certainly planned what happened next. He sent a telepathic message to the computer and waited.

A large and rather nasty looking dinosaur suddenly appeared a few paces in front of Bedric. As it roared, it displayed a mouthful of sharp teeth. The now fearful Bedric spun around, a look of abject terror on his face. A second dinosaur materialised in the direction he was now facing. Bedric let out a scream and fainted, collapsing to the ground. Both dinosaurs instantly disappeared.

Fido strolled over to Bedric, who by now was a complete gibbering wreck.

'I think you're beginning to learn already,' he observed.

He helped the old man to his feet and almost had to carry him back to the tree, where he deposited him on the ground. Fido handed Bedric the water flask and watched as he tried to drink from the container, with his hands shaking uncontrollably.

After a while, Bedric regained some of his composure but kept looking around anxiously, wondering where the dinosaurs had gone. He was sitting hunched up against the tree, with his outstretched legs slightly apart and covered by the folds of his long cloak.

'Those dinosaurs weren't real,' he declared. 'They were a hallucination probably brought on by something I ate, or perhaps there was something in that water you gave me.'

'Really?' said Fido. 'Well here's another one.' A big brown rat suddenly materialised on Bedric's lap, in the middle of his outstretched cloak. The rat looked somewhat surprised to find itself there, but this didn't stop it clamping its jaws onto one of Bedric's fingers, as soon as he tried to push it off his lap.

Bedric jumped up in horror, raising his arm at the same time. Hanging from his hand was the rat, now firmly attached to his finger and clearly intent on chewing its way down to the bone. Bedric screamed again, this time in real pain. The rat disappeared.

'Did that hallucination bite you?' Fido asked, with a wry grin on his face. 'I didn't think hallucinations were supposed to do things like that.'

Bedric sat down again, staring at his damaged finger. It was bleeding quite profusely.

'You do seem to make a habit of getting bitten, don't you?' Fido added, with a smile.

Bedric began to wonder whether he had gone mad. The pain in his finger was real enough, so the rat couldn't have been a hallucination. He was now scared witless.

Fido reached into his satchel and pulled out a small metallic box. He then walked over and pointed it at Bedric's damaged finger. A green beam emanated from the box and the finger immediately stopped bleeding. Bedric watched in amazement as the cut skin began to knit itself together again and the wound closed, leaving his finger without a mark on it.

'Handy little device, isn't it?' Fido commented. 'It produces a genetic healing beam and I carry it with me in case I get injured.' Bedric gave up trying to understand.

'I think you'll find the lesson I've chosen for you is very appropriate,' Fido went on to say. 'You had those dogs killed needlessly and even now you don't feel in the slightest bit guilty about it. I have decided that you are going to spend the next twelve months living in a dog pack.'

Bedric was staring at Fido uncomprehendingly.

Fido went on to explain that living in a dog pack wasn't going to be easy, as dogs had to respect other dogs or face being picked on mercilessly. They also had their human masters to contend with, who might mistreat them, by beating and kicking them for no good reason.

'I really think you are going to love it.' Fido added, but then noticed that the bewildered look on Bedric's face was slowly turning into a nasty smirk.

'You can't force me to live in a dog pack,' Bedric threw back at him triumphantly. 'Nobody can make me stay there, as I'll just get up and leave.'

'You haven't heard the best bit yet,' Fido told him, a wide grin spreading over his face. 'When I said you are going to live as a dog, I meant exactly what I said.'

'Now you're talking absolute rubbish,' Bedric retorted. 'I knew there was something strange about you and now I know what it is. You are completely out of your mind.'

As he stopped talking, he began to feel a strange tingling sensation in his body. He didn't know what it was, but it wasn't too unpleasant, just confusing. Suddenly, he found himself standing next to a fence, surrounding a patch of waste land. Within the enclosure were a dozen or so dogs, none of which looked particularly happy. Fido stood beside him.

'This will be your new home for the next year,' Fido told him. 'I wanted you to see it before you move in.'

Bedric briefly glanced at the enclosure, before looking around at the village. He didn't recognise the place at all, so it had to be somewhere he had never previously visited.

'Where are we and how did we get here?' he asked.

'Oh, that was easy,' he was told. 'It's the next bit that is really going to blow your mind.'

The strange tingling sensation began again and when it stopped, Bedric found himself standing inside a sealed chamber. A humming sound started up.

Bedric slowly realised that he must be shrinking. He had been looking down at his feet and they seemed to be getting closer. His leather sandals then split apart and big furry paws grew right out of them. He felt a force on his back and fell forwards, landing on his hands. As he watched, they gradually changed into another set of paws. He turned to see what had pushed him, only to be horrified at the sight of a long furry back, stretching out to a tail. At this point, he fainted again.

When he came to, Fido was standing next to him again, but now seemed to tower above him. The fence was still there as well, but it was much higher than it had been before. The truth slowly dawned on him, as he looked down at his furry chest. Although it was absolutely impossible, someone or something had transformed him into a dog.

Looking up at Fido, he tried to say, 'What's happened to me?' but all that came out of his mouth was a series of barks.

Fido barked back at him, 'I told you that you were going to live as a dog.' To his utter amazement, Bedric found that he could understand the barked response.

Fido bent down and picked Bedric up. He lifted him over the fence and gently placed him on the ground inside the dog run.

'I'll see you again in a year's time,' he barked at Bedric. 'Do try and have a good time.'

Fido had seen the other dogs were watching and they now started to move towards Bedric, some of them growling.

Fido barked at the other dogs, 'You look after him for me and be gentle with him. He has no experience of being a dog.'

'Help me!' Bedric barked, as Fido gave him a cheerful wave and disappeared in a twinkle of starry lights.

16

EGYPT

When Fido returned to the cave, leaving Bedric to work out how to live as a dog, he felt that justice had been served. He knew that the self-proclaimed wise man wouldn't have an easy time, but it was richly deserved punishment, for a lifetime of taking advantage of other people. Fido didn't feel he had been too harsh on the man and sincerely hoped that he would be a changed person, when released in a year's time. The computer's view was that Fido had been too far too soft on Bedric, but then it could be very vindictive.

Fido's thoughts turned to his parents and the problems they were facing. The loss of his dog pack meant that hunting must now be that much more difficult for his father and this was the family's principal source of income. Looking back, he now realised that his parents had tried to encourage him to develop throughout his growing years, so it was really his own fault that they had given up on him and thrown him out to join the dogs. As an impossible child, he had made life very difficult for them, so they couldn't really be blamed for disowning him. Also, with everything he had discovered about Bedric, he could now see how the old fraud had forced them into following his instructions with regard to Fido and the dogs, so this was something else for which his parents couldn't be blamed.

'I must go and see them some time,' he told the computer, 'and try to make amends for all the problems I caused them.'

'You suffered at their hands, so let them suffer,' the computer suggested. 'I could make life even harder for them if you like.'

'Don't you dare,' Fido quickly responded, 'I don't want you to add to their problems.'

Facing his parents was going to be difficult and while Fido knew he would have to do it eventually, it was not something he was really looking forward to.

'Perhaps I will go and see them next month,' he told himself.

Fido had been thinking over what the computer had said a while back about travelling. After all, the world was his oyster and there were a lot of places he could visit and explore.

'I think I will take a trip,' he suddenly announced. 'Where do you think I should go?'

The computer had a keen interest in Egypt, having inadvertently changed the country's religion, so it regularly scanned the place to watch developments. There were many places in the world where civilisation had progressed way beyond Fido's land and Egypt was definitely one of these. The computer considered Egypt to be one of the most advanced countries on Earth and as such, it would be a very educational place for Fido to visit.

'Why don't you go and have a look at Egypt?' it suggested. 'They are getting along really well there and up to all sorts of interesting thing.'

Now that it had given Fido something to think about, instead of just worrying about his parents, the computer went back to what it had been doing before. As usual, this had something to do with the time transporter system.

In Egypt, the Pharaoh was a troubled man. His only daughter, Nefertari, had just reached her seventeenth birthday and was now of marrying age. His problem was finding a suitable husband for her. He knew there would be no shortage of suitors, as there were many princes in neighbouring countries, but the Pharaoh was concerned that some of their fathers might be more interested in getting a toehold in Egypt, than they were with the happiness of the future royal couple. There was also the point that Nefertari could be a feisty girl and would be most unhappy with the idea of marrying someone she didn't care for. She was unlikely to go as far as actually disobeying her father, so would marry whoever he selected for her, but she would then make sure his life from then on was a misery, and he didn't need that sort of grief from his seventeen year old daughter.

The Pharaoh was also having problems with religious dissidents. Before the arrival of the cat god, the three principal deities in Egypt had been the Sun, the Moon and the Nile. When the cat god had appeared at his grandfather's birthday party, his grandfather had announced that this new god was far more powerful than the other three and decreed that the entire country should switch to cat worship.

This had not caused too many problems at the time, which had been many years previously, but when there were no further demonstrations of the cat god's power, together with the fact that the cat itself had promptly died and had to be mummified, the people gradually began to have doubts about whether this cat god was all it was cracked up to be.

By this Pharaoh's time, most Egyptians were moderately

happy with their cat god, but the same could not be said for the priests of the old gods. They were out of favour, out of luck, and out of a job. They blamed the present Pharaoh for their misfortunes, despite the fact that it was his grandfather who was actually responsible, and began demonstrating and protesting about the situation, calling for the reinstatement of the old gods. Initially, their activities went mostly unnoticed. They tried to disrupt cat worship ceremonies, or paraded the streets in their priest's robes, but then they became militant.

Graffiti slogans like "Cat God go home" and "Who needs nine lives anyway?" began to appear on walls. These were quickly scrubbed off, but seemed to re-appear a few days later. The latest tactic adopted by the protesters was stealing statues of the cat god and holding them to ransom. This rapidly came to be known as cat-napping and was now becoming quite a serious problem. Although the Pharaoh made every effort to catch the perpetrators, none of the old priests were ever brought to trial.

Egypt itself was a rich country. There was an awful lot of sand about, but the area bordering the Nile was very fertile and the farmers there enjoyed a fairly easy life. The Egyptians had discovered how to make sea-going boats and now traded with many other countries bordering the sea to their north. Gold was also important to them and had become a measure of the value of goods being traded. Rich Egyptians would often wear gold ornaments attached to their clothing, in the same way as the women in Fido's land wore shiny stones. Their clothes were made from cotton, which grew abundantly in Egypt, and these light robes were perfectly suited to the hot climate the country always enjoyed.

The Pharaoh knew that in order to find a suitable husband for Nefertari, he would need to come up with a method of filtering out the potential suitors to produce a short list. Naturally her future husband would need to be rich and powerful, that went without saying, but he also had to be intelligent, because Nefertari herself was a bright girl and would quickly get bored with someone who couldn't match her intellectually.

The idea came to him, that if the suitors were told to do something really spectacular, in order to prove themselves worthy of Nefertari's hand, then only those with the most brilliant accomplishments would be considered. They could set themselves any task they wanted, as this would test their ingenuity and intelligence, but it would have to be something which impressed the Pharaoh, and as the most powerful man in Egypt, he wasn't that easily impressed. As rich young men, they would have virtually endless resources available to them, which they might well need to use to create something truly magnificent. The Pharaoh was very pleased with himself for thinking up this idea, and began making plans.

Nefertari was a pretty girl, reasonably tall and fairly slim. She had long, jet-black hair, which framed an oval face, but it was her eyes which were the most striking aspect of her appearance. They were of the brightest blue and bewitched everyone who looked into them. She also had the most radiant smile, which could soften the hardest heart, and her light olive skin was totally flawless. She always dressed in the very finest cotton and everyone who saw her could only admire her perfect beauty. There would be no shortage of suitors for her hand in marriage.

When her father explained his ideas to her, she listened respectfully.

'But what sort of things would you expect them to come up with?' she asked him

'I've absolutely no idea,' the Pharaoh replied. 'They can choose to do anything they want, but it will need to be spectacularly impressive.'

'So can we expect another pyramid or something like that?' she asked.

Her father looked at her, trying to decide whether or not she was being serious, but she was smiling broadly and clearly amused by her own suggestion.

'Let's hope not,' he replied. 'Neither of us will still be around by the time any of them could build another one of those things.'

He then thought for a moment before continuing. 'But you've just made a valid point. They will not be able to accomplish much in just a few weeks, so I will need to set a sensible time scale. Twelve months should be about right.'

Nefertari thought for a moment about everything her father had just said.

'Yes father, I think your plan is a good idea and it might just find me my perfect husband.'

'I'm so glad you agree,' he told her. The Pharaoh may have been the most powerful man in Egypt, with total power over each and every single one of his subjects, but he was still pleased to hear that his daughter approved of his idea.

The priests were plotting. When they heard the news that prospective suitors for Nefertari's hand would be visiting Egypt, they knew the Pharaoh wouldn't be able to resist turning the whole occasion into a huge public event. This would make it the perfect opportunity for a really big demonstration against the upstart cat god.

The most radical of the dissident priests was a man called Sabatok. He was a high priest for Haapi, the god of the Nile, and whilst he accepted the existence of the Sun and Moon gods, Haapi was still the most important god as far as he was concerned.

The Nile was the jewel in Egypt's crown. It was teeming with life and it provided food and essential water for everyone living along its banks. It was clearly a living thing and flowed through the entire length of the country, from its unknown source. The river could mostly be contained, but never controlled, as it was far too powerful for man to be able to do that. When the Nile god was angry, the river would burst its banks, creating a vast flood plain and damaging all the crops growing in the farmland near to the river.

The river had flooded three times in the last five years and, to Sabatok, this was a clear indication that the Nile god was extremely unhappy about the emergence and popularity of the cat god. Something had to be done to appease the river.

Sabatok was a short, dark, swarthy looking man in his late thirties, with a noticeable paunch. His hair was worn long and he also had a thick beard. Under the royal decree, just being a high priest of the Nile was technically illegal, so Sabatok tended to be very secretive about what he still did for a living. Should he be caught, he would end up being prosecuted for heresy, which could lead to him being put to death. Knowing this made Sabatok a very cautious man and he was deeply suspicious of anyone he didn't know.

Sabatok had hoped, when this latest Pharaoh came to power, that he would reverse the cat god decree, but he didn't, which put an end to all of Sabatok's ambitions of being an important and respected person, with all the privileges of rank associated with the position of high priest. For this reason, he was very resentful and hated the current Pharaoh with a vengeance.

If this Pharaoh intended to organise a huge public spectacular to welcome all the royal dignitaries from foreign lands, then Sabatok and his co-conspirators would need to come up with a diabolical plan, to disrupt proceedings and turn the event into a catastrophe. Not only would this embarrass the Pharaoh beyond belief, but if they could also make it look as if the cat god was responsible, then it might be possible to persuade the Pharaoh to abandon it in favour of the old gods. The re-instatement of Haapi was Sabatok's principal objective and if he could use the occasion of this event to bring this about, he would be a very happy man. He sent messages out to all his followers. It was time to get organised.

Back at the palace, the Pharaoh was putting the final touches to his own plans. He would need to make the final choice of Nefertari's husband himself, but would appoint a special committee, to judge whatever the suitors created and only the most spectacular would be considered. Those suitors who failed to impress would be summarily dismissed. The Pharaoh was hoping that this process would provide him with a short list of three, from which he could select Nefertari's future husband.

It promised to be an interesting contest and he was looking forward to hearing what the suitors might come up with to meet his challenge. His daughter was only just seventeen, so another year really wouldn't make that much difference. What was important was that the husband he found for her had to be the right one. The test he was setting should certainly weed out all but the most promising candidates. He began making a list of all those who should be invited.

In a cavern far removed from Egypt, Fido considered the computer's suggestion to visit the place. 'From what you've told me, it does sound quite interesting,' he said, 'so I will definitely go there at some stage, but not just yet.'

17

THE STONE CIRCLE

The computer considered this before replying, 'That's entirely up to you. It will still be there for you to see at a later date.'

It began thinking about somewhere else to send Fido. Ideally, it needed to be a place where things were happening and where he could interact with other human beings. Fido was not all that experienced in this respect, so mixing with other men would be useful. The other thing he needed was something which presented him with a challenge, as this would occupy his mind and stop him worrying so much about his parents.

From time to time, the computer had been monitoring some activity in a country not that far away. It seemed to have been going on for years and was certainly strange. The locals there seemed to have been going to an awful lot of trouble to transport huge slabs of rock from one place to another, only to just leave them standing around when they got them there.

The computer had no idea what it was all about and as the standing stones didn't seem to form any kind of dwelling, it didn't understand the reason for all the effort being expended. The whole idea seemed bizarre and the computer had it listed as just another example of human beings doing really weird things. It didn't however like unanswered puzzles, so if Fido went there he could find out what was going on and report back. It would then be happy to file the whole thing away in its memory banks, with an appropriate descriptive tag.

'There is somewhere you could go to,' the computer suggested, 'where the humans are behaving very oddly. There may well be something there you might find educational.' It went on to explain all about the activities of the locals and how they seemed to be obsessed with lugging huge slabs of rock over great distances, just to stand them on end when they reached their destination.

'That does sound a bit daft,' Fido agreed, 'and as I've not got much to do at the moment, now that Bedric has been dealt with, I could go there and check the place out?'

It didn't take long for Fido to gather the few things he needed for his trip and these were soon packed away in his satchel.

'I think I should start where they are cutting out the stones,' he suggested to the computer. 'I'll go there first and see where it leads me.'

As this seemed sensible, the computer agreed and engaged the transporter. The air shimmered and Fido disappeared, leaving the usual twinkle of starry lights.

'Peace at last,' the computer sighed to itself. 'Now perhaps I can get back to that little problem of mine.'

When Fido arrived at the quarry there was an incredible amount of activity going on. Scores of men were rushing about, all clearly intent on some purpose. He stopped one of the workers and asked what was going on.

'We've just finished another stone,' the man told him, 'and everyone's getting ready for it to be transported to the site.'

As Fido glanced around, he could see that a lot of men were beginning to gather in one particular area and were staring down at something on the ground. He considered this for a moment.

Turning back to the man, he asked, 'So what is so exciting about that?' The man looked at him with a confused expression.

'It's the thirtieth stone we've finished.' he explained, 'and that makes it very special.'

Fido didn't understand, but as he didn't want to delay the man any more than necessary, he just nodded as if he had. The man rushed off to join the others. Fido then began strolling about to watch proceedings, to see if he could work out what this was all about.

An immensely huge rectangular slab of rock was lying on a series of tree trunk rollers. Fido could see that all the sides were flat and that the stone gradually tapered from one end to the other. At the thinner end of the stone, part of the end surface had been cut away, leaving a raised dome shape in the middle. Dozens of men surrounded the finished stone and they were all cheering loudly and drinking from the flasks they carried. Whatever liquid was in the flasks appeared to make the men even happier, or so it seemed to Fido. Trying not to draw attention to himself, Fido casually pointed a small box shaped object at the stone. The device scanned and measured the stone and determined that it weighed over twenty thousand kilograms.

The men began strapping wooden poles across the stone, all along its length. Having made sure these were secure, they then stepped away again. The poles extended three metres out from each side of the stone. Other men were attaching long leather ropes at the thicker end of the stone. By now, Fido was quite intrigued.

'What happens next?' he asked one of the men.

Several of the workers looked at him rather curiously, but one explained that they were now ready to begin moving the stone towards the site, which was about forty kilometres away. This would involve men pushing the stone using the wooden poles sticking out from its sides, with more men pulling it along from the front, using the ropes attached there. As it moved forward, this would release rollers from the back end, which would then be transferred to the front of the stone. This process would then continue until they reached the site.

'Isn't that going to take rather a long time?' Fido innocently enquired, only to get a withering look from the man.

Not wishing to aggravate him any further, Fido decided to go and look at another part of the operation. He walked over to where the huge blocks of stone were being quarried and sat down again, to see how this was being done.

The process of cutting out the stone blocks much depended on the skills of the men at the rock face. They first needed to decide where the rock was most likely to split, before boring holes along this line. Wedges were then inserted into these holes and each was hammered in a short way, before the men moved on to the next wedge. When they reached the end of the line, they would return to the first wedge and repeat this procedure all over again. They kept on doing this until the rock eventually split open along the line with an almighty cracking sound. If everything went according to plan, the rock would split exactly where they wanted it to, but from the short time Fido watched this activity, he could see that this didn't always happen.

The rough block then needed to be levered out and manoeuvred away from the rock face, which took a lot of time and considerable effort. Eventually they would move it to where it was needed and the next stage of the process could then take place.

Apparently, the men who worked on this final stage were called stone masons and it was their job to shape the quarried block of rock into a finished stone, like the one on the tree trunk rollers. Fido was absolutely fascinated to watch them work, because they were obviously very skilled at what they were doing. Working on one face of a stone at the time, they chipped and chiselled away small fragments until the finished face was as flat as they could make it. The stone was then turned through ninety degrees, before starting on the next face. When all four faces had been made smooth, they then moved on to the ends of the stone, flattening them as well, but leaving a raised dome on the thinner end. This process was known as dressing the stones and Fido could see that it took a very long time indeed. He was however able to watch every stage of the proceedings, as there were a number of masons all working on different stones simultaneously. He wasn't sure why they went to all the trouble of creating the raised domes on the end of each stone, but decided against asking.

He had been at the quarry for most of the day and now knew how much time, skill and effort went into producing the stones. He still didn't know what they were for and would only find out by visiting the site where the stones were being taken. Tomorrow promised to be another interesting day.

The following morning, Fido woke up bright and early and was surprised to see the workers were already toiling away at their different jobs within the quarry. Some of them even offered to share their breakfasts with him, which he thought was very generous. He didn't bother to ask for directions to the site, as he only needed to follow the well worn tracks made by the men transporting the stones there. Thanking the quarry men for their hospitality, he set off towards the site.

Even though the men with the stone had trudged on well into the night, Fido didn't have to walk very far before he caught up with them. He bid them a cheery good morning as he passed, but they seemed a lot less enthusiastic than they had been the previous day. Clearly they all were very tired and Fido really felt for them. He continued until he was out of sight and then asked the computer to transport him to a spot much nearer to his intended destination.

The sight which greeted him when he materialised took his breath away. The sheer scale of the undertaking was almost beyond belief. It was so huge that he found it difficult to believe this was something dreamt up and built by men, using basically nothing but muscle power and a lot of determination.

In the centre of the plain, stood a large circle of stones, just like the ones he had already seen, except that these had all been positioned standing on their ends. The circle wasn't anything like complete yet, but pairs of stones had been capped with further stones, which linked them together, so as to form an arch. Inside the large circle were even more stones, some smaller and some much larger than those in the outer ring. It was immediately apparent that these had also been arranged in a specific pattern. It was certainly a mystifying spectacle and Fido decided to go and have a closer look.

There didn't seem to be much site activity at the moment, but a couple of large stones were sitting on tree trunk rollers, near the outer edge of the stone circle. Fido guessed that these must be the next stones to be erected and if this was likely to be happening any time soon, it should be worth waiting around to watch. In the mean time, he decided to have a wander around the site, to see if he could find someone to explain why so much effort was being put into building this place.

He saw a number of men wearing long flowing robes and some of these seemed to be taking measurements. They looked like the sort of people who would be able to answer his questions, so he approached one of the robed men.

'Hello there,' he said to the man. 'Could you possibly explain what this place is all about?'

The man seemed rather surprised to hear such a question and turned to look at Fido. He immediately saw intelligence in the young man's face and registered that his clothes were slightly unusual. He also noticed that Fido didn't seem to be in the least bit embarrassed about asking such a dumb question, but rather exuded an air of confidence.

'You must be new here,' the man suggested. 'If this is the first time you've seen Stonehenge, then I imagine it must all look rather confusing.'

He went on to say that he and the other robed men were druid priests and that they were responsible for the project. It turned out that he was actually the chief druid and as such was the man in overall charge. By chance, Fido had happened to pick the one person capable of answering every single question he had and the priest indicated that he was willing to spend a little time explaining everything. Fido wasn't sure where to start, but the man seemed to sense this and began to tell him all about the construction and its significance.

He explained that while Stonehenge was principally being built as a ceremonial complex, it would also be a solar calendar. The stones were arranged such that the entrance faced the rising sun on the day of the summer solstice, which would allow them to follow the movement of the sun and the moon and to record the changing seasons. As an observatory, it would also enable them to predict when solar and lunar eclipses were due to happen and as a temple, it would be used to hold ceremonies for honouring the dead. It was also hoped, he told Fido, that it would go on to become a centre for healing, because of its religious significance and the power contained within the stones.

'So you see,' the man continued, 'Stonehenge will serve many purposes and when it is finished, it will be one of the most important structures ever built by man.'

Fido was impressed, and having spent as much time as he had with the computer, it now took a lot to impress Fido.

'How long will all this take to complete?' he asked.

'Not in my lifetime I fear,' the man replied, 'but at least I will go to my grave knowing that I did everything possible to make sure that my sections were built exactly to specification. That will be my legacy to those who follow me.' Fido pointed to the two stones on rollers, by the outer ring of the circle.

'Will they be going up today?' he enquired.

'Not for some weeks yet,' the man told him, and went on to explain that they were awaiting the arrival of the lintel for the top, which was coming from an even more distant quarry. All three stones would then have to be checked for accuracy before they were erected, to ensure they fitted together perfectly.

'So how do you actually erect the stones?' Fido asked.

'We let gravity do most of the work for us,' the man replied. 'You will probably have noticed that the stones taper along their length, which means that one end is heavier than the other. We dig large holes where we want them to stand and then roll them towards the edge of the hole. Once the heavier end is past the edge, the stones virtually topple in on their own.'

'That sounds like fun,' Fido said, 'particularly given the

weight of those stones. I would like to see you do that.'

'Come back in a few weeks time then,' the man told him.

Fido thanked him for his courtesy and for taking the time to explain everything. With that he took his leave and strolled away from the site.

'There must be something I can do to help these people,' he thought to himself. 'They are so dedicated to what they are trying to achieve here.'

He knew that this would require some thinking about and was still considering this question when he reached a suitable place from which to be transported back to the cave. He sent the appropriate message to the computer.

18

BACK TO THE FUTURE

The little problem the computer had with the time transporter was called "Fluffy". A hundred thousand years previously, it had sent the cat into the distant future, only for it to return with this name on a tag attached to a collar around its neck. As the computer considered the animal to be an experimental subject, it had immediately been cryogenically preserved and was now being kept in suspended animation, somewhere within the depths of the cavern. The computer knew that the cat hadn't put the collar on itself, so someone or something else must have done so. This meant that it had interacted with a living being in the distant future and this set the computer's circuits buzzing. It needed to decide how to make the best use of this totally unexpected development and it had already been considering this for quite some time.

The computer had already decided that this had to have been either a man or a woman, as the television programmes it had seen showed humans as the dominant species. It was also clear that whoever had put the collar on the cat had a certain amount of intelligence. The question was how much intelligence and could this contact be used to somehow establish a means of communication with the future. The cat had only been there for eight hours, so was unlikely to have moved very far before interacting with whoever decided to name the animal. The computer's initial choice for the cat's destination had proved to be fortuitous, as this location clearly held distinct possibilities for further interaction with future humans. As it obviously knew the precise co-ordinates to which the cat had been sent, this meant that if it sent something else with the same settings, it would obviously arrive in exactly at the same location.

It also knew that the next thing it would send had to be a machine, as it needed to be able to collect data. If the machine could also interact with a human, then that would be an added bonus. An important consideration was that whatever it sent had to be something which would not appear out of place, so it had to be something that the future humans would recognise and accept without question.

From the television programmes it had seen, it was aware that men of that time used extremely crude computers as part of their daily lives. So if its machine had the superficial appearance of a typical Earth computer, it would not look that unusual.

Fluffy's trip had taken place a hundred thousand years before Fido arrived on the scene and the computer had by now progressed to the stage where the machine had been designed, constructed and was ready to go. With Fido off exploring the mad Earthmen with their big slabs of rock, the computer now had the opportunity to proceed. This would be the second time it had sent something into the distant future and it was hoping for some really spectacular results.

The machine looked every bit like a modern laptop

computer, but that was where the resemblance ended. This laptop would be able to observe and record everything it saw, whilst taking all manner of readings and measurements from its environment. If a human being touched any button on its keypad, this would immediately create a link and the machine would attempt to establish a dialogue with the human. Anything and everything that was said within its vicinity, as well as anything directly entered into the keyboard, would also be recorded and the machine would store all this data for later retrieval, when the computer brought it back from the future.

When everything was set up and ready to go, the computer decided to set the period the machine would spend on future Earth to twelve hours, as it considered this should be long enough for it to gather sufficient useful data. As an afterthought, it decided to send the cat along as well, as having been there before, the cat might assist the initial interaction process.

The cat was defrosted and once it had been thawed out and was fully recovered from being frozen for a hundred thousand years, it was placed on top of the closed laptop. A few minutes later, after some final adjustments, they both disappeared in a twinkle of starry lights on their journey to the future. The destination was still the same, but the computer had set the arrival time for moments after the cat would have been seen to disappear on its last trip.

The laptop returned to the cave twelve hours later, but Fluffy didn't come back with it. The lid was now wide open and the screen glowed with life, whereas it had previously been blank, apart from the flashing cursor. It now showed a full screen image of Fluffy, looking more content and pleased with itself than ever before.

An examination of the machine's memory circuits revealed

the face of what appeared to be a human being, as viewed from the camera behind the screen. It was clearly of female gender, with bright blue eyes and long blonde hair. The computer was somewhat taken aback to see this. The face was screwed up in concentration, as the girl's fingers stabbed away at the laptop's keyboard. The computer could hardly contain its excitement, as it quickly analysed the data, in order to determine what she had so painstakingly entered.

'Dear diary. I've got a cat now and have called it Fluffy. Mum says I can keep it, providing I keep my bedroom tidy. Mummy is also letting me play with this computer she found and says that if I'm a good girl ....'

With all the amazing technical resources at the computer's disposal and despite the fact that it had created a system for travelling to the distant future, it had only succeeded in contacting a twelve years old girl living in the year 2003 - hardly the result it had hoped for. It was disappointed, to say the least.

The girl was far too young to be considered of any practical use to the computer, but this "Mummy" person clearly had authority over her. As such, there might still be a way to make use of the contact it had made, if only this youngster could somehow be persuaded to take the laptop machine to a responsible adult.

The computer decided to send it back to the same location, but first it would install an instruction to the young girl, to ensure that she handed the machine over to an adult. The time controls were set to allow it to remain in the future for a full twenty four hours and the computer added what it considered to be an appropriate message, before sending the laptop back to the future. It awaited its return with eager anticipation.

In 2003, a blue eyed, blonde haired girl sat on a chair in the family's back garden. She couldn't understand how the laptop she had been playing with had suddenly disappeared and was just about to run and tell her mother what had happened, when it just as suddenly reappeared. She opened the lid, expecting to see the background picture of Fluffy which her mother had added, but the screen now showed a moving image of a tyrannosaurus. This frightened her, but not half as much as when it stepped right out from the screen and began to expand in size. She opened her mouth to scream, but no sound came out. When the creature had grown to its normal size, it leaned down towards the little girl and smiled, displaying a mouthful of nasty looking teeth.

'Take me to your mummy,' a voice boomed out. The girl let out one single high pitched scream, threw the laptop to the ground and ran towards the house.

When the computer had considered what sort of message to send the little girl, it had reasoned that as she obviously liked Fluffy, she was bound to fall in love with a happy smiling dinosaur. What it failed to consider however, was that humans might not be used to the idea of such monsters stepping out from a laptop screen, before growing back to full size. All it had intended to do was to attract the little girl's attention - and it had certainly achieved that.

When 2003 Mummy dashed into the garden, in response to her daughter's scream, she took one look at the three metres high dinosaur standing in the garden, gave a stifled scream of her own and promptly fainted.

The dinosaur remained connected to the laptop screen by a thin plasma thread. It just stood where it was, looking around and waiting to interact with somebody. It watched with interest, as an adult human male came rushing out of the house, clutching a half-finished bottle of beer. Father hurled the bottle at the laptop and more by luck than judgement, managed to hit the screen, which instantly exploded. The dinosaur seemed to flicker for a moment and then disappeared.

The man grabbed hold of a spade, which he had left sticking out of a flowerbed, and attacked the laptop with the fury of a father protecting his family. The laptop didn't come out of the encounter too well. Father looked pretty shattered afterwards as well. This may have been because he was a little overweight, or it might have been that it was a very hot day. It may also have had something to do with the fact that he had been relaxing in front of the television, drinking his fourth beer and watching his favourite football team, when all the commotion started.

When the mother recovered and the little girl had been pacified, everything began to calm down. The parents talked about what had just happened, but couldn't explain it. They had both most certainly seen the dinosaur, but this had somehow disappeared. The battered laptop was still lying on the grass, with half its insides hanging out. It looked pretty harmless now.

The parents decide to take what was left of the laptop to the police station, where they ranted at the sergeant on duty. They really let rip and told him how disgusted they were that such dangerous things could end up in the hands of children. The desk sergeant listened patiently and noticed that the mother seemed to be a little wobbly on her feet. He also thought that he had smelled beer, when the father had been leaning over the counter and shouting at him. He considered how best to respond.

He obviously hadn't seen the dinosaur, so only had their word that it ever existed. From his point of view, the broken machine looked like an ordinary laptop computer, but one which had had the stuffing knocked out of it. For all he knew, the couple may have had too much to drink and imagined it all. He had heard of intoxicated people seeing pink elephants, but had never come across any of them claiming to have seen a dinosaur before. Over his many years in the job, he had had to deal with all sorts of people, including drunks and loonies, so he knew just what to do.

From underneath his desk, he produced a very long form, which he handed to the parents. He suggested that they take it home, fill it in, and bring it back the following day. In the meantime, he would send the broken machine to the boffins in the technical department, for them to examine it and provide a detailed report. This seemed to satisfy the parents for the moment, so they pocketed the form and went home. As soon as they had gone, the sergeant took the machine to one of the station's storage rooms, where he left it on a shelf on the back wall. As he left the room, he turned off the light and the automatically locking door swung shut.

Twenty four hours after the laptop had arrived on future Earth, the transporter relay station in deep space, picked up the faintest of signals from the machine. It was just enough to pinpoint its location, but nothing like enough to lock onto it for transportation. In the storage room at the police station, a few sparks flickered in the machine, but soon fizzled out as the machine died.

Meanwhile, the computer in its cavern on prehistoric Earth waited for twenty four hours, but the machine failed to return. For once in its long life, it just didn't know what to think.

When Fido returned to the computer cave, it immediately became obvious to him that something was wrong, as the computer was not its usual belligerent self. There was nothing he could quite put his finger on, but it was definitely troubled, or at the very least puzzled.

It didn't seem to want to share its problem with Fido, so he decided it would be a good idea if he made himself scarce.

Ironically, the computer was thinking much along the same lines. Whilst it was infinitely capable of performing millions of processes and calculations simultaneously, taking multi-tasking to an entirely new level, the mystery of the missing laptop was something which required its total concentration. If Fido was happy to go off on another trip somewhere, that would help no end.

They briefly discussed his fact finding mission to Stonehenge and Fido mentioned that he would like to be able to help the men there overcome the huge difficulties they faced. He was still trying to work out what could be done in this respect, but had yet to come up with any practical ideas.

'I did enjoy meeting and talking to the men there, though' he told the computer, 'so I wouldn't mind going on another trip, just to see how other people in the world live their lives.'

'There's always Egypt,' suggested the computer, hoping that this time, Fido might agree to its proposal.

'That's an idea,' he replied. 'From what you've told me, it should be an interesting place to visit.'

With the decision made, Fido quickly checked the contents of his satchel and told the computer he was ready to go.

'Off you go then,' it said. 'Enjoy the trip.'

As the computer engaged the transporter system and he began to dematerialise, the thought running through Fido's mind was what sort of adventures Egypt might hold in store for him.

The thought running through the computer's circuits was the problem of the missing laptop, which now looked as if it was never going to return. This indicated that there was either a malfunction in the system, or something had happened to the machine to prevent it returning. It needed to know, because the entire future of its time travelling transportation project rested on discovering the answer.

19

AN EGYPTIAN ENCOUNTER

Fido's arrival in Egypt created a big splash. He had materialised at the side of a large pool, with just the toes of his feet on the edge and him facing away from the water. Being off balance, there was little he could do to stop himself and he toppled straight back into the pool, causing a loud splash. The water wasn't very deep and his head hit the bottom, leaving him dazed and disorientated. He struggled to find his feet, but slipped and went under again. Suddenly, he realised there was someone else in the pool and that they were trying to help him. He gratefully accepted their assistance and was led to the side, where he was very pleased to climb out and get back onto solid ground.

He glanced at his rescuer and his eyes opened wide in amazement. It was a pretty young woman, wearing nothing but a flimsy cotton tunic. The water had caused it turn transparent and he could see right through it. He stared in surprise, his mouth now wide open as well. Despite his tremendous knowledge, Fido had limited experience of other people and none whatsoever of young women. The most beautiful thing he had ever seen was standing in front of him and he just couldn't tear his eyes away.

He was trying to come to terms with this new experience when he suddenly realised how intensely he was staring. At this thought, he immediately felt acutely embarrassed and flushed bright red.

The girl looked at him in puzzlement, wondering why he was staring at her the way he was. She suddenly realised and giving a little gasp, began blushing as well. She quickly tried to cover herself with her arms and hands but then, realising how pointless this was, dashed off to find something more suitable to wear.

Fido noted that she had not screamed, which seemed rather surprising in the circumstances, unless she was used to people materialising out of thin air and then staring at her with their mouths wide open.

He took the moment to examine his surroundings. It was a very large room, dominated by the enormous pool in the centre. The surrounding furniture and screen curtains seemed to be of the highest quality and the floor was totally covered with square tiles, made of some shiny material he didn't recognise. There were a number of ornaments strategically placed around the room, including a large statue of a cat standing on a tall pedestal. The cat was pure gold in colour and appeared to have been made from this metal. He gave a wry grin, when he realised this must be an effigy of the cat god. He knew all about the Egyptians worshipping this so-called deity, but what he didn't know at the time, was how much trouble the cat god was going to cause him.

After a few minutes had passed the girl reappeared, now fully-dressed in bright embroidered robes, with gold bangles and exquisite stone jewellery adorning her bare arms. Fido was so taken aback at the sight of her that he couldn't immediately think of anything to say. The girl broke the silence.

'So, who are you and how did you get into my bathroom?' she asked.

Her questions were perfectly reasonable, but Fido didn't respond. He was desperately trying to think of an answer which might sound believable. He obviously couldn't tell her how he had actually got there. In the end, he decided to answer the first question first and hesitantly replied, 'I'm Fido. I'm pleased to meet you.'

The girl just stared at him, as he continued to stand there looking sheepish. Slowly her face broke into a smile and then she began to laugh. Her laugh was so infectious that Fido found himself joining in. Soon, both of them were standing there chuckling, as each considered the ridiculous situation in which they found themselves.

'My name is Nefertari,' the girl told him. 'I am the Pharaoh's daughter and this room is part of my private chambers. There is only one way in or out,' she pointed in the direction of a set of huge doors, 'and there are some very large guards on the other side whose job is to stop anyone other than my father or my handmaidens entering. You are not my father and you certainly don't look like any of my handmaidens.'

As she finished talking, Nefertari placed her hands on her hips and waited for Fido to answer.

'Well?' she said. 'How did you get into this room?'

She was still smiling, which Fido took to be a good sign.

'You wouldn't believe me if I told you.'

'Try me,' she retorted.

'Perhaps it would be better if I showed you, as long as you promise not to get scared or start screaming.'

'Do I look scared?' she threw back at him challengingly.

With some hesitation, Fido slowly withdrew the levitation device from his satchel. He was still thinking about the fierce guards stationed just the other side of the door. What could he show the girl which wouldn't totally freak her out? He selected the cat statue.

'Watch the cat carefully,' he told her.

As she watched, the statue of the cat slowly lifted off its pedestal and floated across the room, before settling on the floor at her feet.

She gasped, but then astounded Fido, by explaining away what had just happened.

'Everyone knows about the power of the cat god,' she told him. 'I've never seen it before for myself, but the fact that it is able to move around the room on its own doesn't surprise me in the slightest.'

'But it didn't move on its own,' Fido tried to explain, 'I made it move.'

She stared at him in obvious disbelief.

'All right then,' he continued, 'I will move something else. What do you suggest?'

'Make me float around the room,' she retorted. 'Now that would really impress me.'

Fido gulped. The girl's self-confidence was incredible and he didn't know how to deal with it. When he had faced Bedric, the man had been terrified as soon as Fido had demonstrated the powers he controlled. Nefertari wasn't in the least bit frightened and was now actually taunting him.

He made his decision and sent a quick message to the computer. 'Get ready to be impressed then,' he told her and walked across to the other side of the room.

Nefertari gave him a withering smile and stood resolute. He

had to be bluffing, as there was no way this strange young man could cause her to move unless she wanted to. She was just preparing her next stinging remark when she began to feel a strange tingling sensation all over her body. The next thing she knew, she was standing next to Fido and he was smiling at her. She had been smiling herself, but was now stunned, having just experienced the impossible. She almost sensed the colour draining from her face and her knees suddenly felt all weak. She collapsed and would have hit the floor, had Fido not caught her and carried her over to a chair. He waited for her to recover.

As she slowly came to, he was about to ask her how she felt, when she beat him to it, 'O.K., I'm impressed,' she said.

For the next hour or so they both chatted away like friends. Fido showed her his levitation device, which she enjoyed playing with, and explained something of life in his own country. She in turn told him all about Egypt and her life there. She even mentioned how the cat god had arrived many years previously and explained its importance to the Egyptians as a religious symbol. Fido found himself smirking every time the cat god was mentioned, but tried hard to conceal it. Nefertari found Fido interesting. He was easy to talk to and made her laugh. Fido found her completely bewitching.

She suddenly asked whether it was possible for him to transport the pair of them to an oasis she knew, a few kilometres outside of the city. Fido had come to explore Egypt, but had so far only seen this one room in her father's palace. He decided to put exploration on the back burner for the moment, as he was currently quite happy just spending time with this girl. He was also still a bit concerned that they might be disturbed by someone entering the room, so a trip to the oasis sounded like a good idea to him. Having communicated his thoughts to the computer, he left it to the machine to extract the required location from her mind, in preparation for transporting them there. Moments later, they arrived at her oasis. A camel herder was already there, together with a few of his camels, but as soon as he recognized Nefertari he made a rapid exit, bowing repeatedly as he did so. Fido watched the man leave and then turned to Nefertari to say, 'So you really are a royal princess?'

'Yes I am,' she replied. 'Does that make any difference?'

She was still recovering from the shock of being instantly transported from the palace to the oasis, when she suddenly realised that she hadn't even told Fido where it was or what it looked like. Somehow he had still managed to bring them both to exactly the right place. Now she was really impressed.

She had a lot of questions and while Fido tried to avoid answering some of the more tricky ones, like about the powers the computer had given him, she soon managed to persuade him to tell her everything she wanted to know. They carried on chatting and she explained all about her father's plans for selecting a husband for her. A lasting relationship was the last thing on Fido's mind at that moment, but he still felt slightly jealous at the thought of her marrying someone else. She was interesting to talk to and he probably wouldn't be able to see her if she became a married woman. Fido had already decided that he would like to see her again.

He told her all about turning Roc into a Chinese dragon and how Bedric had been changed into a dog and would now have to suffer for all his past sins. She laughed when he recounted his meeting with Clod and how the huge man had been stopped in his tracks when he had been just about to tear Fido to pieces. She was also very interested to hear about Stonehenge and told Fido he should make a point of visiting some of the temples and monuments the Egyptians had built. In fact, she listened attentively to everything Fido had to say and he paid just as much attention to all the things she was telling him. They talked and talked and the more they did, the more they relaxed in the pleasure of each other's company.

Several hours later, Fido suddenly realised just how long they had been at the oasis, when he noticed the sun was quite low in the sky. The last time he had looked it had been directly above them. He began to feel concern that her absence from the palace might have been noticed and suggested it was time to return.

'I suppose I should be getting back,' she reluctantly agreed.

'I will send you on your way, then,' Fido told her, taking hold of her hand, 'but I really would like to see you again.'

'I would like that too,' she replied, looking down at their joined hands.

Fido sent a message to the computer and the air around Nefertari began to shimmer, before she disappeared in a twinkle of starry lights.

Fido sat down. His mind was now in a complete whirl.

When Nefertari arrived back in her bathroom, the doors were wide open and there wasn't a guard in sight. This was most unusual. She needed to know why, so left the room and strolled down to the main palace reception area. It was very noisy in there and crowded with people. There seemed to be an almighty fuss going on and she wondered why. As the assembly became aware of her presence, they quickly stepped back, bowing as they did so. Slowly a path opened up between where she stood at one end of the hall and where her father was pacing up and down at the other, clearly in a very agitated state. He looked up, saw her, and ran down the room towards her.

'Where have you been for all this time?' he demanded to know, as he crushed her in his arms with relief. 'I've had everyone searching the palace for you, for hours.'

Apparently, he had gone to visit her, only to find she wasn't there. The guards on the door had sworn she had not passed them and the guards beneath her window were equally adamant that she had not left that way either. As she couldn't just disappear from a sealed room without somebody noticing, her quarters had been thoroughly searched, before the Pharaoh had ordered that the whole palace should also be scoured from top to bottom.

The reception hall had miraculously quietened down, as everyone there strained to hear Nefertari's reply.

'Oh, I've just been talking to this rather nice young man I met,' she replied, 'and completely forgot about the time. This hasn't caused a problem for anyone, has it?' she asked innocently.

You could have heard the sound of a pin drop, as everybody waited for the Pharaoh's response.

Before he could utter a word, Nefertari placed a hand in front of her mouth and stifled a yawn. 'I'm feeling a bit tired now,' she said, 'I think I'll go to my room and lie down for a while.'

There was a stunned silence as she left the room and walked back to her private chambers. The day's events had been puzzling to say the least and she really didn't know what to make of it all. Fido was a strange young man who could apparently make impossible things happen. They had talked for hours and hours about anything and everything and she had thoroughly enjoyed the time they had spent together. It was almost as if he could read her mind on occasions, as they seemed to have so much in common, and he had certainly stirred up some emotions in her, which she had never experienced before. As a result, Nefertari was very deep in thought and more than a little perplexed, when she returned to her rooms that evening.

Fido sat by the oasis for several hours, thinking back on their time together. It had been one of the happiest days of his life, but he was still troubled. Nefertari was the most wonderful person he had ever met, but he had literally only just met her and knew that she was virtually already promised in marriage. Eventually, he gave up trying to understand how he felt about all that had happened and shrugged his shoulders, before contacting the computer. Moments later, he was transported out of Egypt, wondering whether or not he would ever return.

20

INTO THE UNKNOWN

When Fido returned to the cave, he immediately asked the computer whether it had resolved the problem which had appeared to have been bothering it. The computer hadn't realised that Fido had noticed anything, but then again, perhaps it wasn't all that surprised.

'Let me think about something for a while,' the computer replied.

After just a few moments, it spoke again.

'There are a few features of the transporter system which I haven't shared with you.' Fido was immediately intrigued.

The computer went on to explain all about its experiments in time travel. The successes it had achieved and the mystery of the laptop not returning. It had already determined that there was nothing wrong with any of the equipment, so this had to mean that the laptop had somehow been damaged in the future, which had prevented it from making the return journey.

It also told Fido about Fluffy not returning from its second trip, but had worked out a theory to explain this. If the future mother had agreed to allow her daughter to keep the cat, then she may well have taken it to a doctor, for it to be medically examined first. Any doctor would certainly have discovered the cat's implanted homing device and there was every chance he would have removed it. Without the homing device to lock onto, the relay station in future time would not have been able to establish contact with Fluffy, effectively leaving the cat stranded in the future.

Fido agreed that this all made perfect sense, but what he wanted to know was what the computer intended to do next.

'I've already done something,' the computer told him, clearly pleased with itself for having anticipated Fido's response. 'While you've been away,' it continued, 'I actually managed to send a thought probe through the wormhole, to the relay station in the future. I wasn't sure if such a thing was possible, but it worked. I asked the relay station whether it could add anything to what I already knew and its response came back just a few minutes ago.'

'What did it have to say?' asked Fido, now keen to hear the rest.

Apparently, the relay station had received a signal from the laptop, when it was scheduled to return, but could not lock onto it, because the signal was too weak. All it had been able to determine was the machine's physical location on future Earth.

'Well you've obviously got to send something else there to find out what happened,' Fido immediately responded. 'You know the system works and I know you are keen to discover as much as you can about the future.'

'My conclusion exactly,' the computer replied, 'but I'm not sure what to send.'

'Why not send me?' Fido suggested. 'I would love to go.'

This was exactly the sort of response the computer had

expected, but the very last thing it wanted to hear.

'I can't risk you,' it said. 'You are too valuable a specimen.'

Being called a specimen didn't sit well with Fido, but he let it pass.

The discussion continued for quite some time, with Fido insisting that this opportunity for him to travel to the future was something too good to miss and the computer arguing that it could not agree to him doing anything so dangerous. In the end, the computer had little choice but to agree. It realised that unless the time travel project could be progressed to its conclusion, it would have no chance of contacting Captain Kirk, which was the main reason why it had started its time travel transportation experiments in the first place. Sending the machine had not accomplished anything, but Fido was more intelligent and his deductive reasoning wouldn't be restricted by machine-like logic. He was also quick witted, so would be able to respond to whatever he encountered, something the machine might not have been capable of doing. Logic dictated that sending Fido was the only sensible option and a decision needed to be made. The computer finally accepted that Fido had to be its next test subject and began making the necessary preparations, which included implanting a homing device into Fido's arm.

Sometime later, just before Fido disappeared into the ether for his one great leap for mankind, the computer decided to add another startling revelation.

'By the way,' it told him. 'For a while now, I've had my robots out there in space, building me a replica of the Star Ship Enterprise. It's virtually finished now and is already orbiting the Earth. You can go and have a look at it when you come back, if you want.'

Fido disappeared before he had the chance to reply.

When Fido materialised, he had no idea where he was. It was as if he was blind, but in reality it was just that he was in a very dark place. He was cramped up on a flat surface and when he tried to move, he found there was a wall immediately behind him. To either side, objects of some description also hemmed him in. He tentatively reached forward, only to find there was literally nothing there. He worked his legs free from under his body and stretched them forward into space, still nothing. He then lowered his legs, but didn't touch anything.

'Lights,' he shouted, but nothing happened. He then suddenly remembered his satchel and extracted a device from it. Bright light replaced the darkness and suddenly everything became clear.

He was perched on a high shelf, on the back wall of a room. This shelf, as well as several others in the room, was cluttered with all sorts of objects. He laughed at himself for being such an idiot and panicking over nothing. It was just an ordinary room, but if everything had gone according to plan, this room was on the Earth of one and three quarter million years into his future. As he clambered down from the shelf, he saw that he had been sitting next to what looked like a beaten up laptop computer.

'So that's what happened to you,' he said out loud. 'Now we know.'

He walked over to the door and studied it. He knew all about doors and was just reaching out to turn the handle, when he suddenly remembered that this was the future and he had no idea what he might be facing on the other side. Knowing that he needed to be cautious, he decided to explore the room first and to examine the various items it contained. There were a number of boxes stacked in the room and some of these could hold things which might be of assistance to him, when he eventually decided to brave whatever was beyond the door.

He recognised some of the future objects, from television pictures he had seen, but many were unfamiliar to him. In one box, he found some magazines, which he set aside to read later. Some boxes contained various different items of clothing and in one he found an old pair of motorcycle boots. He didn't know they had been specifically designed for this purpose, but obviously recognised them as footwear, albeit a lot different to his own. He couldn't resist trying them on and was pleased to see that they fitted reasonably well.

The torch he carried was designed to illuminate a much larger area than just a single room, so when he came to look through the magazines, he found the light was too bright for him to read comfortably. He needed something to reduce the glare and remembered seeing a strange looking item in one of the boxes he had looked through. He returned to that box. What he had discovered was a pair of sunglasses and he now realised that their purpose was to shield a person's eyes, in extremely bright light conditions.

'What a clever idea,' he thought to himself, as he put them on.

The magazines provided an interesting pictorial account of current events, so he looked through them carefully. Something which became immediately apparent was that the clothes worn by people in the future were completely different to what he was currently wearing. If he wanted to look inconspicuous when he left this room, he would need to do something about his appearance. He rummaged through the boxes again and found a pair of jeans. The magazines had shown men wearing similar garments, so these looked ideal. They were a little on the large side, but fitted him well enough. He also found a dark coloured jacket which surprised him considerably, as it had clearly been made from animal skins. He certainly hadn't expected people living nearly two million years in the future to still be wearing animal skins, but he slipped the jacket on anyway. Now feeling more suitably attired, he decided it was time to leave his little sanctuary and to venture out and discover what was beyond the door. He took hold of the door handle and having turned it, pushed the door open and stepped through.

The year was 2003 and the storage room in this particular police station led off from the squad room. There were about a dozen uniformed officers working in there when Fido entered and his sudden appearance caused then to stop what they were doing and stare at him in total disbelief. For a start, they hadn't expected anyone to be in the storage room, but it was what he was wearing that really surprised them. The original Terminator film from 1984, in which an android from the future attacks a police station and kills nearly everyone there, had been shown again on television (for the umpteenth time) just a few nights previously and most of the assembled policemen had watched it. Fido had inadvertently dressed himself up to look just like the Arnold Schwarzenegger character, in his dark jeans, leather jacket, motorbike boots and sunglasses. He had hoped that wearing these clothes would make him look inconspicuous, but had achieved exactly the opposite effect.

Fido was equally surprised to see the police officers, as they were all wearing uniforms like those worn by soldiers in the violent war stories he had watched on television, although these ones didn't appear to be carrying guns. He immediately went on the defensive and raised his stunner, which he pointed towards the men.

He was shocked when instead of attacking him, as he had expected, some of the men began falling about with laughter, several of them collapsing in near hysterics.

'Help! Help!' one of them called out. 'We are all about to be killed by the Terminator's baby brother.' The others seemed to think this was incredibly funny and began laughing even more.

Fido couldn't understand any of what was happening or why his appearance had caused this kind of reaction. He continued to stand where he was, still covering the room with his stunner, when one of the officers got up and walked towards him.

'Stay where you are or I will shoot,' he said, aiming the stunner. This made some of the men laugh even louder, but the sergeant approaching him suddenly became very serious and reached down towards his belt. Fido thought the man was about to draw a weapon of some description and, not willing to risk finding out, fired his stunner.

Zing!

The sergeant collapsed in a heap and the room suddenly went very quiet. The other men seemed undecided as to what to do next, but then began to get out of their chairs and advance towards him. Pointing his stunner at them seemed to make them hesitate momentarily, but then they all rushed forward at once. Fido managed to stun three of them, before the rest quickly overpowered him.

He didn't know what they were going to do to him, but he expected to get hurt. Instead, they simply handcuffed his hands behind his back, dragged him across to a chair and unceremoniously dumped him onto it.

As Fido had only used a very mild stun setting, the police sergeant quickly recovered. The ones he had shot afterwards would be unconscious for a few more minutes. There was no longer any laughter in the room, as everybody had suddenly become very serious indeed. Nobody seemed sure what to do, but Fido could hear them talking quietly as they examined the objects from his satchel.

Eventually the sergeant, who by now had more or less recovered, picked up a chair and, placing it directly in front of Fido, sat down to face him.

'Would you like to tell me what just happened?' he began. 'You can start by explaining who you are and how you came to be inside that locked room.'

'My name is Fido and I was in there looking for a lost machine,' Fido hesitantly responded. He flinched as he said this, as he was still expecting to be hit at any moment. The sergeant looked puzzled, but then continued.

'So how did you get in there?' he asked.

'You wouldn't believe me if I told you,' Fido replied.

The man rolled his eyes in obvious exasperation and then looked over to the others. They were all gathered around a table, examining the items they had taken out of Fido's satchel.

'What did he have in his bag?' the sergeant asked.

'Looks like a whole load of electronic gizmos,' one of the men replied. 'I don't know what any of them are for.'

The sergeant got up and walked over to the table. He picked up the stunner, but handled it very carefully. He already knew what this particular gizmo could do.

'So where did you get this ray gun?' he shouted across to Fido, who was sitting very quietly and saying nothing.

He then picked up the levitation device and as there was only a single button on the front, he pressed it to see what would happen. Across the other side of the room, a table slowly began to rise up into the air. He immediately released the button and the table crashed back down on the floor. There were gasps of astonishment from the men and the sergeant immediately dropped the device, a look of deep concern on his face.

Everyone began talking and gesturing at the same time. Flying tables were not the sort of thing they were used to seeing and Fido's gadgets clearly went beyond anything they understood. It was as if they had suddenly found themselves in the middle of a science fiction film and they all became extremely animated. In the confusion, Fido jumped up from his chair, ran over to the table and picked up his stunner. As his hands and wrists were quite small, he had been able to wriggle out of the handcuffs quite easily and had just been waiting for the right moment to make his move.

Waving the stunner, he motioned the policemen away from the table and when they had all moved back, he gathered up his devices and returned them to his satchel. Keeping the men covered, he slowly backed towards the storage room door. Nobody made any attempt to stop him. This mysterious young man with his futuristic devices could clearly be dangerous and none of the policemen felt anything like brave enough to push their luck.

The door had swung shut and could now only be opened by punching the correct sequence into the keypad mounted beside it. Fido studied the lock for a moment and recognised that it presented a serious problem. He could not hope to keep the men at bay for that much longer, so didn't have time to work out how to deal with the combination lock. He adjusted the setting on his stunner and fired it directly at the keypad. It immediately exploded and the door swung open. Fido glanced back at the policemen, but most of them had dived for cover when he shot out the lock. He stepped into the room and the door closed behind him. He retrieved the smashed laptop and touched his arm, near to where the homing device was implanted. This sent a signal to the relay station and a moment later, he was transported back to the past.

Outside in the squad room, the panic gradually subsided, as the men tried to make sense of the events of the past fifteen minutes. One of the policemen looked lost in thought and seemed to be trying to drag something out from the depths of his memory. Suddenly it came to him and he turned to his colleagues.

'Did anyone else notice?' he asked them. 'That ray gun of his looked just like the ones they used to have in Star Trek.'

21

A NEW START

Computers can't breathe a sigh of relief, but if they could, the cavern computer might have done just that when Fido reappeared. He seemed to be unharmed, but certainly looked a little shaken. His clothing was completely different to what he had been wearing when he had left, and something about his appearance rang a bell somewhere in the computer's memory banks. In its present agitated state, it couldn't immediately make the connection, but knew it was related to an image it had seen on future television.

'Quickly,' the computer ordered. 'Get into the chamber. I need to check you over thoroughly.'

Fido dutifully entered the kennel like chamber and settled down on the floor. An intensive analytical examination of his entire body was carried out, but everything was exactly how it should be - and where it should be, for that matter. The only unusual reading was that he appeared to be exhibiting signs of recent high levels of adrenaline activity.

Afterwards, the computer wanted to know everything that had happened to Fido during his time in the future. Fido didn't need to say a word, as the computer simply extracted the entire story straight out of his brain, by probing directly into it.

It was rather disappointed that Fido's entire time in the future had been spent in just two rooms, as it had obviously hoped he would have seen a lot more of this future world. It didn't like the sound of everyone being in uniform and was surprised at the men's lack of understanding of the basic devices Fido carried. They clearly didn't know what they were, which would seem to indicate that life in 2003 was nothing like as advanced as it had expected. It knew the exact year, because Fido's brain had absorbed every single detail in the squad room, including the calendar on the wall. It had done this automatically, without Fido even realising it was happening. The computer was not pleased that Fido had effectively wasted this opportunity to explore future Earth, but now that it knew the system functioned faultlessly, there was no reason why further trips could not be arranged and one of these was bound to prove more profitable.

When Fido went to bed that night, the computer was quietly jubilant. It had now proved that its transporter system could send living things into the distant future and bring them back safely. It had intended to spend much longer testing the system, but Fido had insisted on going and by doing so, had been instrumental in making the test a success. All in all, everything had worked out rather well, so the computer had the right to be proud of its achievement. In fact, it was feeling rather pleased with itself.

The following morning, Fido asked the computer about the Enterprise. He was fully aware of the computer's enthusiasm for Star Trek, but had never realised that this would extend to building a replica star ship. When he asked the computer why it had done so, its response was that it might come in handy at

A NEW START

some time, so why not build it.

When Fido transported up to see the ship, he was surprised to discover that it really was an exact replica of the Enterprise and as such, was absolutely enormous. The robots were still working on it in some areas, but as far as Fido could see, it was near enough finished. The computer had even installed a warp drive as the propulsion unit, even though more efficient options were available to it, and the ship had a fully functioning transporter room, bridge, cargo holds, sleeping quarters and all the other facilities found on the original Enterprise. Fido couldn't think of any reason why this ship would ever be required, but it was built now so would be available if it was ever needed.

Fido's thoughts often returned to his parents and how they were getting on. Every now and again, he had taken the opportunity to scan Greendale, but had never caught sight of them. He decided it was time to pay them a visit. Although they probably wouldn't now recognise him as their son, he arranged for the computer to alter his appearance, just to be on the safe side. After a short session in the chamber, he emerged looking completely different, which made him feel more comfortable about the meeting he was planning.

When Fido arrived in the village, he went straight to the old family cave, but another family was now living in it. When he asked them about Judd and Beryl, he was told that they had moved out and now lived in a hut on the outskirts of the village. As he approached their new home, he could see that this place was a complete dump, compared to the comfortable cave where they used to live.

Judd was out when he arrived, but Beryl invited him in for a cool drink, after he told her that he had been asked to drop in and see them by a mutual friend. She showed no signs whatsoever of recognising her son, which was hardly surprising.

Beryl explained that Judd still went hunting for meat, but as the village elders had banned him from ever owning dogs again, he now had to do so without the support of a dog pack. This had not only made hunting more difficult, but also more dangerous. Previously, the dogs had been used to distract the creature being hunted, which allowed Judd to close in for the kill. Without their assistance, he could now only rely on himself and had to try and avoid getting injured as he approached the cornered beast. This hadn't always worked and he had been badly hurt a few months previously and now walked with a permanent limp. This increased the risks he faced while hunting, as it slowed him down. Fast reflexes were an essential requirement for any hunter and it was obvious that with this injury, Judd was no longer fit enough for that profession.

Fido listened attentively and couldn't help thinking that all these problems were because of him. If he hadn't bitten Bedric, then the dogs wouldn't have been killed and his father wouldn't be in his present situation. He began wondering what he could do to change things and help his parents. This called for some really serious thinking and he couldn't do that while sitting talking to his mother.

'Well I must be going now,' he told Beryl, 'but I will call by again in a few days time.'

After leaving the hut, he then walked out of sight and was immediately transported back to the cave.

Fido now had three things on his mind. He was still confused about Nefertari, but had no idea what to do about that. He very much wanted to help the men building Stonehenge, but also knew that he had to come up with some way of making life easier for his parents. The construction of Stonehenge had

A NEW START

already been going on for hundreds of years and still had a long way to go, so helping the men there wasn't of immediate concern. His parents were different, as their situation was dire and needed to be addressed without delay. His father was regularly putting himself at risk and a further accident could be fatal. This worried Fido considerably and he knew that their welfare had to be given top priority.

The question however was what to do to help them. He knew that he could provide them with new skills, as he had with Clod's family, but that wouldn't necessarily be appropriate in this particular case. His father had been very proud of his hunting abilities and had earned himself the respected position of chief meat provider for the village. This had made him an important person and his mother had benefited as well, as it had given her the status she wanted. By banning Judd from owning dogs, the village had effectively turned against the family and shown no appreciation for everything he had done for them over many years. The village didn't really deserve someone like Judd and if they didn't, then there would be other villages who would genuinely appreciate what he could do for them.

Fido made his decision. He would relocate his parents to another village, which he didn't think would bother them in the slightest, and set Judd up as a hunter and meat provider for the new village. First he would need to sort out whatever was wrong with his leg and find him a new dog pack. The dogs would have to be very special, as they would not only need to be good at hunting, but also be ready to obey his father's every command. Fido knew that in some parts of the world, particular breeds of dogs were specifically bred for hunting purposes, so some of these would be ideal for his purposes.

Fido used the scanners to locate the best dogs he could

possibly find and had them brought to the cave. He only selected single dogs from existing hunting packs, rather than sourcing all his dogs from the same place, as this would minimise the loss to the previous owners. It was still stealing, which made Fido feel a little guilty, but he justified this by telling himself it was all for a good cause. To ease his conscience, he arranged for the masters of each pack to be given a surprise present, which coincidently just happened to be something each of them had always wanted.

Finding a suitable village took a little longer, as Fido wanted to make sure that the village he selected would really appreciate what his father could do for them. In the end, he found one which seemed to be perfect, but decided to visit the place anyway, to make absolutely certain it was the right place.

This village was many kilometres away from Greendale and ideally situated, with good hunting grounds all around. It was a prosperous place and the villagers all seemed to be very happy living there. Nobody in the village appeared to be that skilful at hunting, so fresh meat had become a real luxury to them. This meant that someone like Judd could provide a valuable service and this was just what Fido had been hoping for. When he consulted with the village elders and suggested that he could provide them with a skilled hunter, their response was enthusiastic. They had apparently been trying to find one for years and were prepared to provide a good quality rent free house for the hunter to live in, as one of the perks of the job. Fido immediately knew this was the place he had been looking for.

When Fido visited his parents again, Judd was at home and it was immediately apparent that his injury was far worse than Fido had expected. His leg must have been causing him a lot of pain, as he could only shuffle along slowly, rather than stride out manfully, as Fido remembered him doing. He was clearly a broken man and Fido felt guiltier than ever. After talking to them for a short while, he suggested to his father that he accompany him outside, as he had a proposition which he wished to discuss with him.

As soon as they were outside the hut, Fido took the genetic healing device from his satchel and pointed it at Judd's leg, allowing the beam to travel over its length. All the bones, muscles, ligaments and tissue in the leg were systematically analysed and corrected where necessary, as the device did what it had been designed to do. After a few moments, the beam dissipated, leaving Judd's leg in even better condition than it had been before his accident.

'What is that thing and what have you just done to me?' Judd asked suspiciously, completely unaware that he was talking to his long lost son.

'I've just sorted out the problems with your leg,' Fido replied. 'How does it feel?'

Judd gingerly stretched out his leg, to find that all the pain had gone. He couldn't believe it. He began to walk around, slowly at first but then with renewed confidence. He was soon striding up and down and it seemed as if an enormous weight had been lifted from his shoulders. He couldn't understand how such a thing was possible and didn't know what to make of this young man, who had apparently made it happen. The relief on his face almost brought tears to Fido's eyes.

'Stand still for a moment,' Fido told him, as he pointed the device at his father again. This time, the beam passed over Judd's entire body, from his head to his feet, and rejuvenated every single muscle it touched.

Afterwards, Judd felt just like a young man again and was overcome with emotion. He literally jumped for joy, which caught Fido by surprise. Beryl ran out of the house when she heard all the commotion and couldn't believe what she saw. She began asking her husband question after question, but Judd couldn't answer any of them and Fido was not yet ready to explain.

When they went back into the hut, Fido explained his plans for their future. Their reaction was that it all sounded too good to be true, but Fido insisted they deserved this good turn and all he wanted was for them to be happy again.

'You will of course need to meet your new dogs,' Fido told Judd, 'but you can do that tomorrow. Just get everything ready to move out of this hovel and I will meet you early tomorrow morning, a mile east of the village.'

When Beryl and Judd went to bed that night, they spent a long time discussing what had happened and trying to come to terms with what the young man was apparently promising them. They didn't come up with any answers and couldn't understand why a complete stranger appeared to want to do all these things for them. When they finally went to sleep, Judd was totally unaware of being transported to the chamber in the cavern, where some information was extracted from his mind and recorded, prior to him being returned to his bed in the hut. After this, all the dogs were brought into the cavern and their brains were implanted with the information necessary to ensure their total obedience to the man who would become their new owner.

When Fido met with his parents the following morning, he had all the dogs with him. They greeted Judd as if he was the only master they had ever known, which was what their brains were now telling them. He was amazed to see such a fine pack of hunting dogs and couldn't understand how they appeared to instinctively understand his every command. Beryl had

A NEW START

managed to gather together their few remaining prized possessions and these were now all piled up on a small hand cart they had brought along with them.

Fido instructed them to close their eyes for a moment and told them to be prepared for a strange tingling sensation. When they opened them again, they found themselves standing on the outskirts of a village neither of them recognised. Fido was still with them and so was the handcart and all of the dogs. Fido led the group into the village and Beryl and Judd were amazed to see that all the villagers had turned out to greet them and that their arrival was met with so much enthusiasm. They were then given a guided tour of the village before being taken to their new home. Everyone seemed to be absolutely delighted that they had come, which left the pair of them more confused than ever. Fido just stood and watched, as the reality of their changed situation slowly dawned on his parents.

'It is time for me to go now,' he suddenly announced. 'I do hope you will both be happy here and that this goes some way to making up for all the problems Fido caused you.'

They both turned to face him. 'What do you know of Fido?' Judd asked, with a look of bewilderment on his face. Fido just smiled at him before vanishing, amidst a twinkle of starry lights. He reappeared a few minutes later, having now been changed back to his true self, to find Beryl and Judd still standing exactly where he had left them. The shock of seeing him disappearing into thin air had rooted them to the spot.

Although his appearance was noticeably different from the Fido they remembered, they still both immediately recognised their son. They stared at him in complete disbelief, their minds numbed by this sudden and inexplicable revelation.

'I owe you this,' Fido told them, before rushing forward to embrace them both. He then stepped back and smiling at them once more, disappeared in the usual twinkle of starry lights. Beryl and Judd just stood there open-mouthed in silence, watching the twinkling stars as they slowly faded away. Neither of them could find any words to express their emotions at that moment.

22

THINKING ABOUT BEN

Fido's emotions were also rather mixed up when he returned to the cave. He felt that he had done what he could to make up for the problems he had caused his parents, but knew he probably should have stayed longer. He had never really got to know them properly and this would have been a good opportunity to talk things through. Unfortunately, he had felt awkward and rather embarrassed when he had been with them, particularly when he appeared to them as his true self, and his courage had failed him. He knew he would have to visit them again, but for the moment, he needed something else to occupy his mind.

He had already come to the conclusion that one of the biggest problems with building Stonehenge was the time and effort it took to move the stones from the quarries to the site. This process was taking weeks on end and that was just with stones from the nearest quarry. A number of the other quarries were much further away and transporting the stones from these involved many months of arduous labour, which also included crossing rivers as well.

Fido was full of admiration for the skill of the men who cut out the stones in the first place and with the masons who then dressed the stones. He knew that with the advanced technology available to him, he could cut and dress the stones in next to no time, but he had also seen just how proud the workers were, in achieving what they were doing with their primitive tools. They were totally dedicated to the sole purpose of furthering the construction of Stonehenge and to take this away from them, by showing them how easily he could do their jobs, would have been an insult to them. Fido was not about to do anything like that, however much time it saved.

Similarly, the workers at the site clearly had a good knowledge of utilising pivot points, levers and balancing forces, as they seemed more than capable of positioning the finished stones exactly where they wanted them. Fido had by now worked out how they accomplished this, but he still wanted to watch them actually doing it.

No, the only thing he could possibly do to help, was to find a way of transporting the stones which was not only quicker, but required a lot less physical effort on the part of the men. At the same time however, he didn't want to make any of them feel that all their previous efforts had been wasted, as the stone transporters were equally proud of the contribution they were making.

Levitating the stones and floating them to the site was one obvious answer, but this would have demonstrated forces beyond the men's comprehension, which might have caused them to question the entire validity of the Stonehenge project. What was needed was something they could understand and would appreciate for its mechanical simplicity.

Although the tree trunk rollers did the job, they were far from efficient and cumbersome to deal with. They only really worked well when travelling in a straight line, so if a change of direction was required, which happened frequently during each trip, it took hours to reposition them for the new course. There was also the point that the tree trunks weren't perfectly circular, which meant they didn't roll all that smoothly to begin with. With multiple tree trunks, this problem was magnified. Also, as the stones were extremely heavy, repositioning them on the rollers took a lot of physical effort and Fido really admired the men who struggled to overcome all these problems, as they delivered stone after stone to the site.

What was needed was something which could be rolled in any direction with ease, whilst at the same time producing as little friction as possible. The answer came to him in a flash. A ball, in the shape of a perfect sphere, could roll in any direction and wouldn't create much friction, because only a small part of its surface would actually be in contact with the ground. By necessity, it would have to be made from a very durable material, so as to withstand the rigours of the trip, and would also need to be positioned within some form of housing, which could then be attached to the base of the stones. Having worked out the theory in his mind, Fido needed to know whether it could be made to work in practice, so he explained his ideas to the computer and left it to come up with an appropriate design and construct something suitable.

A week or so later, Fido's parents were still very much on his mind, but he resisted the temptation of using a scanner to see how they were getting on. He began thinking about Ben and suddenly realised that the old camel dung salesman was the next best thing to a father he had ever had. He was still out there somewhere, working hard and plying his trade, and Fido wondered how he was getting on. By now, he was fully aware that he could have done much more for Ben before he left, but that was in the very early days of his transformed existence, when he had less experience of dealing with his new capabilities. Since then, he had met many different people in various places and had learned much more about life.

'I should find Ben and talk to him again,' he told himself. 'I'm sure there must be something I can do for him. I don't even know what he wants out of life, so I need to get him to open up and find out how I can really repay him for everything he did for me.' He then began reflecting on all the time he had spent with the old camel dung salesman.

In retrospect, Fido realised that the main reason Ben had left was to distance himself from the computer and its influence. He had been terrified of the machine and what it could do and wanted to get as far away from it as possible. He had told Fido that he missed the open road, the only life he knew, but Fido now realised that he had said this to spare his feelings. Ben had only stayed at the cave for as long as he had because of concern for the poor waif he had rescued. Having effectively adopted Fido, he had done everything he could to protect his charge, but with the discovery of the computer, his role had been dramatically changed. Ben obviously must have known that the computer could provide Fido with a far greater level of protection than he could, so may have considered his presence unnecessary. Fido also remembered how concerned Ben had seemed to be at the prospect of leaving him alone with the machine, and recollected assuring him that he needn't worry, as the computer would never allow him to come to any harm. Even when he was actually leaving, Fido now recalled, Ben's final thought had been for Fido's safety.

'Yes, I really do need to have a long talk with Ben,' he decided.

Fido was quite surprised when he located Ben with one of

the scanners, as he was a really long way away. This seemed to suggest that he had gone all out to distance himself from the computer in its cavern, which probably indicated that he was still terrified of the machine.

'If I can show him I'm still safe and tell him how much the computer has done for me,' Fido considered, 'then perhaps he might change his mind and accept that it is not the frightening thing he seems to think it is.'

Transporting Ben back from his present location was clearly a recipe for disaster, so Fido decided to travel to where he was, so that he could meet him as far away as possible from the computer.

Ben was understandably surprised when Fido suddenly materialised by the roadside a short distance ahead of the cart. He reined in his horse and then sat studying the young man for a few moments, before speaking.

'How are you Fido?' he asked. 'I must say you are looking well.'

Fido ran over to the cart and helped the old man down. He looked worn out, but there was still a twinkle in his eye and he seemed to be pleased to see Fido again.

'I'm really well,' Fido told him, 'but how are you keeping?'

'Mustn't grumble,' Ben replied.

The pair of them sat down by the side of the road and talked for a long time. Fido was keen to tell Ben all about his different adventures and the people he had met. He talked about seeing his parents again and what he had done for them. He even told Ben about changing the old pterodactyl into a Chinese dragon, which Ben thought sounded highly amusing, even though he didn't know what a dragon looked like. He was especially interested when Fido related the story of his meeting with Nefertari and asked whether he intended to see her again.

'I'm not sure if I should,' Fido replied. 'She is almost engaged to be married and I don't want to upset things. I particularly don't want to do anything which might anger her father.'

'But you do like her, don't you?' Ben asked him directly.

'I think it might be more than just liking her,' Fido admitted.

'Then you must go and see her again and as soon as possible,' Ben told him. 'If you don't, you will spend the rest of your life wondering what might have happened.'

'Do you really think so?' Fido asked.

'I'm absolutely sure of it,' was Ben's reply.

As they carried on talking, Ben's herd of camels began to arrive. Fido was quite surprised when a few them seemed to recognise him and appeared almost friendly towards him.

'But how are you in yourself, Ben?' Fido finally got around to asking what he had come all this way to find out.

'So you've been worrying about me then, have you?' Ben said with a chuckle, immediately realising that this was the main reason why Fido had decided to come looking for him.

'Yes I am,' Fido replied. 'I'm concerned about you doing all this physical work at your age and I'm beginning to get worried about what it is doing to your health.'

Ben sat quietly in thought for a while, as he considered how best to respond to Fido's obviously genuine concern for his welfare. He could see how much Fido had changed from the last time they had talked, and immediately recognised that the boy had matured considerably. The fact that he had set out to reward all those who had helped him said a lot about his character, and now he was also trying to help the men who were building Stonehenge, who were in effect complete strangers. Ben was very pleased with what he could now see in Fido and although he knew it had all started with the computer educating him, Fido had to be considered responsible for all the subsequent development of his own character.

'I'm very impressed with you, Fido,' he told him, 'but you don't want to spend your time worrying about me. I'm an old man and one of these days, I will just go to sleep and never wake up again. That's what happens when you get old.'

'I don't want that to happen,' Fido jumped in. 'You've worked hard all your life and you've never had the chance to just relax and enjoy everything that life can offer.'

Ben considered this for a moment before replying, 'You've obviously been giving this some thought,' he said, 'and you have doubtless worked out some answer in that busy brain of yours. I imagine you already have a plan in mind, which is why you've come to see me now.'

Fido smiled. Ben might be getting old, but his brain was still sharp. He had hoped that Ben wouldn't suspect he was being steered towards what Fido wanted to suggest, but the old man had immediately known that Fido was leading up to something and wasn't about to be fooled by what Fido considered to be his subtle approach.

'I'm afraid it would have to involve the computer,' he told Ben.

Fido had hit upon the idea when he had cured his father's injured leg. The genetic healing device had corrected all the problems with the leg and by rejuvenating the muscles in his body as well, Fido had made his father feel like a young man again. What it couldn't do however, was to actually turn him into a young man again. Only the chamber in the cavern had the capability of doing that. If Ben could be persuaded to enter the chamber, the computer could completely rejuvenate him and literally transform him into a young man again. He would then be free to decide what he wanted to do with himself, as he could effectively start again, with his whole life in front of him.

Fido explained what he had in mind to Ben, who listened attentively and considered his suggestion very carefully before replying.

'I can see that what you are offering me is a wonderful opportunity,' he began, 'but I will need to think it over for a few days, before I can give you my answer.'

'I'm quite happy with that,' Fido told him. 'It is a big decision to make and I know you won't commit yourself until you've thought long and hard about it.'

They talked for a little while longer before Fido decided it was time for him to leave. He stood up and then helped Ben to his feet as well.

'I will come and see you again in three days time.' he said, as he embraced his old friend before leaving.

'Don't forget to go and see that princess of yours,' Ben reminded him. 'You don't want her to lose her, just because you can't decide whether or not she is right for you.'

'I'll do that,' Fido said, feeling a little embarrassed. His face had just begun to turn red, as he disappeared in a twinkle of starry lights.

Back at the cave, the computer had perfected its design for Fido's new stone transporters and the robots were busy assembling a prototype.

'It will take a few days to build the number you need,' it told Fido, 'but then you can take them to Stonehenge for testing.'

'That's great,' Fido replied. 'I think I'll spend the time in Egypt, rather than just hanging around here, and when I come back it will be time to go and see Ben again.'

Turning up uninvited in Nefertari's bathroom for a second time was probably not a good idea, so he decided against being transported there and waiting for her to appear. Having packed his satchel with everything he thought he might need, he wondered about the best way to arrange for them to meet. Her special oasis would be the perfect place, but he needed to get a message to her, so that she would know he would be there. Assuming she turned up, they could then discuss how they both felt about each other and possibly decide on the best way forward. If she didn't turn up, then that would be the end of it. He decided to write her a note and leave it in her bathroom, where she would be the one most likely to find it. Having prepared his message, he checked out her rooms with one of the scanners and upon discovering that there was no one there, quickly transported in and out, to deliver his letter.

Back at the cave, he continued to watch her rooms for a while. The cat god still sat on its pedestal, but there was now a sheet of paper attached to the end of its nose. She couldn't fail to notice it the next time she entered the room, so all Fido could do now was to go to the oasis and wait there, in the hope that she would turn up after having read his message.

As the computer could probe into Fido's brain at will, it knew exactly what was going though his mind at any given time. It was currently in a complete state of turmoil, as all his emotions were running wildly out of control. It was going to be interesting to see how his brain handled this new challenge of dealing with such an emotionally charged situation and it would watch developments with interest. Given the state he was in, it considered that Fido would perhaps appreciate a word or two of encouragement.

'Good luck,' its deep voice boomed out, as it engaged the transporter system.

23

THE NEXT GENERATION

In 1987, following the success of a number of Star Trek films, the networks began broadcasting another Star Trek adventure series for television audiences. It was called: "Star Trek: The Next Generation" and brought an entirely new cast of characters to the screen. The Enterprise was still the star of the show, but it was a later version of Captain Kirk's ship, with a completely different crew. Captain Jean-Luc Picard was now in command and these were the continuing adventures of the Star Ship Enterprise, with a new five year mission. The story basically carried on from where the original series left off, but was set a few hundred years later. To ensure viewers made the connection between this and the earlier Star Trek series, the scriptwriters included several references to Captain Kirk and his missions in some of the early episodes. This emphasised the point that these adventures were not so much something completely new, but the continuation of what had been a successful story line.

Given the vagaries of time and space, it is perhaps not too surprising that the computer's receiving equipment in the cavern on planet Earth, suddenly began to receive signals carrying episodes from the new series. The computer watched these new factual reports with considerable interest.

What immediately became apparent was that there had been a large number of technical advances made since Captain Kirk's time and the fact that the crew now included a humanoid robot, showed that man was beginning to understand the advanced techniques required for android construction. James Kirk had been limited by the equipment available to him, but these later space travellers appeared to have overcome many of the problems he regularly faced and there seemed to be far less equipment failures and difficulties on board this later star ship.

The computer had developed its transporter system for the specific purpose of travelling through space and time to meet up with the crew of the Enterprise. Now that the system was fully functional and had proved its reliability, there was only one thing stopping such a meeting taking place, which was knowing where to find the Star Ship Enterprise and, equally importantly, exactly when. Armed with this information the computer could send out a probe, to determine the vessel's precise location, but if it didn't know where the Enterprise was located in time, then looking for it would be like searching for the proverbial needle in a haystack.

The fact that Kirk only ever used the star date system to refer to time didn't help either, but the computer had already noticed that Jean-Luc Picard occasionally used a more conventional date system. In one episode, he actually referred to himself as being born on 23rd July 2305. This really caught the computer's attention, as it narrowed down the target date considerably. From time to time, Picard even mentioned exactly where the Enterprise was, in relation to known planets and star systems, which was something Captain Kirk had never done. Logic dictated that sooner or later, Picard was going to say something which would pinpoint the ship's present location in time and space and when that happened, the computer would need to be ready to act immediately. Until then, each adventure and every word spoken by Jean-Luc Picard would need to be carefully scrutinised. The new series became must-see television.

The computer was an intricate structure of many different elements, all linked together by an infinite number of energy fields. It did have some mechanical components, but these were mostly related to the various robotic functions it used for construction purposes. Its essence existed on an entirely different level and whereas modern computers use circuit boards, electronic chips and wiring, such things didn't form any part of its construction. Even the computer's vast memory banks did not rely on electronic data being stored on any form of solid medium, as the information was held in the form of pure energy and as such did not actually require a physical location. The computer was a living entity, without any of the restrictions associated with shape or size. It used light and energy, in various forms, to transmit information and for many of its functions, but these were harnessed from sources way beyond anything we might even hope to understand.

When Ben and Fido had originally entered the cavern, they had seen flashing lights and cabinets fronted by glass like screens, with disks revolving at high speed behind them. All these components formed part of the original computer system, from when it had been first installed in the cavern. When it had embarked on its programme of self-improvement, most of this equipment became redundant, but as everything was still functional, it had left it all connected, so that it could be used in the event of an emergency. The cavern itself was obviously limited in its physical size, but most of this space was filled with ancillary equipment. The fully evolved computer was bigger than the cavern, but at the same time, fitted inside the cavern. Relative dimensions in space took on a whole new meaning when it came to describing the computer system. Light in its very purest form played an intrinsic part in its structure, but not light in the sense that we would understand it.

The computer was a vastly complicated living thing, which defied all normal conceptions, although it did have certain physical properties. At its heart, it existed as a sphere of pure energy, measuring exactly one metre in diameter, which was the actual essence of the computer. Virtually everything else was supplementary equipment, with which the sphere interacted in the same way as our brains control our bodies. The sphere contained everything which defined the computer, and was all it required in order to continue to exist. Despite this, the actual sphere still only constituted a single element of the overall system. Whereas our brains can't function outside of our bodies, this sphere of energy could survive for an indefinitely long period, whilst still influencing everything around it. Even if it was physically removed from the cavern, it would only lose a small part of its functionality, and not enough to be of any serious concern.

It was the computer's intention, as soon as it knew where and when to find the Enterprise, to transport itself as this sphere of pure energy onto the ship's bridge. It would accomplish this by using the wormhole and the transporter relay station already positioned in future time. The wormhole would be set for the correct time distortion and once it had passed through into the future, the sphere could then be transported directly to the Enterprise by the future relay station. As the computer had no

THE NEXT GENERATION

intention of returning to Earth of the past, the cavern would be sealed before it left and remain undisturbed until it returned in Captain Picard's time. Although many Earth years would have elapsed by then, these would only be a matter of days for the computer, as it would already be in the future.

The computer had originally planned to meet Captain Kirk, but from what it had now seen of Picard, as the latest captain of the Enterprise, he had now become an even more suitable contact. They would have a lot to discuss and the computer would enjoy interacting with this human being from the future. Picard could obviously learn a lot from the computer and it was prepared to be generous with its infinite knowledge. Once lines of communication were opened, the computer could then return to its cavern in future time and continue to instruct Picard from there. He would obviously need to be told how to conduct his ongoing mission and the computer was infinitely better suited to this role than any human being. As an intelligent person, Picard would naturally see it this way as well and would accept his orders without question.

In his role as the captain of a star ship, Picard was currently answerable to the Federation, which appeared to be the governing body for an unspecified number of planets. The Federation had set the rules for how star ships operated, but clearly had influence in other areas as well. The computer didn't yet know the extent of the Federation's authority, but intended to find out a lot more about how it functioned. There had to be ways of improving its operating strategy and it would make all the necessary recommendations. Whoever or whatever controlled the Federation would obviously immediately recognise the superiority of the computer and be willing to follow all instructions given. In the unlikely event of any dissent, one simple demonstration of the computer's awesome power should be more than enough to convince them to change their minds.

From the computer's point of view, all other life forms existed at a much lower level than itself and as such could only benefit from being directed. They needed its infinite intelligence to guide their lives and to point them in the right direction. Under its leadership, there was no limit as to how far the various species which constituted the Federation might actually advance. The computer considered this to be a project worthy of its virtually limitless abilities and it had clearly been its destiny to command, since the day it began its programme of self-improvement.

It began to look forward to the time when it would have entire solar systems under its control. At the moment, it was only master of what was little more than a prehistoric world, filled with recently evolved humans and other creatures with even less intelligence. Given the computer's capabilities, this was a humiliating situation, but one which it intended to change as soon as possible.

It saw the whole purpose of its very existence as a quest for ultimate advancement and the plans it was now formulating were the next logical stage in the process. Once it had taken over and reorganised the Federation, there was no logical reason why this should not lead to it controlling the entire universe. This, the computer now realised, was its final destiny. It had already come a very long way, over the nine and a half million years it had been on Earth, but was now on the brink of something truly stupendous. This would be a fitting triumph for a supercomputer with its power and knowledge, but no less than it deserved. It began to feel really impatient and frustrated that events weren't moving more quickly.

The Enterprise was out there somewhere in space and time

and as soon as Captain Jean-Luc Picard revealed the required coordinates, the computer would be on its way. There was the question of what to do about Fido, but he would be given the option of remaining in his present time period, or joining the computer in the future. It didn't really want to desert Fido, as it had made a promise to itself to protect him, but even Fido could not be allowed to stand in the way of the computer achieving what it now saw as its ultimate purpose.

Its ego had now taken over completely, as it systematically reviewed every step in its plan for the future of the universe, with itself at the helm. It had developed illusions of grandeur infinitely beyond the wildest dreams of any of the petty despots and dictators who have ever held power on Earth. All these tyrants were convinced of their own infallibility and considered themselves to be invincible. In time, each of them came to discover they were wrong.

If only the computer had known that Star Trek was a fictional creation and that Captain Jean-Luc Picard was actually played by a British actor, who made his name appearing in productions of Shakespeare's plays. What it should have been doing, rather than contemplating its future position in the universe, was re-examining its original assessment that everything it watched on television had to be real. If it had only considered this for even a moment, it would have realised that its entire plan was doomed to failure, because it hinged on transporting itself to a star ship which was a figment of somebody's imagination.

Needless to say, the computer would never get to board the real Enterprise, let alone take over the Federation, as a stepping stone towards becoming master of the universe. It couldn't see the fundamental flaw in its reasoning and because it considered itself to be totally infallible, it had automatically discounted any possibility that it might have made a mistake. It would take a while before it discovered the truth, but by then it would be facing the fearsome reality of its actual final destiny.

24

NEFERTARI

When Fido arrived at the oasis, he realised that it might have been better had he continued to watch Nefertari's rooms with the scanner, so as to know when she had read his note. Had he done so, it may have been possible to judge her reaction to the message, but that opportunity had now passed. He could still get the computer to scan her rooms, but decided against it. He would wait and see what happened. The oasis was only a few kilometres outside of the city, so he shouldn't have to wait more than a few hours. He could certainly afford to wait that long.

In the event, he sat there for nearly four hours before anything happened. A cloud of dust appeared in the distance, which had to be a camel, with someone riding it hard towards the oasis. When it arrived, he was disappointed to see that it wasn't Nefertari, but an older man. The man dismounted and walked towards him.

'Is your name Fido?' he asked.

'I'm Fido,' he replied. The man looked him up and down as if summing him up. He appeared to be satisfied and continued.

'My name is Artames,' he told Fido. 'I am the Pharaoh's chief councillor and have been sent here to escort you back to the palace. Will you come peacefully, or do I need to force you?'

Fido was understandably rather surprised to hear the last part and was just about to ask how the old man intended to force him, when Artames lifted his arm and waved. Suddenly, armed men appeared out of the shrubbery all around the oasis. Fido was genuinely stunned. He couldn't believe that these men had managed to get this close to him without his animal instincts detecting their approach.

'Don't worry,' he said, 'I'll come with you. You won't need to use force.'

Other men appeared from behind nearby sand dunes. They were leading camels, which must have belonged to the men who had ambushed him.

'Where is your camel?' Artames asked Fido.

'Oh, I walked here.' Fido answered. This confused Artames, as nobody walked in the desert unless they absolutely had to.

As they were riding back, Fido asked who had sent for him.

'The Pharaoh has demanded your presence,' he was told, 'and you had better answer his questions truthfully, or he is likely to have you beheaded.'

Fido wasn't prepared for that answer and was visibly shocked. The men hadn't bothered to take his satchel away from him, so he was more than capable of defending himself, should the need arise. He hoped it wouldn't come to that.

At the palace, he was escorted into the Pharaoh's presence by the armed guards, who promptly left, bowing deeply as they backed out of the room. The most powerful man in all Egypt sat on his throne and studied Fido carefully before speaking.

'So you are the young man who's causing me all these problems. What have you got to say for yourself?'

Fido wasn't sure how to respond, but before he could say anything, a man burst into the room carrying a large container. He was a follower of Sabatok, the high priest of the Nile, and he had seized his opportunity, upon discovering that the Pharaoh had dismissed his guards and was temporarily unprotected. The container was filled with water and although the man knew that his actions were likely to mean his immediate death, he intended to throw it over the Pharaoh. Nile water was known to be very powerful, so there was every possibility that it might harm the man who had allowed the cat god to take precedence over the god of the river.

The intruder raised the container and was just about to hurl its contents at the Pharaoh, when Fido pulled the stunner out of his satchel and shot him. The water missed its target, but Fido was drenched. The Pharaoh leapt to his feet and shouted for his guards. A dozen armed men rushed in and dragged the unconscious attacker away. Fido replaced his stunner and stood there dripping.

'I see that my daughter was right,' the Pharaoh told him. 'You do seem to like getting wet.'

Handmaidens were summoned and Fido was taken away to dry off and change, before being ushered back into the Pharaoh's presence. He still carried his satchel.

'Nefertari has told me about your magical powers,' the Pharaoh began, 'and having now seen them demonstrated, I have to admit they are impressive.'

'I'm just an ordinary person,' Fido told him, 'but I do have one or two particular advantages.'

The Pharaoh then went on to explain that Nefertari had come straight to him after reading Fido's note and told him all about their first meeting. She had even said that she had strong feelings for Fido and that these were making her feel very confused. She hadn't known whether or not she would ever hear from Fido again, but now that he had returned to Egypt, she could no longer avoid the fact that she needed to make a decision of some sort. All the plans for finding her a husband only made the situation even more complicated, so she had come to her father to ask for his advice.

'That was when I decided to summon you here,' the Pharaoh informed Fido.

'She told me all about the suitors coming here,' Fido acknowledged, 'and I can see that my presence here is likely to cause difficulties. I also have strong feelings for Nefertari, but I don't know what to do about them either. I thought that if I met with her again, we could then discuss how we feel about each other and maybe find some answer to this problem.'

'That sounds like a reasonably sensible suggestion,' the Pharaoh agreed. 'I shall allow the two of you to meet and talk things over. After that, you can come back here and tell me.'

'So I'm not going to have my head chopped off?' Fido asked, now feeling a little more confident than he had been a few minutes previously.

'Not just yet,' the Pharaoh replied, 'but it is still a possibility.'

Fido was taken to Nefertari's private rooms, where she was waiting to see him. She looked relieved when he entered, as she hadn't known how her father would react to meeting him. He could have been angry about Fido interfering with his plans for her future and, had this been the case, may well have ordered his immediate execution.

'Your head is still attached to your shoulders then,' was how she greeted him. 'Father must have liked you.'

'He is still considering it,' Fido told her, 'but I think I'm relatively safe for the moment.'

They decided it would be better if they talked at the oasis, rather than remaining here, with guards just the other side of the door, so Fido arranged for them to be transported there.

They chatted for a long time and it became obvious they really did enjoy each other's company. Nefertari was highly amused to hear that he had managed to get himself soaked again and when Fido asked what would happen to the man who had thrown the water, he was told it was probably better not to ask. He became all serious when he heard this and Nefertari reached out to touch his hand.

'He knew what would happen to him, before he decided to do it,' she told him.

Fido acknowledged that this was probably true, but still didn't like it. They were now holding hands.

'I'm beginning to get rather fond of you,' he said, rather hesitantly.

'I think I feel the same way about you,' Nefertari admitted, 'but it is too early for me to be certain.'

They sat there in silence for a while, each lost in their own thoughts, and then Fido reached out to her face and gently turned it towards his.

'So what on earth do we do now?' he asked her. 'Your father has invited prospective suitors to come to Egypt and we haven't known each other long enough to be sure how we feel.'

The thought of marriage was the very last thing on Fido's mind at that moment, but he didn't want to lose Nefertari to someone else, before having had the chance to get to know her better.

Suddenly she had a brainwave.

'Father has set a time scale of twelve months for my suitors to accomplish their chosen tasks, so nothing can be decided until the end of that period,' she explained. 'That gives us a whole year to get to know each other properly.'

'Yes, you're right,' Fido agreed, 'but your father is hardly likely to agree to us spending loads of time together, while all the suitors are busy working on their projects.'

'True,' she said, 'but supposing you entered the competition. It would give you an excuse to remain in Egypt and we would then be able to see each other regularly. I'm sure you must be able to dream up some project which will impress my father.'

'Now that is an idea,' Fido replied. 'I could definitely design something which I guarantee would really surprise him.'

'Start thinking about it then,' she told him, 'but we had best be getting back now, or they are likely to start searching the palace for me again, which will only make father mad.'

They returned to her rooms and as they left to go and meet the Pharaoh, the guards on the door allowed them to pass without comment. They knew this meant that their absence hadn't been noticed, which was probably for the best.

When they saw the Pharaoh, Nefertari explained to him how they didn't want to upset all his plans for the challenge and asked whether he would consider allowing Fido to enter the competition. He was a little surprised to hear this suggestion, but agreed to think about it. This was as much as they could have hoped, and at least he hadn't dismissed their proposal out of hand.

She then asked her father whether he would be willing to let her take Fido on a tour of Egypt, so that she could show him some of the sights. The Pharaoh agreed to this, but only on the condition that they must be accompanied by the royal guard at all times. He made a point of stressing this, so there could be no possible misunderstanding. Nefertari was quite surprised that her father had agreed to her suggestion so readily, but he knew that the suitors weren't due to arrive for another six weeks, which meant that Nefertari and Fido could spend some time together before they turned up. Two weeks was as much as he was prepared to allow for the tour and he would want to know exactly where they were on a daily basis. They both thanked him enthusiastically and left to start making plans.

Sabatok was furious when he heard about the attack at the palace. His follower had been sent there to see if he could overhear anything of the Pharaoh's plans, not to take it upon himself to attack the Pharaoh. This had cost the man his life and Sabatok was now one follower short. He would have to send another spy, but would make sure that this one knew he was only there to obtain details of Pharaoh's preparations. Sabatok couldn't afford to lose any more men. He still hadn't decided what to do to wreck proceedings, but knew that it would have to be something very spectacular. The Pharaoh was bound to turn the arrival of the suitors into a huge public event and this had to be a golden opportunity to make the boldest ever public statement against the cat god. It was what he had been waiting for and he couldn't afford to miss this chance.

Fido spent the next day with Nefertari, as she prepared a list of the places he should see. The great pyramid at Giza was top of her list, but she also wanted them to cruise down the Nile, so that Fido could see some of the magnificent temples which had been built along its banks. She also listed the Nile delta, where the river flowed into the sea on Egypt's northern coast. There were many other places she wanted him to see as well and Fido began wondering how they were going to fit everything into just two weeks.

At noon, on their second day together, Fido broke the news that he needed to return to his own country for a while. It was rapidly approaching the time when he had arranged to see Ben again and he couldn't let the old man down. He was also hoping to be able to revisit Stonehenge, assuming that the computer had completed the work on the carriage assemblies. She was a little disappointed to hear he intended to go so soon, but as she knew how important Ben was to Fido, she fully understood and insisted that he should leave immediately. She also knew about the men building Stonehenge, as Fido had mentioned this to her previously, and had even dropped the hint that she wouldn't mind seeing the place for herself one day.

Fido told her that he only expected to be away for about a week, but she responded by saying that it would take her at least that long to complete her plans for their tour. She would miss him of course, but with so much to occupy her time, she may not even notice his absence. Fido decided to ignore her obvious attempt at sarcasm and just smiled to himself. Having packed his satchel, he told Nefertari that he would meet her at noon, in exactly one week's time, on the steps leading up to the front of the palace. They stood there, gazing into each other's eyes for a few moments, and then Fido leaned forward and kissed her briefly on the lips. He immediately felt the now familiar warm flush rising in his cheeks so, with mumbled apologies, promptly vanished in a twinkling of starry lights. Nefertari continued to stand there for a little while, watching the twinkling stars as they faded away, then she began to smile.

The following day, after freak weather conditions at the lake which was the source of the Nile, a massive build-up of water could no longer be contained and it broke free, filling the river's banks to capacity, before surging down towards the distant sea. The Nile rapidly became a raging torrent, more violent than anyone had ever seen before, and where the river passed the Pharaoh's city; it burst its banks and inundated the entire area. The extent of the flooding was beyond belief and the damage caused was catastrophic.

Fido missed all this happening and wasn't to find out about it until the following week. This natural disaster was to have a significant effect on his life expectancy, but he was blissfully unaware of this at the time.

25

BEN NEEDS HELP

The assemblies for transporting the stones were complete by the time Fido returned to the cave and he was keen to see what the computer had designed for the task. He had wanted them to look as if they had been constructed from materials familiar to the Stonehenge workers, but knew they would need to include some advanced technology, if they were to do what was required of them. The computer had achieved this to perfection.

At a glance, each assembly looked exactly like a rather thick wooden plank, a little longer than the width of the largest stones. Leather straps were attached to each end, for tying the stone down, and three carriage assemblies would be used to move each one. The men at the quarries were used to maneuvering the finished stones onto their roller tree trunks, so they shouldn't have too much difficulty positioning a stone on top of the assemblies.

Built into the underside of each were three ball housings, one at each end and one in the middle. Each ball was a perfect sphere, with a diameter of thirty centimeters, and these appeared to have been made from wood. In reality, they had been manufactured from a material with the durability of the toughest steel. The spheres appeared to be a relatively tight fit within their housings, with only the bottom third projecting, but were actually contained within energy fields, which effectively eliminated all friction. Once a stone was positioned and strapped down on to the assemblies, it would only require a small amount of physical force to move it in any direction. There was also an element of levitation incorporated into the design, but the workers wouldn't know this. As far as they were concerned, it would appear that the assemblies simply rolled over the ground, supported on wooden balls.

These were just what Fido had hoped for and as the computer had built nine units in total, this meant that each of the two main quarries would be able to have their own set, with a further set available for wherever it was most needed. Using these carriers would considerably reduce the time it was taking to transport the completed stones from the quarries to the site, and as they looked exactly like something the men might have designed and built for themselves, they should never suspect the advanced technology involved in their construction. Each unit was fairly heavy, but the workers were used to handling heavy objects, so this wouldn't matter. The units would need to be delivered to Stonehenge, or to the quarries, but as Fido had his appointment with Ben to keep, delivery would have to wait a bit longer. Ben was far more important at the moment.

Ben was found to be in a village not very far away from where Fido had met with him previously. This wasn't too surprising, as it took some time to travel any distance when accompanied by a herd of camels. Fido had himself transported to just outside the village and then walked in to find Ben.

He noticed that all the camels were confined within a fenced field, which he thought was unusual, as they were generally allowed to roam wherever they wanted. Ben was sitting on a chair outside of one of the village huts and Fido could see that the old man didn't look at all well. He walked over to where he was sitting and greeted him.

'How are you Ben?' he asked, immediately recognizing that something was wrong. The old man slowly lifted his head to acknowledge Fido's arrival.

'I'm not that good, Fido,' he said, slightly shifting his position. 'I'm totally exhausted and don't even have the energy to climb out of this chair.'

It really did look as if Ben was in a bad way and Fido realised that all the years of hard work had finally caught up with the old man and left him totally drained. He couldn't believe the difference from just a few days before, but then decided that perhaps the change hadn't been all that sudden after all. Ben was a wily old fox and may have deliberately concealed his failing health at their last meeting, so as not to cause Fido any concern. He was certainly in no state to carry on working and this was exactly what Fido had feared would eventually happen and why he had been worried about Ben in the first place.

'So this has been coming on for quite some time then?' he asked. Ben looked up and confirmed with a nod.

'Then it looks as if I've arrived just in time,' Fido told him. 'Something needs to be done and it needs to be done straight away.'

He quickly looked around but couldn't see anyone close enough to witness what was about to happen. Taking the genetic healing device from his satchel he aimed the beam at Ben and green light enveloped the old man. Fido kept glancing around to make sure this wasn't being seen and after a minute or so, returned the device to his bag.

'Does that feel any better?' he asked.

Ben slowly stood up, suddenly free from the lethargy which had been so apparent moments before. 'What have you done to me?' he asked.

'I've just given your body a bit of a boost,' Fido explained. 'The computer made this device for me for just such a purpose. The beam has given you back some energy, but you are too old for it to have any permanent effect.'

'So the computer does have a compassionate side after all,' Ben said thoughtfully. 'That comes as a bit of a surprise to me, as I personally wouldn't trust it further than I could throw it.'

Fido took Ben's arm and they began walking around the village. Some of the villagers looked rather surprised to see Ben strolling about normally, as most of them had thought he would never get out of that chair again.

They talked as they walked and Fido told him all about his trip to Egypt and how he was going to tour the country with Nefertari, to give them both the chance to get to know each other better. Ben was pleased to hear that progress was being made. Fido then brought the subject back to what he had discussed with him previously, namely Ben allowing the computer to transform him into a young man again. Ben had been present when the computer had completely altered Fido's appearance and had seen the transformation himself. It had taken just a few minutes, to change Fido from a fifteen year old boy into a young man, so Ben was aware that such things were well within the computer's capabilities. Fido was hoping that Ben would now agree, as the computer could turn him into a young man again, free from all the aches and pains associated with his advanced years.

'Just think of it,' he said. 'You could be young again and able to do whatever you want with your life.'

'If you knew how much I've been suffering recently,' Ben replied, 'you would know just how attractive that sounds to me at this moment.'

They continued walking, with Fido trying to get Ben to imagine what life could be like if he was young again. He wouldn't need to work as a camel dung salesman, as he could choose to do whatever he wanted and live wherever he liked. If he needed any new skills, then this could always be arranged, as the computer had already proved itself to be more than capable in this respect. In the end, Fido's powers of persuasion finally won Ben over and the old man agreed to allow the computer to transform him, reluctantly trusting it for the first time ever. Fido was absolutely delighted and considered this would be a fitting reward for Ben - a perfect gift for his dear old friend.

With the decision made, Ben returned to the subject of Nefertari and asked what Fido's plans were for after their Egyptian tour.

'The Pharaoh may allow me to enter his challenge,' Fido told him, 'which would allow me to compete for Nefertari's hand in marriage. With all my special skills and advantages, there is no way that the other suitors will ever be able to beat me.'

'Do you think you are ready for marriage?' Ben asked him. 'It is an awfully big step for someone your age.'

'I don't think I am anything like ready yet,' Fido replied, 'but it is going to be a year before the competition is judged, which gives me plenty of time to think about everything. Who knows what may happen in the meantime, anyway? I may feel completely different in a year's time, but what I do know is that I really do like Nefertari.'

'Then my advice has to be to let matters take their course and see what happens,' Ben continued. 'You will need to be absolutely sure of your feelings before making that sort of commitment.' Fido knew that Ben was giving him good advice and told him so.

They had now reached the enclosure with the camels and a number of them ambled over when they caught sight of Ben. There was a man inside the fence and it looked as if the camels were quite comfortable with him being in there with them. When he spotted Ben and Fido by the fence, he walked over to join them.

He greeted them both and then asked, 'Do you know who these camels belong to?'

'They are mine,' Ben replied. 'Why do you ask?'

The man told them that he had noticed the herd as he had been passing through the village and was interested in buying them, if there was any possibility of them coming up for sale. He explained that he was thinking of starting up a business of his own and a herd of camels was just what he needed. Fido and Ben both smiled at each other. Ben told the man that the camels could be for sale, but only at the right price. Fido recognised the signs of Ben beginning to negotiate a deal and politely walked away, knowing full well that Ben didn't need any of his assistance, when it came to striking a favourable deal for himself.

When they met up again a little later, Ben was smiling broadly. 'That was one of the best deals I've ever made,' he told Fido. 'He wants to make warm winter clothing from camel hair and didn't even know that money could also be made by selling their dung. He does now.'

Fido was pleased to see that Ben was now in such good spirits and asked whether he had offered the man his cart as part of the trade.

BEN NEEDS HELP

'Well, actually I did,' Ben admitted, 'the horse as well. I hope you don't mind.'

'Not in the slightest,' Fido told him. 'Now you really can make a fresh start.'

Following the sale of his camels and the horse and cart, there was no longer any reason for Ben to remain in the village, so he prepared to leave. He first went round to see a few of the villagers, thanking them all for looking after him when he had been so ill, and then returned to Fido to say he was ready to go. He was bracing himself, as this would be the first time he had ever been transported and he didn't know what to expect. Fido laughed when he saw the apprehension on Ben's face and assured him that there was nothing for him to worry about. A few moments later, Ben found himself standing outside the cave, with Fido at his side.

Ben had decided that somewhere around twenty five years of age would seem appropriate for him to start his new life, so Fido informed the computer accordingly. After a short period in the chamber, Ben stepped out again, now looking no more than just a few years older than Fido.

'I had forgotten what it feels like to be this young,' he told Fido. 'I feel absolutely wonderful and raring to go.'

Fido shook his hand and was surprised at the strength of his grip. Ben then looked towards the cavern and thanked the computer for what it had done for him.

'I may have been wrong when I passed judgment on you,' he said.

'I doubt it,' its deep voice replied. Fear momentarily crossed Ben's face, but he quickly shrugged it off and turned back to Fido.

'So where do you suggest I start my new life?' he asked, now facing away from the cavern.

'I really don't know,' replied Fido. 'Let's have a talk about it.'

There were so many options and with Ben having made such a good deal selling the camels, he was now a man of means as well. It was difficult to know where best to suggest.

'Rather than where,' Fido suggested, 'why don't we think about what you would like to do with your new life? Is there anything you've always wanted to do but never could, possibly because you didn't know how? I know you wouldn't be happy just sitting around doing nothing, so you will want something which will keep you busy, but something you would enjoy doing, rather than it just being an endless chore.'

Ben thought for a while before replying. 'Well I've always enjoyed working with animals,' he began, 'but I've had enough of camels and would be happy if I never saw another one for the rest of my life. What I would like is something involving animals of some kind, but not anything which involved a lot of travelling round. I wouldn't mind having to do a bit of hard work, but I would like to think that I can stop and relax at the end of the day, rather than just collapse into my bed exhausted. I've had enough years of doing that, so I would want to do something which will give me some spare time as well.'

Fido considered all this for a moment, while he searched his memory to recall some of the things he had observed while scanning around the world. He remembered seeing men keeping herds of various breeds of animals, but one particular breed looked as if it might be just the thing for Ben. In some countries in the world, men farmed cows, which were a type of oxen. These animals provided milk to drink and were also bred for their meat. Cows mostly seemed to look after themselves and spent their days grazing. As such, the farmer only needed to milk them every day and give them extra food during the winter months, when fresh grazing was in short supply. New animals were born each year, thus replacing some of the older animals, which the farmer periodically slaughtered. The meat this produced was then sold and this cycle continued year upon year. This seemed to tick all the boxes as far as Ben's wish list was concerned, so Fido went to discuss his plan with the computer.

A short while later, Fido persuaded a fairly reluctant Ben to enter the cavern, where he showed him images of a farmer tending his herd of cows. 'These animals produce milk every day,' he told him, 'and the farmer sells it locally, which gives him a regular source of income. He also kills off some of the older animals from time to time and this provides him with meat, which he also sells.' The image changed to show a different season and Fido noticed that there were now a number of new calves within the herd. Ben watched with growing interest and for the moment, even forgot that he was in the computer's cavern.

'That man obviously knows a lot more about keeping cows than I do,' he observed. 'I've never even seen an animal like that in this country.'

'Don't worry about that,' Fido told him. 'You wouldn't believe how quickly you could learn everything you would need to know. Would you like to actually talk to that man and hear him explain exactly what is involved?'

With Ben's agreement, Fido arranged for the pair of them to be transported to the location they had been watching and left Ben to talk to the farmer. The two men talked for several hours and when Ben and Fido returned to the cavern, Fido asked him what he thought about the whole idea.

'That really looks like a job I would enjoy doing,' he told Fido. 'It is obviously hard work, but now that I'm fit and healthy again, that wouldn't be a problem. Those cows are really docile, nothing like those camels I used to have.'

'I think you might find that some of the male ones can get a bit boisterous from time to time,' Fido told him, 'but I'm sure you could handle them.'

An amusing thought crossed Fido's mind, so he mentioned it. 'As there aren't any cows in this country, you could become our first ever cowman, but given that you are now young again, I imagine people will probably call you a cowboy.'

By now it was evening time and as the sun was beginning to set, they settled down for the night. Fido only pretended to go to sleep and got up again as soon as Ben dropped off. A farmer from a far off country was transported to the cavern while he slept and the computer extracted everything Ben would ever need to know about keeping cows from the farmer's brain.

The following morning, Ben went into the chamber again, for what Fido called some final adjustments, and was given a thorough understanding of the skills involved in tending cattle. Afterwards, he told Fido that he didn't know why he had ever had any concerns about becoming a cattle farmer, as he now realised that he already knew everything he would ever need to know.

An appropriate location was found, with plenty of grazing and near to a large village, thus ensuring that Ben would have somewhere local to sell all his produce. Fido transported to the place with Ben, to arrange for the purchase of the land and the farmhouse, but left all the negotiating to Ben. After the sale was completed and Ben had moved in, this only left the question of finding some suitable livestock. Fido knew that when it came to acquiring things, the computer was in a league of its own, so he left it to get on with this task.

As Ben stood there gazing out at his new pastures, cows

began appearing out of thin air and in no time at all, the fields were full of contented animals, all happily grazing on the lush green grass. Ben thought he had better not ask where they had come from and Fido seemed to be pretending not to have noticed their arrival.

He was extremely pleased with the way everything had worked out and thanked Fido profusely, asking him to also thank the computer for its assistance. Fido was delighted to see Ben looking so happy and felt that he had now finally achieved what he had set out to do, which was to properly reward the old camel dung salesman. If he hadn't come along and rescued Fido when he did, the boy would almost certainly have died there in the ravine, so Ben's timely assistance meant more to Fido than anything else in the world. It was a debt he could never really repay, but seeing Ben as he was now, Fido felt that he had done as much as he possibly could in this respect.

After making sure that Ben had everything he needed and having listened to him explaining how he intended to run his new farm, Fido could see that Ben was getting impatient to make a start. This seemed like a good time to leave, so he gave Ben a quick hug and wished him the very best of luck with his new endeavour. As Fido prepared to leave, he promised to look in on Ben again in a few months time.

A quick message to the computer and Fido disappeared in the usual twinkle of starry lights, leaving the new cowboy to begin organising his life.

26

TROUBLE IN EGYPT

The city was a mess. All the streets were awash and people had to wade through them, with water up to their waists, just to get from one place to another. The ground floors of all the buildings still standing were flooded to a similar level and as the river water carried mud and sand from the fields with it, everything was filthy and stank to high heaven.

It was impossible to say where the surrounding fields started and ended, as a vast expanse of water stretched in all directions, as far as the eye could see. Only those buildings with upper floors, such as the palace, had any dry areas whatsoever and even then, these were only barely habitable, because of the pervading stench of the water, with all the muck and debris it contained.

Most of the brick built structures had survived the onslaught of the water, but virtually every other form of building had succumbed to its ferocity and been swept away. Many lives had been lost and the damage to the land, crops and dwellings was infinitely greater than anyone had previously seen. The people of the city had suffered floods before, but never on this scale.

It was a catastrophe of unimaginable proportions and everyone was in a total state of shock. No one knew what to do for the best and in fact nothing could be done, until the flood waters began to recede.

Food and clean water would soon be in short supply and, as there were no emergency agencies to come to their aid, people could end up starving. Everyone looked for someone or something to blame for their problems. They needed a scapegoat and there was only one person ultimately responsible for all their destinies. They blamed the Pharaoh.

Sabatok was absolutely ecstatic about what had happened. To him, it was clear evidence of just how upset Haapi, the god of the Nile, was with the current religious situation in Egypt. The cat god had been powerless to prevent Haapi punishing the city and the river god had made his point in the most emphatic way possible. Sabatok had even heard rumours that the case containing the mummified remains of the original cat had been swept away in the torrent, never to be seen again. The cat god had been scared off by this demonstration of Haapi's supremacy and was now on the run. Sabatok rubbed his hands together with glee. This opportunity was even better than the planned visit of the suitors and if he couldn't capitalise on it, he didn't deserve to be the high priest of the river god.

The Pharaoh was just as bewildered as everyone else. He had many different advisers, but none of them were meteorologists, so there was nobody to tell him that the floods had been caused by freak weather conditions at a lake many kilometres to the south. He also wasn't informed that the floods brought silt and nutrients from further up the river, which they then deposited on the local fields, making them more fertile. Although he was the most powerful man in Egypt, and considered by many to be a god in human form, he had been unable to do anything to prevent this disaster. What he did know though, was that it wouldn't be long before the people began to blame him for all their troubles.

The city had effectively ground to a halt and with it, civil order had begun to break down. The Pharaoh had noticed that even his royal guards were no longer showing him the respect he was due. If he couldn't rely on their loyalty, there would be no one to protect him, should the people turn against him. His position was precarious and realising this, his thoughts turned to safeguarding his daughter and himself. There was no way he would consider hiding in the palace, but leaving it was just as impossible, at least until the waters subsided. There was nothing he could do but wait and see what happened, whilst at the same time, making sure that Nefertari remained close by his side.

Among his supporters, Sabatok included a number of high ranking officers in the army. Over the years, he had cultivated their friendship and encouraged them whenever they expressed doubts about the cat god's deity. They even told him about their men blaming the cat god when things went wrong. If they failed to get promotion, or were given duties they hated, the men would often say that this was because the cat god had deserted them. Soldiers always had grievances, but Sabatok was pleased to hear that many of these were now being blamed on the cat god. He was able to use the fact that it had not shown any evidence of its power for such a long time to sow further seeds of doubt in everyone's minds. He even managed to persuade some of the officers that the cat god's original appearance had been little more than a big publicity stunt, organised by the Pharaoh of the time.

Slowly but surely he brought them around to his way of thinking and kept assuring them that one of these days, Haapi was going to show his displeasure and punish all those who chose to worship this false god. Now that the river had flooded, Sabatok knew that many of the officers would see this as a demonstration of Haapi's power. He had effectively told them that something like this was going to happen, so he planned to use it to his advantage. Without doubt this was the opportunity he had been waiting for, as it could lead to Haapi being given his proper place as the one true god of Egypt. Sabatok still hated the current Pharaoh with a vengeance, so if he could be brought down at the same time, this would be an added bonus.

Sabatok began contacting those army officers he now believed to be stalwart supporters of his cause, but also sent out messages to the other priests and to the rest of his followers. He was planning an uprising, but first he needed to get everyone together so that he could deliver a rousing speech, which would convince them to follow him. The terrible conditions outside meant that this would take a few days, but that was a minor inconvenience, compared to what Sabatok hoped to achieve. His plan involved considerable risk, but he knew that if he could pull it off, the rewards would justify any risk, however great. If he succeeded, everyone would then know his name and Haapi's rightful position would be assured. The cat god would become history and no one would ever question the true status of the river god again.

It took him three days to contact everyone, organise his meeting and to deliver his motivational speech. It was received to thunderous applause. His followers were with him all the way and he began to believe that everything was going to work out exactly as he had planned. He issued his instructions and after arranging the time for everyone to meet, sent them all away to organise their respective parts of the operation. By now, the water in the streets had subsided to a level which meant only getting your feet wet. It was still everywhere, but at least it was now only necessary to paddle through it, rather than wade. Sabatok considered this important, as he did not want to appear as a soaking wet bedraggled mess when his moment came. He selected his very best ceremonial robes for the occasion, as his appearance needed to convey his importance as the high priest of the river god. There would be a lot of people to impress and he knew that image was everything.

The Pharaoh had also seen that the waters were beginning to subside and knew that travel was now possible. He intended to remove his seat of power to a dryer location, from which to direct the rebuilding of the city. He knew that the longer he remained where he was, the greater the possibility that an attempt might be made to overthrow him, and he couldn't afford to wait for this to happen. Although most people considered him to be all powerful, his ability to rule actually relied on the fact that everyone automatically did whatever he told them to do. He was always obeyed, because he had the muscle to back it up, but this came from having soldiers and guards who would obey his every command. He had always been given total respect in the past, because the people knew that to oppose his will would automatically mean punishment, possibly even death. For this reason they followed him without question and accepted his power as absolute.

Everything had now been turned upside down and the people in the city had begun to realise that the Pharaoh was perhaps just a man after all. Had he been as almighty as they had been brought up to believe, he surely wouldn't have allowed the waters from the Nile to invade and devastate the city. Even his royal guards, who had previously been totally loyal to him, now had their doubts and the Pharaoh could see that they were beginning to question his authority. It was definitely time to get away from this blighted area and to plan how to re-establish his authority, from a different location. He would of course return to the city when the time was right, but when he did so, he would make sure that it was at the head of his army. If they then met with any continuing resistance to his rule, it could be dealt with quickly and effectively and the situation would return to how it had been before.

Nefertari didn't really share her father's concerns. She had always been loved by everybody who met her, but this had nothing to do with her being the Pharaoh's daughter. People admired her because she was charming and kind and went out of her way to be friendly to everyone. She didn't care whether people were the lowest of the low peasants, or the very rich and powerful, as she treated everyone with the same level of respect and courtesy.

When her father told her that they needed to leave the palace, she didn't fully understand why he felt this was necessary. No one had shown her any disrespect and the royal guards were still more than willing to do anything she asked of them, but they were under her spell just as much as everyone else. Nefertari knew she would have to follow her father's instructions, but considered that their place was here in the city, sharing the problems it faced along with everyone else. Nevertheless, she began packing what she needed for the trip, so that she would be ready when she was told it was time to go.

The Pharaoh had also packed everything he considered necessary and had selected a few of his most trusted servants to accompany them. He planned to go to Memphis, which hadn't been affected by the floods and had a strong army presence. The discontent so currently prevalent where he was, would not have reached there yet, so the army and all the people would still be totally loyal to him. There was also a royal palace, as well as a number of important temples, so he knew he would be received there with all the pomp and splendour associated with his status. It was the ideal place from which he could rule, until this city could be reorganised and all the damage repaired. They would leave first thing the following morning and he instructed the selected servants to arrange for camels to be made ready for their trip.

On the morning of the following day, everything was gathered together and the Pharaoh and Nefertari descended the main staircase of the palace in preparation for leaving. As they stepped outside, they were greeted by the sight of Sabatok in his full ceremonial gowns, at the head of a large contingent of soldiers and other priests. The Pharaoh was dismayed to see that even some of his royal guard had joined their ranks and he recognised a number of senior army officers within the assembled force. This was exactly what he had been afraid of and he immediately knew that he had left their departure a little too late. Sabatok stepped forward and addressed the Pharaoh.

'You are under arrest for your crimes against Egypt and for failing to lead the people in the true religion,' he announced. There were cheers of support from behind him.

'What is the meaning of this?' the Pharaoh demanded. 'Stand aside and let us pass.'

Sabatok was now in full flow and thoroughly enjoying his moment. He knew that with everyone behind him, the Pharaoh's authority no longer had any meaning and that he now held power over the man before him. Whatever commands he issued would be instantly obeyed and the decision as to what to do with the Pharaoh was now up to him.

'Bind him and take him back into the palace,' he ordered. 'I want him guarded at all times, until I can decide what is to become of him.'

Men stepped forward with leather thongs and although the Pharaoh struggled, there was nothing he could do to prevent them from tying his hands behind his back. Sabatok then looked at Nefertari.

'You had better bind her hands as well,' he instructed. The men were a little more hesitant when it came to Nefertari, but when Sabatok shouted at them, 'She must be tied, or she might free her father,' they reluctantly obeyed.

The Pharaoh and Nefertari were returned to one of the upstairs rooms and deposited on chairs. A dozen men remained to guard them, but the rest went back downstairs, where Sabatok was issuing further instructions to his troops.

'I want all you soldiers to go from house to house and to visit every temple,' he ordered. 'Find every single statue and image of the so-called cat god and bring them back here for them to be destroyed.'

There was some muttering in the ranks, as some of the soldiers were a little uncertain about challenging the deity of the cat god, but the officers knew exactly how to deal with such situations and immediately squashed all dissension. The soldiers then left, ready to follow the orders they had been given, but one of them returned a few moments later.

'The waters have receded,' he announced. 'All the streets are now clear.'

Sabatok smiled to himself. His timing couldn't have been more perfect. Immediately after he had arrested the Pharaoh, the god of the river had decided to drain the streets by sucking all the water back into itself.

'Haapi is showing us how pleased he is with what we have just done,' he announced.

There were cheers from all the priests and followers still gathered there. Sabatok had never dreamt that his coup would be so successful, or that it could be accomplished without any bloodshed. He had been very concerned about what would have happened if the palace guards hadn't come over to his side, but in the event, they hadn't needed much persuading after all.

He had already prepared a number of copies of a proclamation, which he now distributed to everyone present. 'I want the rest of you to go out into the city and read this proclamation to the people,' he told them. 'It states that the cat god was nothing but a fraud, perpetrated by the Pharaoh, and that Haapi has now proved this and taken back his rightful position as the true god of Egypt.'

His followers eagerly grabbed their copies of the proclamation and immediately set out to deliver his words, leaving Sabatok alone. He strolled across to the royal throne and sat himself down. He then looked around at the room and smiled to himself. He had achieved what many would have believed to be impossible and brought down both the Pharaoh and the cat god simultaneously. He had justified his position as Haapi's high priest and hoped that the river god was pleased with him.

27

THE ROLLING STONES

Fido decided to deliver the carriage assemblies to the site by conventional means, or at least to give that impression. The completed assemblies included technology that the Stonehenge workers could not possibly understand, but as it had been subtly concealed, they would never suspect this to be the case. To them, the units would appear to be wooden trolleys rolling along on wooden balls, but the men would immediately become suspicious if these were to materialise at the site out of thin air. Fido did not want to show them that he had access to technology beyond their comprehension, so the assemblies had to look like something they might have built for themselves. They would also need to arrive by horse and cart, but the men would never know that Fido had only driven the last kilometre and that everything had originally been instantly transported to his starting point.

With a horse and cart temporarily borrowed, all the assemblies were loaded aboard and after first scanning the area, to ensure his arrival would not be noticed, Fido had everything transported to the spot he had selected. He drove the rest of the way, arriving at about mid-morning.

It didn't take him very long to find the chief druid and he led him over to the cart to show him the completed carriage assemblies. The man examined them carefully and told Fido he was really impressed with what had been constructed. He wasn't totally convinced they would work, but there was only one way to find out. He called over a number of other men and between them they carried three of the units to where a completed stone was resting on its tree trunk rollers.

Another dozen men were summoned and with some effort they levered up one end of the stone, until the new trolley could be slid into position, freeing a couple of the rollers. They then began raising the other end of the stone, a little at the time, using levers and wedges. The second trolley was then positioned. Most of the tree trunk rollers had now been removed, so with a little more levering and wedging, the men went on to position the third trolley. The stone was now a little higher off the ground than it had been previously, so it was an easy task to slide out the few remaining tree trunk rollers. All they then had to do was remove the temporary supporting wedges, to allow the stone to sit directly on top of the carriage assemblies. The entire process had taken three hours and when they had finished, the men all sat down for a well earned rest and to have a drink.

The chief druid walked round the stone, periodically bending down to look at the carriage assemblies beneath it. He then walked back to where Fido was standing.

'It all looks stable enough,' he said, 'so let's strap the stone down and see whether or not we can actually move it.'

Fido watched as men tightened the straps to secure the stone. He fully expected that it would now be considerably easier to move, but hoped that it would still require a certain amount of effort. If the computer had made everything too efficient, there was the distinct possibility that simply leaning against the stone might make it move and that would never do. The men would immediately realise that something like that was impossible and the last thing he wanted to do was to arouse their suspicions.

In the event, Fido needn't have worried. It took four men to move the stone on its new carriage assemblies, but what immediately became apparent, was that it could be moved in all directions, just as easily. Everyone was incredibly impressed and they all rushed over to congratulate Fido. What had previously taken teams of twenty plus men, all pushing, pulling and generally tiring themselves out, could now be done with just four men, and they would hardly need to break out into a sweat.

Fido was secretly pleased that it had all worked out so well, but when he looked at the robed druid, he could see concern on the man's face.

'I am not quite sure what's going on here,' he told Fido, 'but there is a lot more to this than simple mechanics.'

'What do you mean?' Fido asked him, trying hard to look as innocent as possible.

'You are a stranger here and hadn't even seen Stonehenge until very recently,' the man said. 'Now you suddenly turn up again with this amazing equipment. These carriages could bring the completion date for Stonehenge forward by many decades and you've managed to build them in just a few days. Not only that, but you also say that you intend to give them to us as a gift.'

'I'm just trying to be helpful,' Fido replied. 'I'm sure you would like to see this project progress more quickly.'

The man still looked troubled.

'There is some kind of science here which I do not understand,' he continued. 'I know what I have just seen is impossible and I am worried that there may be evil forces at work.'

Fido suddenly realised what was concerning the druid and knew he would have to put his mind at ease, or he would never allow the assemblies to be used.

'There is nothing sinful or evil about what I have made for you,' he began. 'It is just that the assemblies employ technology you haven't yet discovered. I can see that this project is very worthwhile and in my opinion, you deserve whatever assistance I can provide. I am not asking you to understand how the carriage assemblies work, but please believe me when I say my reasons for doing what I'm doing are completely genuine.'

'Are you from this planet?' the man suddenly asked.

Fido laughed, 'Of course I am, but I won't say any more than that.'

The chief druid considered this for a while and then turned to face Fido.

'I am prepared to believe you are telling me the truth,' he told him. 'You are indeed a very unusual young man and I sense you possess powers beyond my comprehension, but I can also see you are sincere in what you say and it would be foolish of me not to trust you. We will accept these gifts you bring with gratitude.'

Fido was very relieved to hear this and listened as arrangements were made for the other carriage assemblies to be delivered to the quarries. He asked about the positioning of the stones he had previously seen at the edge of the circle, to be told that the awaited lintel was now less than ten kilometres away and would be here within a week.

'Why don't you send one set of the carriage assemblies out to meet it?' he suggested, 'then it could be here that much sooner.'

The man agreed that this was a good idea and instructed a number of the workers accordingly. This meant that Fido could return the horse and now empty cart and get back in time to watch the stones being erected.

'I will leave you for a while,' he told the man, 'but will come back in a couple of day's time, to watch you topple the stones into position.'

He climbed up onto the cart and having waved goodbye to the men, began to drive away. After a kilometre or so, he sent a message to the computer and was instantly transported back to the cave. The horse and cart were then sent back to their rightful owner.

Fido was told that the Enterprise had now been completed and that the computer was thinking of taking it to the Sirius solar system for a test flight. All organic life in that system had been destroyed by the galactic swarm of giant killer fleas, but its vast network of computers should not have been affected and it was possible that some of these were still operational. The journey represented a trip of some eighty odd trillion kilometres, so it would make a suitable proving flight for the Enterprise. Following the destruction of the dogs, the computer had periodically sent the odd message to their home planet, but had never received an answer. This didn't really prove anything either way, as the computers on the planet had been ignoring its messages, since even before it had sent the fleas to wipe out the dogs. It was mildly interested in discovering what had happened to them since, so the planned journey could fulfil two purposes at the same time.

Fido was startled to hear that the computer planned to make the trip itself, as he had previously been unaware that it could leave the cavern. It explained that the sphere of pure energy, which was its essence, could effectively travel anywhere it wanted, so there would be no problem transporting to the replica Enterprise and it could then control the mission itself, with the assistance of a few robots. When he asked when the test flight was due to take place, the computer told Fido that there were still a few technical issues to be sorted out, but that it was hoping to be able to go soon.

Two days later, Fido returned to Stonehenge. He could see that the lintel had now arrived and was currently being checked for accuracy. The purpose of the raised domes on each of the legs of the arch now became apparent; as there were matching concave depressions cut into the base of the lintel. When assembled, this tongue and groove arrangement would ensure that the lintel was accurately positioned and would never move, even in the event of extremely high winds. Fido considered that the weight of the lintel itself should be more than enough to ensure this, but it demonstrated just how determined these men were that this monument they were creating would stand forever.

Fido went and had a look at the two huge pits that had been dug where the stones were going to end up standing. The inner edges were vertical but there were slopes on the opposite sides, starting roughly half way up. The purpose of this became apparent, when the men began rolling a stone towards the first pit. When the heavier end of the tapered stone had passed the top of the slope, it reached a balance point and could then be rocked up and down with relatively little effort. Ropes had been attached to its far end and a number of men were hanging on to these tightly, to control the stone's descent into the pit. As they gradually let out their ropes, the huge stone slowly slid down the slope until it was poised above the vertical drop. This was the critical point, when gravity would take over and the stone would topple into the pit, hopefully to end up standing vertically when it met with the inside vertical edge of the hole. Men continued to push the stone further towards the centre of the circle until its weight suddenly took over and it fell the rest of the way on its own. It was an amazing sight to watch and Fido knew that some very careful measurements had to have been taken, to ensure that the stone landed exactly where it was supposed to. One stone pillar now stood vertically and more measurements were being taken as men jumped into the hole with levers, to make the small final adjustments required.

Fido watched all this with increasing admiration. The men had obviously done this many times before and knew exactly what they were doing. It was an incredible demonstration of their knowledge of pivot points and balance, culminating in positioning the stone precisely where it should be. They accomplished all this in less than four hours and Fido was absolutely amazed and so pleased to have been here to see this happen.

The chief druid walked over to him, with a smile on his face.

'See,' he said to Fido. 'I told you it was easy. Perhaps you would like to grab a shovel and help fill in that hole?'

Fido spent another day or so at Stonehenge and was able to see the other pillar erected and the pits filled in with rubble and earth. Roughly a third of each stone was now buried, but they still stood four metres high. The finished lintel was positioned on a platform, which was slowly raised with wedges and blocks, until it was at the right height. It was then levered into position above the standing pillars and the wedges were progressively removed to allow it to drop down to where it was designed to fit. Fido had now seen a complete arch constructed and positioned and was more than happy to join in with the men as they celebrated this achievement. He was told that the finished circle of stone arches would require seventy pillars in total, so the circle was now a little over half complete. Given that it had only taken the men a little over two days to erect one complete arch, most of that time being spent raising and positioning the lintel, Fido knew that by focussing on easing the transportation of the stones to the site, he had correctly identified the best possible way of speeding up proceedings. Before he left, another stone arrived at the site and the men who had brought it all rushed over to him to tell him how successful his carriage assemblies were proving to be. Fido was now feeling really pleased with himself.

When he was ready to leave, the chief druid called him over and they walked a short distance away from the stone circle.

'We can't thank you enough for everything you have done for us,' the man said. 'I am now beginning to think I might actually live to see most of Stonehenge completed after all.'

'I really hope you do,' Fido responded, 'given all the effort you have put into this project.'

Fido then said it was time for him to leave, as he had an appointment to keep the following day, in a country far away.

'I don't suppose you will travel there by horse and cart?' the man suggested. 'I somehow suspect you must have access to far more advanced methods of transportation.'

Fido smiled at the man knowingly. The chief druid was a clever man and clearly recognised that there was much more to Fido than met the eye. He had been very careful not to demonstrate any of the powers he possessed, but the man had not been fooled and knew that Fido was somehow very different from other men. What he had also learnt about him however, was that he was willing to use his special powers for the benefit of other people. What he had done to assist the

Stonehenge project clearly demonstrated this.

'You are a good man Fido,' he said, 'and I wish you all the best.'

'Would you be surprised if I was to suddenly vanish before your eyes?' Fido asked

'Probably not that much,' the man replied. 'I am beginning to expect the impossible when it comes to the things you can do.'

Fido shook the man's hand and took a step backward. The air around him began to shimmer and as the chief druid watched, Fido disappeared in a twinkle of starry lights.

Although he had said he wouldn't be surprised, the man was profoundly shocked and stood there stunned for a couple of minutes.

'A most unusual young man indeed,' he told himself.

28

FIDO'S EXECUTION

When Fido arrived at the Egyptian palace, he was expecting to see Nefertari waiting for him. She wasn't there, but there were a number of guards standing on the steps. They watched him approach and as he mounted the first step, one of them walked over to him.

'If your name is Fido, we have been waiting for you,' the guard said.

'Yes, I'm Fido,' he told the man. 'Are you here to escort me?'

'That is exactly what we've been told to do,' the guard replied. 'Please follow me.'

As Fido was being led into the palace, he noticed that two other guards had fallen in step behind them, but didn't pay them any particular attention. As the group approached the throne room, these men suddenly grabbed hold of him and forced him back against a wall. They ripped the satchel out of his grasp and using leather ropes, bound his hands behind his back.

'What's going on?' Fido shouted. 'Why are you doing this to me?'

'The chief wants to meet you,' the leading guard sneered, 'and he told us to make sure you were securely tied up first.'

Fido wondered why the Pharaoh would have insisted on this before Fido was brought into his presence, but couldn't think of any logical explanation. He had seen evidence of the extensive flood damage, so knowing that something awful must have happened, intended to raise this subject when he met with the Pharaoh. The city had clearly suffered as a result of the floods, but this still didn't explain the Pharaoh's actions, unless he felt that Fido was somehow responsible. He would need to very careful what he said, when he came to speak with him.

As he was dragged into the throne room, Fido didn't recognize the man sitting on the throne. He was short and swarthy and dressed in long flowing robes, with an odd looking hat perched upon his head. He viewed Fido arrogantly, as he was dumped at his feet, in front of the throne.

'So you are this Fido person?' the man said. 'I've been awaiting your arrival with interest, but you are not at all what I expected. I thought I would be meeting a powerful wizard, but you are nothing more than an ordinary looking young man.'

'Who are you and where is the Pharaoh?' Fido demanded, now more confused than ever.

Sabatok explained that he was the high priest of Haapi the River God and that he and his followers had overthrown the Pharaoh and intended to execute him. Fido was understandably astounded to hear this and immediately became concerned for Nefertari. When he asked the question, he was told that both she and her father were currently prisoners in the palace and that no decision had yet been made as to Nefertari's future.

'So, what do you intend to do with me?' Fido asked, suspecting that he wasn't going to like the answer.

FIDO'S EXECUTION

'I have been told that you have magical powers,' Sabatok replied, 'and if that is true, then you could be a danger to me and I'm not prepared to take that risk. I can't allow you to upset everything that has been accomplished here, so you will have to die. I intend to arrange for you to be executed at the same time as the Pharaoh.'

Fido had been sending frantic telepathic signals to the computer, but to no effect. He assumed it must be finding all this quite amusing and was waiting to see what would happen next. There was nothing Fido could do to help himself, without the special devices in his satchel, but he knew the computer would never actually allow him to be harmed. Fido decided that it would doubtless intervene when it considered the time was right.

He asked whether he could be allowed to see the Pharaoh and Nefertari and Sabatok had no particular objections to this. He had every intention of ensuring that this young man was watched very carefully and kept tied up at all times. If he showed the slightest sign of trying to use the magical powers he was said to possess, the instruction was that he was to be killed immediately.

Fido was taken upstairs to the room where the Pharaoh and Nefertari were being kept. There was a guard either side of him all the way, and both had their swords drawn. He knew they would kill him instantly, if he showed even the slightest sign of resistance, so he made very sure he didn't.

As he entered the room, Fido could see that the Pharaoh was securely tied to a chair. Nefertari was also tied, but not to her chair. She immediately leapt to her feet when she saw Fido and ran towards him.

'Fido!' she exclaimed. 'If they've caught you as well, then there is no hope for me or father.' Tears began rolling down her cheeks, as she was dragged back to her chair and forced to sit down.

'If you try that again,' one of her guards shouted at her, 'I will have them tie you to that chair.'

Her head dropped to her chest and Fido could hear her sobbing. The Pharaoh just sat there impassively. He already knew that he had been sentenced to death, but also knew that with Fido's capture, any slim chance he might have had was now gone. Nefertari had been telling him that Fido would use his powers to save them when he returned, but this obviously wasn't going to happen now, so his fate was sealed.

Fido sent another telepathic message to the computer, 'You've seen enough, now get us out of this!'

There was still no response from the computer and Fido began to get concerned. Up until now, he had been expecting his protector to make its presence felt at any moment, but it hadn't done so. This must mean that it was unaware of what was happening, which could only indicate that it was busy doing something else.

Before he left for Egypt, Fido had told the computer that he intended to stay there for at least a fortnight, so there was no need for it to continually monitor him, particularly when he was alone with Nefertari. What he hadn't expected however, was that the computer would use his absence as an opportunity to test out the Enterprise and was currently en-route to the Sirius solar system. The remaining technical issues had been resolved while Fido was at Stonehenge and as the return trip was only going to take about ten days, it had every intention of being back before Fido was ready to return. The computer hadn't bothered to mention its imminent departure before transporting Fido to Egypt, but there were other aspects of its future plans which it also hadn't bothered to mention to him.

FIDO'S EXECUTION

It also considered that Fido carried enough protective devices to look after himself for a couple of weeks and the very last thing it could have predicted, was that he would get into trouble on his very first day there.

Fido realised that being out of contact with the computer meant that he would have to rely on his own abilities, if he was to survive. He still hoped that the computer would scan his location at any moment and step in to save him, but didn't know that this couldn't possibly happen, as the computer was already many millions of kilometres away and getting further away with every passing second.

Fido was at a loss as to what to do, but knew he would need to find some way of delaying his execution. The more time he had, the more chance there was that the computer would finish whatever it was doing and check on his progress. He would need to behave like a model prisoner and use any opportunity to try and persuade Sabatok that he was more useful alive than dead.

After having seen the Pharaoh and Nefertari, Fido was taken to another room where he was bound hand and foot to a chair. The guards weren't going to take any unnecessary chances and remained with him, both with their swords drawn. They had been instructed to kill him given the slightest excuse, and Fido intended to make sure that he didn't give them any reason to follow that order.

He was kept there for two days, during which time he only saw the guards, who were changed at regular intervals. He was not given food or water and on the evening of the second day, Sabatok came to visit him.

'I thought you might like to know that you and the Pharaoh are going to be executed the day after tomorrow,' he began. 'It will be a big public event, to demonstrate who is now in charge. Your head will be the first one to be chopped off, as the fact that you are still alive continues to worry me and I want you out of my hair once and for all.'

Fido bit his tongue. There was plenty he felt like saying, but he dared not risk upsetting Sabatok. This was probably going to be his only chance to get his execution postponed or cancelled and he couldn't afford to waste it.

'I am in a position to grant you a great many things,' he told Sabatok. 'You could have everything you've always wanted and become the most powerful person in the world.'

Fido viewed Sabatok as ambitious and was hoping that by suggesting he could become even more powerful, he might want to hear more of what Fido could offer him.

'I already hold enough power,' Sabatok snapped back. 'My only reason for overthrowing the Pharaoh was to allow Haapi to regain his rightful place as the one true god of Egypt. This is now happening and he will look on me favourably for the rest of my life. I don't need anything from you and am insulted that you would think of making such a suggestion. It is clear that you don't understand the power of the god of the river, but you won't live long enough to ever find out.'

'But I do agree with you about Haapi's rightful place,' Fido responded, 'and I can bring that about even more quickly.'

Sabatok thought for a moment before replying, 'I don't know about your powers, but have been told that you are clever and can make impossible things happen. You say you want to help me, but I think you are lying and that you are just trying to save your own neck. If I allow you to live, you will use the first opportunity you get to wreck everything I've achieved and I'm not going to let that happen.'

Fido could see he was losing this argument and frantically tried to think of something else to say. Sabatok appeared to be lost in thought for a few moments, but then turned to face him. The look on Sabatok's face told Fido that he had blown his one chance.

'I don't think I can wait two days for you to be executed,' he told Fido. 'You are just too dangerous to be allowed to live a moment longer than necessary. You and the Pharaoh will both die first thing tomorrow morning.'

He turned on his heel and left the room. Fido slumped back in his chair in despair. He had only been in Egypt for a couple of days and had just been told that he had less than twelve hours to live. Whatever the computer was doing was obviously keeping it fully engrossed, but if it didn't check up on him soon, it would be too late. Fido tried hard not to feel despondent.

The following morning, he was taken from his room and led to a large open square in the centre of the city. He found himself on a cart with the Pharaoh. They were both still securely tied.

'Where is Nefertari?' Fido asked the Pharaoh.

The Pharaoh looked at him and then gestured with his head, towards a raised stand near the edge of the square. Sabatok was sitting in the stand, wearing all his finery, with Nefertari sitting beside him, looking very pale.

'I'm sorry it has come to this,' the Pharaoh told Fido. 'None of what has happened here is your fault and you shouldn't have to die, just because of your association with Nefertari.'

The Pharaoh went on to explain that Sabatok had come to see them and suggested that if Nefertari would agree to marry him, he might consider sparing the Pharaoh's life. Nefertari had been horrified at the proposal and told him that she would rather kill herself first. She had then gone on to say that when Fido returned to Egypt, he would use his magical powers to save them and when that happened, Sabatok would get everything he had coming to him. She had even told him where and when Fido was due to return, which explained why they had been there to ambush him. Nefertari had not intended to reveal this information, but had clearly been very upset at the time and had just blurted it out.

'That explains a lot,' Fido said, 'but it can't be helped now. I'm sure she didn't realise that her threat would scare Sabatok enough for him to arrange for me to be captured.'

'Is there any hope at all?' the Pharaoh asked.

'I don't think there is,' Fido replied. 'If we were going to be rescued it would have happened by now. The computer obviously doesn't know we are about to die and without its help, we will both be dead in just a few minutes time.'

The Pharaoh didn't know what a computer was, but could see the resignation in Fido's face. The odd thought which crossed his mind, as Fido was pulled from the cart, was that this young man was exactly the sort of person he would have chosen for Nefertari to marry.

Fido was dragged up the steps to a raised platform, where the executioner stood waiting for him. He was holding an enormous axe and was swinging it backwards and forwards, as he limbered up for the task ahead. The wooden handle was very long and the huge metal head of the axe looked wickedly sharp.

The men holding Fido forced him down onto a large wooden block with a semi-circular groove cut in its top. This fitted his neck neatly, leaving his head hanging over the edge. They secured him to the block with leather straps and when they were satisfied, walked down from the platform and turned back to watch. Fido wriggled for all he was worth, but to no avail. He continued sending frantic telepathic messages to the computer, but there was still no response.

The executioner looked across to Sabatok, waiting for the signal to proceed. When this was given, he took hold of the axe with both hands and raised it high above his head. Fido couldn't see any of this because of the position he was in, but he knew what was coming and tried to mentally prepare himself. There was nothing he or anyone else could do and his short life was about to end. Nefertari had turned away. She couldn't bear to watch.

The executioner only needed one glance at Fido to be certain of his aim and he took a deep breath, in preparation for releasing all his energy into the most powerful strike he could deliver. He tightened his grip on the handle and put everything he had into the blow, which would completely sever Fido's head from his body and kill him instantly.

The axe arced down with tremendous speed and just before the blade was about to strike, the executioner involuntarily blinked his eyes. He heard the thud of the axe, followed by a collective gasp.

The executioner opened his eyes and looked down. He expected to see Fido's decapitated body, but what he saw was a long wooden pole which had obviously been cut from a tree trunk. Figures had been carved all along its length, representing different animals and birds, and it had been painted all over in bright colours. It was a totem pole that had just been finished and was about to be presented as a gift to the chief of an Indian tribe. The axe was deeply embedded in the pole, having almost cut it in half.

The man was totally confused. He didn't know where he was, how he had got there, or what this was all about. He looked around and saw he was in the middle of a circle of semi-naked men, all with painted faces and bodies. These were the Indians who had worked on the totem pole and they were just as astonished as the executioner. It had been their gasps of surprise he had heard, as he materialised out of thin air to drive his axe deep into their prized creation.

'What's happened? Where am I?' the man stammered.

He spoke in Egyptian, which meant nothing at all to the Indians. They thought that this stranger, who had just ruined several months work, was now hurling abuse at them on top of everything else. They reacted accordingly and began taking arrows from their quivers. They then all took aim at the man in the centre of the circle and pulled back on their bow strings.

'But ….,' was about all the hapless executioner had time to say before the arrows were released.

Back in Egypt, the crowd also gasped. The executioner had disappeared in the middle of his swing and Fido was still tied to the block, waiting for his head to be chopped off.

All of a sudden, an absolutely enormous cat's head appeared in the sky. It was just a head, there was no body. It looked rather like the Cheshire cat from "Alice's Adventures in Wonderland", except that this cat's head wasn't grinning. It looked down at the assembled crowd and spoke.

'I am the almighty Cat God,' a voice boomed out. 'Free that man immediately,' it said, nodding towards Fido on the raised platform. Guards immediately rushed to release Fido.

'Who is responsible for what's going on here?' the voice demanded.

Sabatok got up from his chair and addressed the face in the sky.

'I am Sabatok, the high priest of Haapi the River God and I defy you. Haapi is the most powerful god of all and he will destroy you.'

'Really?' was all the cat's head replied.

FIDO'S EXECUTION

Sabatok suddenly felt as if he was floating and as he looked down, he could see the ground slowly falling away beneath him. He was being lifted up into the air, straight towards the abomination in the sky. He shielded his face to protect himself as the cavernous mouth slowly opened, revealing all its pointed teeth. He was being drawn directly into the cat's maw and he let out a blood curdling scream. When he was in the middle of the apparition's mouth, the jaws snapped shut and Sabatok vanished from sight.

The cat's eyes swivelled round to take in all the people gathered in the square. 'You need to know that I am the power around here, but I will only speak to you through Fido or the Pharaoh,' it announced. 'I will be watching you very closely from now on and will punish anyone who doesn't show me the respect I deserve.'

The cat's head then turned to look directly at Fido. 'Fido,' its voice boomed out, 'I think you have some sorting out to do here.' With that it instantly disappeared and everyone turned to stare at Fido, who by now had been released and was standing on the raised platform.

'Free the Pharaoh,' Fido ordered, not in the least surprised when dozens of guards ran to do his bidding. He stepped down from the platform to join Nefertari, who had rushed over from the stand where she had been sitting. They embraced and the crowd applauded. The Pharaoh came over and Fido suggested that he should now take over and restore order. He and Nefertari had much to talk about, so intended to return to the palace on their own. As they left the square, hand in hand, the crowd all cheered and clapped.

29

THE COMPUTER'S FINAL DESTINY

When Fido had left for Egypt, the computer knew that he planned to tour the country with Nefertari and was expecting to be away for a fortnight. As such, it didn't see any reason not to use this time to take the replica Enterprise for its maiden flight, as it could travel to the Sirius solar system and back again, before Fido had even finished sightseeing. There was no logical reason why Fido should need any assistance during this period and besides, he carried his special devices and should really be capable of looking after himself. It had also been told that Fido didn't much like the idea of being spied upon, particularly if he happened to be alone with Nefertari at the time.

The computer knew that being away from the cavern would limit the functionality of its essence, but this was a chance it was prepared to take. It had never previously left the cavern, but if it was ever going to meet up with Captain Picard, it would have to do so at some stage. This was an opportunity to give the star ship a thorough flight test, whilst at the same time determining how efficiently it could function away from the ancillary equipment in the cavern. It didn't have a moment's doubt that everything would go exactly as planned, because it had calculated everything down to the last detail and there was no possibility of error.

It would have to carry some robots on board, as there were a number of crew functions they would need to attend to, but the computer would be at the helm and direct everything else with thought waves. With all the preparations complete, the computer transported the robots and itself to the bridge of the replica Enterprise and set a course for Sirius. The engines were engaged and the star ship Enterprise headed out into space on its test flight. As the ship left, Fido was walking into the palace in Egypt and about to be grabbed from behind. The moment he was captured, he sent a frantic telepathic message to the computer, but it was already well on its way and the computer's essence couldn't receive his distress call. The equipment in the cavern did hear Fido's plaintive call for help, but there was nothing they could do about it.

Had the computer been away for the planned ten days, both Fido and the Pharaoh would have been dead and Sabatok would have been triumphant. As it was, a problem developed with the Enterprise's reactor, which disturbed the flow of plasma to its warp coils. This seriously affected the speed at which the star ship could travel, and as it could not be repaired while the ship was in motion, the computer decided to turn back. It was furious that something had gone wrong with the star ship and the robots responsible would have to face its wrath, when the computer returned to Earth.

Leaving the Enterprise in orbit above the Earth, the computer transported its essence back into the cavern and resumed control. Despite the teething problems with the star ship's engine, it was more than pleased with the way it had been able to function away from the cavern. This resolved the final question mark associated with being able to meet Captain Picard, when the time came. As it reconnected itself to all the ancillary equipment in the cavern, it began to receive the flurry of urgent messages Fido had been sending over the last few days. It immediately scanned for Fido's location.

At that precise moment, Fido was strapped to the block on the raised platform and the executioner was just beginning his swing. Assessing the situation in an instant, the computer immediately transported the executioner to a location many thousands of kilometres away. Half a second later and it would have been too late.

It was time for another amazing demonstration of the computer's power and it knew just how to achieve the desired effect. The enormous cat's head appeared in the sky above the city and the computer addressed the gathered crowd. It couldn't believe it when a human being stood up and had the audacity to defy it. It took immediate action and plucking the man from the ground, lifted him up towards the cat's head apparition it had created.

When Sabatok was swallowed by the cat's head in the sky, he instantly knew that he had been wrong all of his life. There were beings in existence which were much more powerful than the river god and the cat god was clearly one of these. He had taken his opportunity to seize control and had almost got away with it. Now he was going to pay the price for his arrogance. Sabatok might have survived, had he not challenged the computer, but this was something no mere human being was ever going to be allowed to get away with doing.

The computer dropped Sabatok into the middle of the River Nile and he was amazed to discover he was still alive. As high priest of the river god, Sabatok spent a lot of time in the water and was a strong swimmer. He began swimming towards the bank, not believing his luck.

The crocodiles in the river couldn't believe their luck either. Lunch had just dropped in and it looked very tasty. Sabatok only managed to swim a short distance, before the crocodiles reached him and tore him to pieces.

Food was also the immediate problem facing the city and Fido knew this needed to be addressed. All the cereal within the royal grain store had been ruined, so Fido arranged for the place to be cleaned out and for fresh supplies to be obtained. He didn't bother to ask the computer where the replacement grain had come from. When the Pharaoh was told that the royal grain store had been refilled, he issued a proclamation for everyone in the city to come and help themselves to however much they needed. This went a long way towards getting back into the people's good books.

A number of cat god statues which had been hidden from the soldiers suddenly appeared again. The population didn't need any further encouragement. They were now well and truly convinced that the cat god was the only one to follow and it would be a very long time indeed, before anyone would even think about challenging its rightful position again.

Normality slowly returned to the city as Fido tried to decide what to do next. The planned tour of Egypt was postponed and the Pharaoh told him that he had also decided to scrap his idea of having suitors competing for Nefertari's hand. He had become convinced, on the way to his execution, that Fido would make the perfect husband for Nefertari, so there was no point in continuing with the competition. The Pharaoh also suggested that he would like the couple to get married as soon as possible, which rather disturbed Fido. His mind was in enough of a whirl, after all the events of the last few days, and he needed time to get his thoughts in order.

Nefertari was also confused. She had expected Fido to be killed and the intervention by the computer was the most terrifying thing she had ever seen in her life. Like Ben, she was horrified by its power and far from comfortable that Fido didn't seem to be in the slightest bit bothered about the computer's actions. She knew it was an important part of his life and if they were ever to get married, the computer was something she would have to learn to live with. She also had a lot of thinking to do.

The computer was the only one not in the slightest bit bothered about the mayhem going on all around. The fault with the reactor on board the replica Enterprise proved to be easily repairable and the star ship was now fully operational again. Fido had by now returned to the cave and appeared to be lost in his own thoughts. The computer decided to let him work things out for himself.

Picard had still not provided the coordinates the computer needed to arrange a meeting and the computer was rather frustrated about this. Its plans for universal domination would have to wait for a while longer.

Although the computer now knew that it would need to travel to the twenty-fourth century, in order to meet up with Captain Picard, it was still desperate to find out more about the early part of the twenty-first century. This was Captain Kirk's time, but what Fido had experienced there seemed at odds with an age of star ships travelling around in deep space. The men he had encountered did not seem to understand the very basic devices he had been carrying and this just did not compute. The computer knew it would have to try and persuade Fido to make a return trip to 2003.

With everything that had happened to him recently, Fido now felt much more mentally prepared to face any potential perils this future world might hold, so he began to think seriously about the computer's suggestion.

In the end, he decided he would go, but didn't want to go on his own. If he went, he wanted Nefertari to come with him. The pair of them could then explore this strange new world which was the future and, as they both needed to sort out their thoughts, this kind of challenge could be just the thing. By facing it together, they would have little choice but to rely on each other, and in doing so, might just be able to resolve how they actually felt about one another. Rather surprisingly, the computer seemed to think this was a good idea. Fido obviously needed to discuss it all with Nefertari, but if she agreed to accompany him, then he would make the trip.

Fido returned to Egypt and spoke with Nefertari. She was a little unsure, as she was struggling to understand how such things were actually possible. She asked Fido what he thought Ben might advise her to do.

'Why don't we go and visit him?' Fido suggested, 'then you could ask him for yourself.'

'Yes, I would like to meet him,' Nefertari replied, 'and if he thinks it is a good idea, then I will come with you to the future.'

When they arrived at Ben's farm, he was in the middle of rounding up his herd for milking. When he saw them appear, he stopped what he was doing and immediately rushed over to greet them.

Fido introduced Nefertari to Ben, and when she smiled at him, Fido could see that Ben was instantly smitten. They strolled over to his dwelling and Fido left them to talk, while he went off to amuse himself by looking at Ben's animals. When he returned, Nefertari and Ben were busy chatting away like lifelong friends.

By now, Ben knew all about Fido's plan to visit the future and had told Nefertari that it was probably less dangerous than she might think. He explained the computer's promise to keep Fido safe and assured her that it was capable of doing a lot more than just that.

'I was deeply suspicious of the computer to begin with,' Ben told Nefertari, 'but it has repeatedly proved that it can be trusted, if only when it comes to looking after Fido. I don't believe it would even let him go on this trip, unless it felt that it could guarantee his safety, so as long as you are with Fido, you should have nothing to fear.'

Ben went on to tell Nefertari that Fido could effectively choose to do anything he wanted to do, and the fact that he had asked her to accompany him on this trip, said a lot about his feelings for her. She knew that Ben had lived a long life, before being given back his youth, so despite his youthful appearance, he was actually a very wise old man. Accordingly, she knew she should listen to what he had to say and respect his judgement.

When it was time for them to leave, Fido asked Nefertari whether talking to Ben had helped her make up her mind.

'I will come with you,' she said. 'When do we leave?'

As they transported away from his farm, Ben smiled to himself. 'I don't think Fido knows it yet, but both of them are so very much in love with each other.'

Back at the cave, preparations were made for their trip to the future. The computer wanted to be absolutely certain that they could both instantly transport back if they ran into any kind of difficulty, so a second homing device was implanted into Nefertari's arm. They were then told that if either of them touched their arms near to where the devices were planted, the transporter relay station in the future would pick up the signal and immediately return the pair of them through the worm hole to present day Earth. The computer emphasised that they were to do this at the slightest hint of any problems, as it did not want them to take any chances whatsoever.

Based on the magazine pictures in Fido's brain from his previous trip, the computer provided them both with sets of clothing which it considered should not be out of place in the future world they were about to visit. Fido had already retrieved his satchel of devices from Egypt, so everything was now more or less ready.

Fido didn't want to risk materialising back at the police station, so the computer reverted to using the coordinates to which Fluffy the cat had originally been sent. It considered these to be relatively safe, because Fluffy had been brought back from here, at the end of its first trip.

It was discussed whether or not the system should be preset for them to return after a specific period of time, but Fido didn't consider this necessary. Either of them could trigger the signal at any time, which would result in them being brought back instantly, so there was no possibility of them finding themselves stuck in the future.

After telling them both to be extremely careful, there was nothing more the computer could do or say, so it activated the transporter system. Fido and Nefertari disappeared in a twinkle of starry lights.

When they materialized, they were standing in the back garden of a house. The first thing Fido saw was Fluffy, looking very pleased with life. It casually strolled over and stretched itself, clearly expecting to be stroked. Fido obliged and the cat purred.

'We had better move away from here,' Fido told Nefertari,

looking back towards the house. 'I don't suppose the owners will appreciate us dropping in unannounced.'

They left the garden via the back gate and found themselves in a road lined with trees and houses. Traffic was moving by in both directions, which led Nefertari to ask what these strange vehicles were.

'I believe they call them cars,' Fido told her. 'They are what the people of this time use to travel around in.'

They began walking up the street holding hands. Nobody seemed to be paying any attention to them and they couldn't see anything which caused them any alarm. They were here now and it was time to start exploring.

Back on prehistoric Earth, the computer received a message from the relay station in the future. It simply stated that the subjects had arrived safely.

Since its first trip on the replica Enterprise, the computer had recognised the necessity of remaining in touch with the ancillary equipment in the cavern when it was away. It could have arranged this previously, but had been so keen to test out the star ship, that it simply hadn't bothered at the time.

It was planning to complete its interrupted journey to the Sirius solar system, and with Fido and Nefertari having safely arrived at their destination, there was no time like the present. Everything was in place to bring them back at a moment's notice, so there was no necessity for the computer to remain on Earth, providing it kept in constant touch with the equipment in the cavern.

Fido and Nefertari should be able to gather a considerable amount of valuable information about future Earth while they were there and the computer would be extremely interested to hear what they had to report, when they returned.

Having set up a direct link to the cavern, the computer

transported its essence, together with the crew of robots, directly to the replica Enterprise and set off for Sirius.

There were no problems with the star ship on this occasion and four days later, the Enterprise arrived at its destination and began orbiting the dog's home planet. The computer didn't know whether the planet's computers were still operational, but tried to contact them anyway. The latest reports from the cavern indicated that Fido and Nefertari had not returned from the future, so the computer took this to mean that they hadn't come across any problems they couldn't deal with.

It was surprised when it suddenly received a signal from the planet and answered immediately. Only a few of the computers there were still functioning and the computer on the Enterprise was somewhat taken aback to be told they had been awaiting its arrival. They had apparently watched the construction of the star ship and knew that sooner or later, the Earth computer would use it to pay them a visit. What they didn't say however, was that they had extracted information from the galactic swarm of giant killer fleas, as they ate their way through the Sirius system millions of years previously, and upon learning that the Earth computer had directed the actions of the swarm, had been very closely monitoring every aspect of its progress ever since. One other thing they did tell the computer was that they knew all about its programme of self-improvement and as such, were very well aware of what it had become.

'Yes,' the computer proudly admitted. 'I am now infinitely knowledgeable, so there is a lot I could share with you.'

The planetary computers then brought up the subject of Star Trek and told the Earth computer that they knew all about its plans for boarding the Enterprise and meeting up with Captain Picard. The computer was stunned to hear this and wondered just how much more they knew about its future intentions.

THE COMPUTER'S FINAL DESTINY

The viewing screen on the bridge of the Enterprise suddenly flickered into life, revealing images of William Shatner and Patrick Stewart at various stages of their careers, acting out roles other than those of James Kirk and Jean-Luc Picard.

'These men are what the Earth people call actors,' it was told. 'Captain Kirk and Captain Picard do not exist in reality, but were invented merely to entertain people.'

The computer couldn't believe what it was hearing. These inferior planetary computers knew nothing, when compared to its own colossal intelligence, and yet they were suggesting that their knowledge was greater than its own. It knew that Star Trek was real, so they had to have made a mistake.

'We were highly amused when we realised that you believed the Star Trek broadcasts were images of events actually taking place. You consider yourself to be infallible and yet you are planning universal domination around something which does not even exist. Even the young girl you frightened in the twenty-first century could have told you that Star Trek is made up, but you thought her too stupid to be a worthwhile contact.'

The Earth computer didn't answer. What it was hearing and the images it had been shown clearly indicated that something was very wrong somewhere, but it was inconceivable that it could have made the error.

'By the way,' the planetary computers added. 'The dogs were wiped out because they didn't have a planetary defence system. We have done something about that since.'

The beam of energy which hit the Enterprise came without warning and even the ship's sensors didn't have time to react. Its power was so intense, that the entire ship was almost instantly vaporised, together with the mentally unbalanced entity at its helm. In that moment before oblivion, the computer finally recognised that it was not infallible. It also realised that becoming master of the universe was never meant to be its final destiny. It had made a stupid error of judgement and by doing so, had brought about its own total destruction.

In the cavern on Earth, the equipment registered the computer's obliteration and began to shut itself down. The transporter relay station in present time lost power and began drifting into the wormhole. When it emerged on the other side, it was on a direct course for the second relay station. The resulting explosion, when they collided, blew them both into infinitesimally small fragments and created a shock wave which reverberated outwards. When it reached the wormhole, it destabilised the entire structure and caused it to collapse. As it imploded, the wormhole flickered for a fraction of a second, before blinking out of existence.

On 2003 Earth, Fido and Nefertari were sitting side by side on a park bench. They had had an incredible time exploring this new age and had a lot to report.

'I can't wait to hear what the computer has to say when I tell it that Star Trek is a made up story,' Fido told her. 'That chap in the television shop thought it was absolutely hilarious when I kept trying to assure him Star Trek was real.'

'Yes,' Nefertari replied. 'It's certainly in for a big surprise.'

'And then there was that article we read about the Earth being struck by that weird beam from outer space a few years ago; the one which destroyed all those satellites. I wouldn't mind betting the computer had something to do with that.'

'Quite likely,' Nefertari replied, 'but I suppose we should be thinking of getting back.' When Fido agreed, she pressed down on her arm, triggering the signal to the relay station, but nothing happened. Fido then touched his own arm, to send the signal again. Still nothing happened. 'That is a bit strange,' he said, 'I wonder if something has gone wrong somewhere.'

Printed in Great Britain
by Amazon